SAILOR ALL AT SEA

A personal tale of conflict and devotion

Richard Trahair

ARTHUR H. STOCKWELL LTD
Torrs Park, Ilfracombe, Devon, EX34 8BA
Established 1898
www.ahstockwell.co.uk

British Library Cataloguing-in-Publication Data.
A catalogue record for this book is available
from the British Library.

ISBN 978-0-7223-4938-0
Printed in Great Britain by
Arthur H. Stockwell Ltd
Torrs Park   Ilfracombe
Devon EX34 8BA

ACKNOWLEDGEMENTS

This modest first venture into writing fiction would not have been possible without the help and patience of several people. Notably I wish to thank Lalla Hitchings for the unenviable task of deciphering and typing a manuscript of three soggy notebooks, largely written in Biro on my knee in the cockpit of a small sailing boat rolling gently at anchor anywhere from Newtown Creek to Blood Alley Lake, usually in the rain.

Thanks too to Giles Milburn, a local connection with professional experience in these things, for suggesting several improvements to the first draft. Also to my daughter Lamorna, herself a keen devotee of boats, for her 'tech-savvy' skills in reproducing my idea for the book cover. Nor can I omit my elder daughter, Emily, whose adoption of the *Swallows and Amazons* approach to boating in her early youth (with a piratical touch) has secured my love of the Frome river and Poole Harbour ever since.

Not least, to my wife, Biddy, I am grateful for her endless patience over my boating trips away from home, without which the inspiration for this novel could never have arisen. Also, I might add, for her challenging and healthy scepticism over the nature of the relationship between the two central characters in the story. She is probably right.

Richard Trahair

CHAPTER ONE

Until that moment my life had been conventional, humdrum even. Fulfilling, but definitely predictable. A little too worthy perhaps – doing all the right things in helping to keep the local community rolling along: giving regularly to charities; chatting to the *Big Issue* seller and not accepting her change for a fiver.

None of that was really going to change, ultimately. My routine would resume its steady course afterwards, at least in the perception of others around me. In reality, if I am honest, I would never be quite the same. The experience of those few days in which I was to be hurled suddenly into crisis, protective devotion and intrigue left me with a heightened sense of fear, exhilaration and a secret loss that remained hidden within me, recognised maybe by my wife alone.

Well, yes, of course she knew. We were already acquainted with an earlier mutual grief and loss that, although no secret, was by now largely hidden. Almost exactly one year into our married life our firstborn and only son, Jamie, had died quietly one sunny afternoon, asleep in his pram in a shady corner outside the open kitchen window.

Cot death, sudden infant death syndrome, was not a widely known label in those days. His had been inexplicable, unheralded, searing our very existence with an anguish that hit us both with the impact of a locomotive collision. Anne and I had sought refuge in one another, mainly in silence as words were inadequate and therefore irrelevant. Over a dark period of weeks labouring into months, we had learnt to read one another's emotions and thoughts with unerring accuracy.

At the time when this narrative begins, Jamie would have been thirty years of age. I tended to feel his absent presence these days when doing the happy things that boys enjoy, but my wife displayed a tougher character and an apparent resilience. She is, however, the wisest person within the radius of my life, exercising a wisdom that will no doubt become evident as this story unfolds. Underneath continues to flow a deep understanding of my obscured temperament, my frequent yearning for solitude. No mood of mine can ever evade the hot iron of Anne's link into my inner core that was forged by the blackened smithy hammer on that dreadful sunny afternoon.

The experience had embedded us in a relationship with deep foundations, strengthened over the intervening years by the arrival in quick succession of four daughters. They had become a balm, certainly, a soothing compress over the wound, but my filial appendectomy remained irreparable.

Anne had coped through friends. I coped alone.

* * * *

And now, I had been retired from the Royal Navy for about six years, with quite a decent pension and the residue of my late father's money from the sale of his business. The navy had been my career ambition from an early age, cultivated by a blissful Cornish childhood messing about in boats, and a naive penchant for the inimitable blue-and-gold uniform.

The reality had proved to be rather different. Not for me the romantic picture of a sailor swashbuckling around the ports of the world through sparkling seas in Her Majesty's service. Certainly I had accumulated plenty of gold, on my sleeve and the peak of my cap, but this duty was almost entirely shore-based at two ends of Britain, in Devonport and Faslane. Still, I probably saw more attractive scenery beyond my office windows than many of my colleagues buried in the darkened guts of their ships, peering at blinking lights and greenish screens in total isolation from nature.

I was definitely a frustrated boatman, and on reaching the age at which a further ring of gold braid on the arm was improbable, I had resigned and bought a boat of my own.

While I had been at Devonport Naval Base in Plymouth, I had often cast a glance at a beamy old converted fishing yawl, long laid up off Mashford's boatyard. She had about her those classic lines of elegant utility that look instinctively right – straight stem, rounded counter-stern, a pronounced sheer line and enough tumblehome to give the impression that she was well fed, amiable and thoroughly comfortable in rough weather. A proper old gaffer – slow, heavy and utterly reliable.

One of my first moves on resigning my commission was to take the little ferry across to Cremyll and make some enquiries. The boat's name was *Peggotty*, and her ancient owner was similarly imbued with Victorian character. Between us, over a foul belching pipe on his part and smoke-smarting eyes on my own, we reached agreement for him to pass *Peggotty* on to my safekeeping in exchange for a reasonable sum. I always felt that this transaction should have been in solid sovereigns and not the arid banker's draft that had impersonally secured my ownership of this quaint vessel.

She could sleep four in spacious comfort, in cabins with full headroom. Apart from a numbingly expensive new suit of sails, old *Peggotty* needed little to render her seaworthy, beyond new electrics, some modern navigation equipment and quantities of varnish. Her venerable Bukh diesel engine had been well maintained.

Now a free man in my early fifties, I had introduced *Peggotty* into our family life with enthusiasm and energy. My wife enjoyed a lazy day on the water and the occasional overnight passage; and two of our four daughters, keen dinghy sailors from a young age, had, with their various friends, begun to master the endearing eccentricities of our new waterborne floating home from home.

On taking the C.-in-C. salute for the last time, I had set up house with my family in Church Knowle, a delightful small village in the Purbeck Hills on the Dorset coast. *Peggotty* had set up home on a deep mooring twenty minutes away downriver from Wareham at the head of Poole Harbour, a tranquil setting of reed beds, oystercatchers, mud and an astonishing number of graceful white swans.

We had gradually established ourselves in the village and had been drawn into much of the local community activity. Impossible to avoid in rather well-to-do rural settlements, but we needed no undue encouragement. Anne is a gregarious person of a disposition that drew her fully into the life of the village and its church. I had cast about for a while, but had found a niche in one or two voluntary groups in Wareham, and in some practical support of the lifeboat station down the road in Swanage, my now honorary naval title having gained me an easy entrée into this and one or two other maritime interests in these coastal towns.

Once a year, however, I needed to put aside all this slightly exhausting community endeavour, and I had already begun regularly to strike through two weeks of my July diary and take myself off, alone, to sail *Peggotty* lazily around the coastline, eastwards to the Isle of Wight and beyond, or westwards to Weymouth and on to the estuaries of Devon and Cornwall.

I took with me no computer, no Internet or email connection, just a mobile phone that was turned off except when I chose to speak to my nearest and dearest. Naturally I had VHF two-way radio for contacting the coastguard and harbour masters and for dire emergency, but otherwise my purpose was to isolate myself totally from my land-based obligations and devote ten days or so to reading, contemplating coastal nature and, of course, listening to Radio 4. *Peggotty* carried on stern davits a ten-foot clinker dinghy, and I would enjoy rowing this little tender up muddy creeks where no large boat could go, until after brushing past overhanging oak branches, and raising questioning looks in the large eyes of grazing cows with their hocks deep in the river ooze, I would turn around and drift lazily back downstream with the current, back to *Peggotty* at anchor in the roads, somewhere on the south coast of England.

In her working life, *Peggotty* would have needed three strong crew to cope with the rough, heavy hemp cordage and saturated canvas sails, relying on strong shoulder muscles and economic necessity. To enable me to run the boat single-handed with the benefit of modern materials, I had rigged up a series of pulley blocks and cleats drawing halyards, topping lift, downhaul, and jib roller-reef back to the aft end of the cabin roof so that I could control everything without leaving the cockpit. How often had I blessed that provision over the years, in those instant hairy moments that loom out of the water on to every sailor sooner or later. Not least did it enable me to cope with that unforgettable experience on the fateful day when my settled life was to be so rudely interrupted in ways that I could never have imagined possible.

CHAPTER TWO

That July morning dawned wet and cold for the time of year. When I poked my bleary head up out of the companionway of *Peggotty* at the turn of the tide, I had second thoughts about my usual routine of a quick plunge over the gunwale and a splashy bathe. Armed with a large sponge, this exercise normally had two purposes – a refreshing start to the day and a wipe-round of the hull to clean mud, scum and green weed from the waterline.

Today, however, I hesitated too long, and confined myself to a brief squeeze of the saturated sponge over my face and neck. With a shiver I scuttled below again to the fug of the cabin to make breakfast and plan the day's passage. I had left Poole Harbour two days previously with the intention of heading east, vaguely contemplating Chichester Harbour as my final holiday destination. In an unpleasantly strong south-westerly I had on the Sunday holed up in Newtown Creek, that charming sanctuary on the north coast of the Isle of Wight, a wildlife idyll now conserved by the National Trust (with eye-watering mooring fees to match) and one of the most delightful anchorages anywhere along the coast of Southern England. Difficult to credit now that it had once been earmarked, in the 1960s, as the perfect location for a nuclear power station. Where I now sat, gently bobbing on the breeze-broken surface of Clamerkin Lake at Newtown, and surrounded by little waders mincing over the mudflats and listening to the black-headed gulls bickering overhead, the creek might well have become a massive coolant tube for embedded cores of lethal plutonium radiation only a few yards away.

This thought was to come back to me sharply a day or two later, with more pressing and alarming association than I could conceivably have anticipated.

The wind was easing a little, and the tide beginning to gather momentum in my chosen direction, up-Channel eastwards. I weighed anchor and headed out into a Solent still very rough from the previous wind against tide. *Peggotty* had no spray hood or wrap-around cockpit dodgers, so familiar on modern yachts, and I was truly getting it in the neck with salt water from fore and aft, and fresh water from overhead. Conditions like these I rather enjoy, so long as the wind is not more than the top end of force 4. If you are warm and dry with plenty of layers and an effective set of oilies it is surprising what testing circumstances can be borne on the water – weather that would be insufferable in the garden at home.

I settled on to a nice reach past Eagle Point, judging my distance from the passage of the Southampton/Cowes car ferry, and swept past the entrance to the Medina river, where Cowes Week was already preparing for its influx of racing super-yachts, those sleek white sixty-foot beasts with intimidating metallic-grey sailcloth and topsides plastered with advertisements for their sponsoring City financiers. I had once encountered an attack from these marine cavalry when I had innocently chosen an old channel buoy as my waypoint, only to discover too late that this was also a Cowes Week race mark. About twenty yards off I suddenly realised that this fleet of monsters was heading my way at 18 knots. All I could do was stop all-standing, and smile sheepishly as they roared past me feet away, their Australian and American crews lining the windward gunwale without a flicker of response or acknowledgement on their lantern-jawed faces.

This morning, there were few people out on the water for fun. Clearing Ryde Sand out through Spithead, I made my way round towards Bembridge, thinking I could then get a decent run north-east across to Hayling Bay and across the bar up into

Chichester Harbour with the tide, and maybe find a perch in Birdham Pool for the night.

The eastern end of the Solent is a tricky place for a small boat. To say nothing of Royal Navy manoeuvres, the cross-Channel ferries and other commercial traffic are all gathering speed as they head out to sea. The vast ungainly cruise ships, like blocks of expensive flats somehow cast adrift from their foundations, glide past and blot out the sun in a total eclipse from my vantage point down at water level. Timing my crossing brings uncomfortably to mind the plight of hedgehogs undertaking a similar challenge on a dual carriageway.

On this occasion I underestimated the tidal flow, and my predicament was not eased by the wind choosing to go round to the north-west and strengthening. Off St Helens I was now taking a broad reach crabwise out into open waters as I set my course for the mainland shoreline. If I was to overshoot the entrance to Chichester and end up in Bracklesham Bay, I would have the devil of a job beating back against wind and tide to get across the bar and up into shelter.

In retrospect I should have nipped into Bembridge Harbour and dropped anchor, and waited for the tide to turn in the afternoon. I say this not merely for the ease of passage single-handed that was naturally uppermost in my mind at the time. Had I delayed my Solent crossing to a more direct route in the afternoon, the extraordinary events that were in fact to unfold that day would never have occurred. Perhaps my retrospective thinking is all too selfish in any case, because my own peace of mind at anchor in Bembridge would have spelt tragedy or mortal danger for a young life that would undoubtedly have passed me by, and which no one else at sea that day could conceivably have prevented.

Shortly after I had tightened sheets and come round out of the lee of the island to begin my cross-passage, the rain really set in, coming at me over the port quarter and drenching the sails in sheets of water. Low cloud was scudding across my view ahead, and visibility was deteriorating. The north-westerly, now clear of the island, was blowing a squally force 5. I had no real anxiety – *Peggotty* with her heavy displacement and ample beam rather relished what to her were modest conditions. After all, I was in inshore waters with no rough seas to contend with, just surface spray and chop. If anything the rain was helping to flatten the water, and of course the tidal flow was following the wind.

My only concern was to minimise my drift out into the English Channel and make enough ground speed northwards – without having to lose pace or direction by falling away or heaving to – to keep a respectful distance from the container ships and car ferries crossing my path, passing into and out of Southampton and Portsmouth.

I was, however, very soon too far south.

Both eastern and western Outer Nab cardinal buoys had loomed off to starboard and vanished in the murk. There was also, I suddenly noticed dead ahead of me, one of those annoying black-plastic gallon bottles that fishermen use as floats for their seabed shellfish pots. Poole Bay is full of them. They are always half submerged in the current and pose a serious threat to small boats as their cord tethers can get wrapped around a propeller or caught up by a rudder, sometimes disabling a craft from any directional control or motive power.

This one was about seventy-five yards off, and had something long and thin floating nearby. Difficult to tell in such poor light and surface spray.

But hang on, I thought, this is an odd place for a fisherman's float. We were in forty metres depth of water here, and almost directly south of the Nab Channel, that narrow neck of water that takes all the deep-draught traffic in and out of the Solent. Maybe it was just a bit of jetsam – marine junk thrown overboard from a passing vessel.

Maybe.

I approached cautiously, trying to leave it to starboard rather than give way yet again. Like icebergs, these floating objects can be much larger than they appear, with sharp bits or loose cordage lurking just beneath the surface of the water. It could even be the exposed corner of a steel tank, or, heaven forbid, a jettisoned container the size of a house. A brief nudge against one of those, and old *Peggotty* would have had her planks stove in and sunk like a stone.

The narrow cigar-shaped item, greenish in colour, was clearly something of little weight, as it was bobbing up and down gently in the swell. It looked about fifteen feet in length.

The black float next to it had a rounded top, and must have been in the sea a long time because even at my distance I could make out long, dark strands of weed growth trailing off it. But as I drew nearer I could see that this globe had an attachment – what appeared to be a dark-grey tube – just breaking the surface.

It was now ten yards off, still visible intermittently as I drew level.

Instantly I recognised it for what it was, as the opposite side of my weed-covered float was revealed as a face.

A very pale face, surrounded by glistening black hair, self-evidently belonging to a girl in a full wetsuit and a black life jacket. A face with its eyes open and its mouth suddenly and soundlessly shouting at me.

Immediately I gybed all-standing, and circled back downwind of her, furling both headsails as I came up into the wind. Turning on the engine, mainsail flapping, I edged *Peggotty*'s bow slowly forward until the girl was abeam of the cockpit on the leeward side.

I reached down to her with both arms, yelling to her to stretch up and grasp my hands. She was quite incapable of doing any such thing as it was patently obvious that all strength had long since deserted her. In any case, it was a pointless instruction, as there was no way that I could have leant down so far and borne her weight up over the gunwale.

Man-overboard techniques in illustrated sail training manuals are all very well, but when the casualty can make no physical response whatever, the options are limited.

Then I noticed that the girl was attached by a long cord and wristband to the curious object floating near her, and which I now saw to be an upturned canoe or kayak.

With my boathook fully extended I could just reach under this cord, which I drew in alongside *Peggotty*'s hull and lifted, bringing the kayak easily across to the boat. I cut the cord about halfway along its length, and secured the craft to a cleat further aft.

I now had in my grip the remaining piece of cord, a physical connection with this girl that was the first of what proved to become for me a close contact of the most disturbing, emotional and yet utterly essential nature in the saving and protection of life – her life and mine.

By raising her arm from the wrist with this bit of line, the girl's shoulders at least were above the surface; and armed with the boathook and a loop formed in the starboard jib sheet, I managed to get the sheet around her under both arms, and slowly winched one end in over the side of the boat, gradually raising the girl's almost lifeless body up the topsides and then heaving her head first over the coaming on to the locker seat. To anyone with normal circulation that manoeuvre would have been agony. To this girl, completely numb from head to toe, it would have meant nothing. Until the bruises appeared the next morning.

I rearranged her powerless limbs into the recovery position along the locker seat, and face down she showed some sign of life by coughing up seawater. At this point I could see that I was going to have to concentrate all my energies on helping my casualty, so I unfurled the jib, backed the mainsail and mizzen and lashed the tiller. Nicely hove to, the movement of the boat settled and I could put my mind to the matter.

To get the poor girl dry and warm seemed to be the priority. Shedding the wetsuit, which was ripped along one thigh, must be the first essential. I dashed below and returned with my double sleeping bag and an old army blanket, which I stuffed into the companionway out of the rain.

Undressing a girl (she looked to be about twenty-two) was something to which I had become unaccustomed for at least thirty years. Upbringing and culture imposed a certain hesitancy. The zip down the back of her wetsuit jammed halfway, and I quickly realised that this was not going to come off in one piece. Once again the mariner's knife which lived in its holster on my foul-weather trousers came into service. Fortunately the inert form before me lessened the risk of injury, and I soon had the wetsuit stripped down on the cockpit sole.

My heart was beginning to thump a bit as it was then obviously necessary to peel off the next layer, a sensible all-in-one bathing costume. A mixture of prudery and what I felt would be the actions of a gentleman prompted me to adopt the same technique, and so with one slow slice up the back from thigh to neck with my knife I now had before me a body that could at last be dried and wrapped. A body which, distracted as I was by the emergency that had reared up minutes ago out of the blue (or more accurately out of the cold grey), I could yet perceive to be trim and fit.

All the protective instincts of the male were triggered within me, mind and body, and in seconds I had the quilted sleeping bag rolled twice around her, the blanket over her head and shoulders, and this human parcel bundled down the steps and on to a saloon bunk, my fleece woolly hat grabbed on the way down and planted firmly over the girl's head of long, dark hair. I fixed the canvas lee cloth to prevent her rolling out, and paused for breath.

Her eyes were closed now, but she was breathing rather grainily. I was not going to get any communication for a while, for certain.

My feverish mind then calmed a little, and I became once again aware that I was navigating and helming a small wooden boat in about the busiest commercial shipping lane of any port in Southern England.

Having been hove to for at least twenty minutes, *Peggotty* had been blown across the now slack tide a considerable distance further south-east. Off to my left, almost due west, I could now see the light on St Catherine's Point, the southernmost tip of the Isle of Wight. I was now well and truly out into the English Channel.

With a shock, I looked at my watch and found that it was

early afternoon. I had eaten no lunch, but was not hungry. More to the point, we were now being drawn into St Catherine's Deep and it was clear that the tide had just turned. The ebb westwards would begin to accelerate, and us with it, unless I chose to fight the tide and resume my reach in an attempt to regain Chichester. That would take hours, and I did not fancy taking the Chichester channel up to Birdham on a falling tide. Far too many sandbanks, and unfamiliar sailing ground so far as I was concerned. It might even be dark by then.

And what of my casualty? Where had she come from and where had she been intending to go? What if she needed serious medical assistance?

I was now in the lee of the island, off Ventnor, and was sheltered from the north-westerly wind. There was no way I was going to beat the ebb tide under sail. Had I the fuel to motor instead, back around? The old Bukh was slow and reliable, *slow* being the operative word.

No, for the moment I must tend to my patient down in the bunk. I remained hove to as best I could, and trusted to my good fortune for the tide to take me westwards. My hazy plan, such as it was a plan at all, was to complete a circumnavigation of the island clockwise, and review some form of strategy once I reached the Needles.

There was not much danger now from marine traffic, only recreational craft on a similar scale to my own, and hopefully they would keep well clear of a drifting sailing boat with no one at the helm.

I went below.

CHAPTER THREE

It was painfully apparent, as I clambered down the companionway, that my efforts to warm up this young woman had been fairly ineffective. She was shivering uncontrollably and her pale face was more drawn and white than ever. She was wide awake now, and her large round compelling eyes were staring intently up at me with an expression that indicated some kind of urgency. She was trying to whisper something to me.

"P-p-papers . . ." it sounded like, but her teeth were chattering so fast that it was hard to discern.

"I'm very much afraid", I said, "that you are suffering from hypothermia. I really think we need to get you medical help right away, and somehow get you into hospital."

I swivelled around to my nav table and reached for the VHF handset. My back was turned to her as I clicked the button for Channel 16 and unhooked the handset. I had pressed the mic button and was forming the words 'pan pan medico', the distress call to the coastguard, when from behind me came an appalling cry of anguish. I whipped around and the girl was raised up on one elbow with the other arm stretched out to me, a terrified look of appeal creasing her face. Just this little movement drained her strength totally, and she slumped back down on the mattress.

"No . . . no . . . please" came muffled and tearful from under the blanket that had fallen back across her head.

I abandoned the VHF set and knelt down on the cabin sole

by her side, wrapping an arm around her shoulders and resting my head against the blanket.

"OK – OK," I whispered, trying to calm her and to relax her violently shaking form, her tremors surely caused by more than cold water and exposure. "But we've got to get you warm."

Perhaps I could hold a cup of hot tea to her lips. Maybe warming her from the inside would help. I had no idea – I was a retired desk-bound naval officer, not a doctor. I lit the stove and put on the kettle, then poked my head outside to check that we were still in open water with no impending hazards. By now, we were well west of St Catherine's and veering away from the coastline, a good two miles off what was probably Brighstone. Hard to tell, as the rainfall was unmitigated and visibility still poor. We had gone about and were no longer hove to, so I reset the sails and tiller once again. *Peggotty* heaves to very well, and I left her to it, returning to my whistling kettle.

I got my patient, little more than a rag doll, sitting more or less upright against the bunk head, and sitting on the edge of the mattress I supported her with one arm around her back and the other with a mug of tea held tentatively to her blue lips. I had not made it too hot, as scalding her throat would not have aided her predicament, and gently gave her little sips which I was relieved to see she was able to swallow. After a few long minutes the mug was drained. So far so good.

She turned her head up to me and tried to speak again.

"The papers . . . kayak . . . please, the papers," I could just about hear her say, her teeth still chattering despite the tea. Her voice was so hoarse from seawater.

The kayak! I had forgotten all about it.

I stuffed a couple of pillows under the girl's head and lifted her down on the mattress flat on her back, covered her form with yet another blanket, and went back up to the cockpit. All this time I had never removed any of my foul-weather gear, or even my life jacket, and I was beginning to feel a trifle warm.

Anyhow, back into the rain and aft I went to see if we still had the upturned canoe with us. Sure enough, it lay alongside, idly tapping against our hull. With a bit of effort I raised one end and let the water drain from underneath as best I could. Then I hauled the thing aboard across *Peggotty*'s counter, turning it the right way up and securing its painter and the remains of the wrist line to the dinghy davits.

This was no recreational canoe or kayak. I immediately recognised the little craft as something very different. I had seen several of these in my time in the navy, and on every occasion they had been manned in grim earnest by fit young men in the Special Boat Service or the Royal Marines. These boats were designed and used for circumstances that usually comprised subterfuge and dark nights.

This one was a single, with just one open aperture and seat, the spray cover long since gone. Fore and aft of the seat position were large circular watertight hatch covers, giving access to storage holds. Several other fittings were fastened to the deck, purpose-made for equipment such as a spade, ropes and small armament boxes.

The aft hold was empty. The forward hold I opened with difficulty, needing the ship's mallet to free the hatch. Inside, after a careful search with the length of my arm, I found a stainless-steel tubular canister, the size of a spent roll of lavatory paper, and a waterproof document case sealed shut. Nothing else.

I screwed the hatches tight again and sat down in the cockpit with one of these objects in each fist.

What the hell was all this about?

I had on my hands an unknown girl suffering from exposure, who was nonetheless excessively anxious not to be placed in safe medical care, and whose primary concern was the retrieval of certain papers – no doubt those which I now held in my hand.

A girl, moreover, who at present was wholly incapable of giving me any explanation. I did not even know her name.

With a quick glance around me to check that *Peggotty* was shipshape and that we were clear of potential hazards, I took my two discoveries back down the companionway steps to see how my mysterious invalid was faring, cocooned as she was in all my bedclothes and prone in my bunk.

I had hoped that the tremors and shakes would have calmed down and that the warmth of the wrappings would have begun to relax her, but this was not the case. Her eyes were closed and her breathing staccato.

I put my hand down inside the sleeping bag, but the air inside was not warm. Clearly her body was not generating enough heat to produce the microclimate in which she could recover. I unwrapped her feet at the other end, and felt her ankles and toes. So cold.

I had some long thick hiking socks in my clothes locker and rolled these on and up her legs, almost reaching her knees.

What next? I was beginning to wonder about my wider responsibility. What if she died on me and I had failed to alert the coastguard or summon any kind of professional assistance? It was not as though we were marooned somewhere out in mid-Atlantic. This was the Isle of Wight, for goodness' sake, and within about six minutes of a coastal rescue-helicopter call-out. I could be in serious trouble.

And yet, her desperate insistence earlier on not to make that distress call, which consumed all her remaining energy and physical resources, must have meant it was of overwhelming importance to her.

Then I remembered something from my training days in Dartmouth all those years ago, part of the sessions on survival techniques and life-raft recovery after 'abandon ship'.

But if I was to adopt this course of action one thing was abundantly clear. We could not go drifting on down-Channel with no one on the helm or keeping lookout. We had to anchor up somewhere, and soon. I inspected the chart and my GPS position.

I was about five miles south of Compton Bay. If I headed north, I could make Freshwater Bay and a safe anchorage there, well protected from the continuing north-westerly. Mind made up, I fired the engine, dropped and gathered in the mainsail, and, steadied under jib and mizzen, motored north as fast as the old Bukh would take us, pushing 6 knots.

Mercifully, the rain at last was easing, and off to my left a bright sun was playing hide and seek with the cloud that was beginning to break up into a separated cumulus pattern. Whenever the sun appeared, the summer warmth flooded out like the beam of a lighthouse. After a while I shed my oilskin trousers. I was starting to feel rather hot, and this was not unintentional as my planned survival technique began to take form in my mind.

Freshwater Bay itself is a delightful semicircle of water fronting the long glass veranda of the white hotel at the top of the beach. On a falling tide, however, some nasty rocks around its fringe begin to break the surface, and for a deep-draught boat I thought it prudent to drop anchor a little outside. There were several dinghies zipping about, a sailboard or two, and a splendid kite surfer performing aerobatics in the air as he shot to and fro along the shoreline, barely skimming the tops of the little wavelets.

I hoisted my black anchorage ball up over the foredeck, and took myself below.

* * * *

At this point in my recording of these events I must admit to some reluctance in describing what followed, in a medium as public as a book. As I write under my own name, I'm conscious of some sensitivity over how my actions may be construed by my readers – not least those who know me well. I do so, however, in the interests of historical accuracy and in setting out truthfully my close engagement with the wider developments that unfolded over the days to come.

Down in the cabin the girl appeared drowsy, but awake. Drowsy, or semi-conscious in a more serious sense, I was in no position to diagnose. The shaking had stopped. She was very still now, and deathly white. Her face and hands were cold to my touch.

Concentrating hard on my inner assurance that what I was about to do was merely standard Royal Navy training instruction, I stripped off all my outer clothing, quickly unwrapped the naked girl from her blankets, and climbed into the double sleeping bag alongside her. As best I could I then packed the two blankets once again around our cocoon, and propped on one elbow looked into her quite expressionless dark-blue eyes.

"Please don't misunderstand what I'm doing," I said. "I am a naval officer, and I am following routine technique for restoring warmth to you in the only way that is now going to be effective." At least, that is what I had carefully prepared myself to say; I cannot remember quite how well I stuck to my script. I was in new territory and frankly quite out of my depth.

Anyhow, with that I gently and carefully intertwined my arms and legs around the girl and resting my cheek against her head, closed my eyes and tried to breathe slowly.

For a moment I thought I had left the old engine ticking over in neutral, but I realised that what I could hear was my heart going clump clump against my chest in a most disconcerting manner.

Within about ten minutes or so we were both fast asleep.

CHAPTER FOUR

I woke to a bright light shining straight into my eyes. A cabin porthole had aligned itself precisely with the late evening sun, now low in the west. I had not moved a muscle since falling asleep, and was feeling a bit stiff in the limbs. I tried adjusting my position slightly without disturbing Sleeping Beauty next to me, but she too opened her eyes. I could see that she took a few seconds to fathom her location, as a light frown creased her forehead. Then her eyes cleared; she looked up at me with the glimmer of a smile, let out a small sigh and closed her eyes again.

Somewhat mixed emotions began to assail me at that moment. Every aspect of my settled, conventional life swam before me in my mind's eye. If my dear wife, Anne, or any other of my family or friends could have seen me now, I did not think I would have survived the mortification and embarrassment.

"This is not what it seems".

And yet. And yet. Surely, I was just responding in an officially sanctioned procedure to a desperate emergency. There was also, I reasoned to myself, the motive born of a biological, genetic instinct to surround and hold small, vulnerable persons, to intervene physically between them and a known danger – such a person was, here and now, mine alone to protect from mortal peril, and from the terror that had lain behind her eyes when I had attempted to contact the outside world.

Mere yards from the shore of a popular holiday resort, from

which only hours ago I had heard the happy, carefree sounds of children playing on the beach, this beguiling person and I shared an isolated world entirely of our own, here in the warm, dark panelled saloon cabin of an old wooden boat idly rocking like a baby's cradle in the gentle swell of the sea. We could just as well have been on the fringe of a desert island thousands of miles from human habitation.

With considerable logistical difficulties, I gradually untangled myself from the intimate embrace of limbs and torsos and slid out of the sleeping bag on to the cabin sole. I was hot, and the temperature under all those coverings had been like that of a greenhouse in June for several hours. My girl (my girl?) had certainly been infused with all that heat. Her calves, under the socks, were warm to the touch and her face had gained colour and life. The small of her back, against which I had lain, was glowing with a thin film of perspiration.

I put my jersey back on, gave myself a moment or two to cool off, and tried to set my brain into a semblance of normality.

So I filled the kettle.

While sitting in contemplation as the water boiled, my glance took in the two items I had salvaged from the kayak and which now lay on the saloon table. Out of curiosity I examined each one. The document case was of thick dark-blue plastic, its flap closed with a small steel lock, the closure reinforced with strong sticky tape taken right around the body of the case in two strips. The tape had a logo on it, repeated several times along its length. This was a circle with the letters 'AWE' within it, topped by a small crown, and 'Ministry of Defence' in small print around its rim.

The canister was not heavy. It felt empty, except that when I shook it there was a feather-light movement of something small inside. It was closed with a screw cap of the same diameter as the tube, and was of polished stainless steel, perhaps with a double skin like a Thermos.

The closure was also sealed with sticky tape around its rim. However, the logo this time was the much more familiar one we all see in hospitals on the doors of X-ray departments – a three-bladed propeller shape in red on a yellow background, warning of the danger of radiation exposure.

I wedged the canister securely into my bookcase on the forward bulkhead, where it would not roll about. Rather absurdly, I suppose, I then washed my hands.

My recovering patient was breathing easily and regularly, lying on her back and well asleep, her mouth slightly open and one graceful arm back behind her head. She looked so peaceful and calm, her face a good deal more healthful, framed in salty black hair – frown-free and smooth now with a faint blush on both cheeks. Who on earth was she, this little lone figure who had so suddenly barged in on my middle-aged existence? What can she have been doing, paddling a commando kayak in a shipping lane with such peculiar cargo in its hold?

I then spotted the time on my watch. At this time of day it was my unwavering practice to telephone home to assure my wife and family that I was still on the water, not under it; to hear the family news; and to catch up with essential domestic administration.

Whatever was I going to say to Anne this evening? I began to ponder what I should report and what I ought to gloss over. One thing that I would certainly do is tell her the truth, and as frankly as possible. Part of the secret of our happy marriage has always been honesty with each other, even when it has put either of us in a bad light. I was not going to be tempted to depart from this discipline now, just to save myself embarrassment or chaff from my faithful and loving life partner. No, I must just state the bald facts fully and frankly, and trust that they would be received in the same spirit.

I somewhat nervously switched on my mobile phone and pressed the button earmarked 'Anne'.

"Hello, my love. It's me. Just reporting in." Oh well, here goes – out with it. "Um, all well at home, darling?"

"Yes, dear, we're fine. Hope you've had a nice day" came the response from my wife.

I cleared my throat. "Actually, my love, I need to tell you that I have been landed with a passenger. She's a young lady who at present is lying down on my bunk in my sleeping bag. I've been trying to—"

"Oh yes, dear?" interrupted Anne. "And I picked up a toy boy in Wareham Market this morning, and we are both having a high old time together in the Priory Hotel. Now, dear, do be serious and listen for a minute because I want you to do something for me and this mobile phone call will be getting expensive. While you are in Chichester, do you think you could look up that nice couple we met at Geoffrey's, who live in West Street. You know, the people with the Labrador puppy. I am hoping they will be able to—"

It was my turn to interrupt. "Sorry, my love, but I'm not in Chichester. I'm at anchor in Freshwater Bay. Events today have not panned out quite as I intended. I—"

"Well, never mind, dear. So long as you are having a nice time. Must dash now, because Sarah's just come in and we're going to Margery's for supper. Speak again tomorrow evening. Lots of love. Bye."

"Anne, darling, I really have to expl—" But she had hung up.

CHAPTER FIVE

"My name is Naomi," she said, a mellifluous alliteration of utmost charm in such an incongruous setting.

She was sitting up in bed now, dressed in one of my long-sleeved shirts and a Donegal sweater (and the hiking socks). The fleece hat had been discarded, and she had swept her hair back behind her neck in a loose knot.

I had made us both bowls of porridge with plenty of muscovado sugar, and mugs of milky coffee. Her white hands were wrapped tightly around her hot mug and were clearly still suffering from poor circulation.

I sat down on the edge of her bunk and waited.

"I need to tell you that I am in great danger." A pause while she gathered her thoughts and gazed a moment through the porthole at the lights of the Freshwater Hotel flittering on the surface of the bay. "I was trying to escape from being followed." A thought struck her. "Do we still have the kayak?"

I nodded.

"The best thing now would be for me to have drowned."

I started to protest at this appalling idea, but she interrupted. "No, no, I mean it would be best if they thought I had drowned, back there off Spithead."

"You mean if they – whoever *they* are – found the kayak upside down with no one in it floating out at sea . . ."

"Yes, exactly." She was beginning to look animated now, this idea dredging up some new energy at last in her expression, her eyes showing something like excitement.

I thought about this. We ourselves in *Peggotty* had more or less drifted with wind and tide hove-to all the way from the Outer Nab around to the point five miles south of us where I started the engine. It was reasonable to suppose that a floating fifteen-foot object might have followed a similar course.

"We could dump the kayak south of here," I said, "and just hope that it looks convincing, assuming of course that the kayak is found. But surely it's more likely to be picked up by someone and reported to the authorities, the coastguard or the police, if it looks as though it was connected with a tragedy of some kind?"

She put a finger on her chin and looked me in the eye. "If so, the people following me would be the first to be informed. There are insiders. I had better explain the whole thing." Naomi stared down into her empty coffee mug. "Did you say you were in the navy?" After a short silence: "What if I'm walking straight into the trap now, with you?"

I said nothing. What could I say? Then I grasped her misunderstanding.

"I'm not in the navy now; I retired more than six years ago. All I can say to you, Naomi, is that you can trust me with your life. I've done my best in that line already," I assured her with a smile, risking a wink at her serious face as she looked up at me in mute and uncertain appeal. "I guess this is my cue to tell you all about me," I continued.

She lay back on the pillows and watched me.

For the next ten minutes I gave her the outline of my present situation – my family, my holiday in *Peggotty*, the picture that I hope I have given my readers in the first chapter of this book. When I had said all that I thought she would like to know, I made to rise from my seat on her bunk, to pick up the porridge bowls and mugs that were strewn around us. Before I could do so, however, a most touching thing happened. Naomi put out her hand, gripped my own and gave me a slow and formal handshake.

I am not an unduly emotional man, but as I turned away towards the galley my eyes were distinctly moist. I needed a discreet wipe with my handkerchief before I could concentrate on the washing-up.

It was now night, and as I tidied up it dawned on me that if we were to jettison the kayak effectively as a decoy, we ought to get on with it. The tide would turn and the position of the abandoned craft look less convincing. But how were we going to put these mysterious shadowy hunters properly off the scent? We needed to provide a clue or two that the boat had not merely been abandoned, but that its occupant and indeed the contents of its storage compartment had come to a sticky end and were not worth further searching.

I put this to Naomi, proposing that we defer her own life story until we had made a decoy plan and put it into action. With this she readily agreed, and immediately had an idea.

She reached for the document case and used my bosun's knife to ease the lock. She then carefully peeled back the 'AWE' tapes and opened the flap. There were several typed papers inside, which she extracted. Then, looking around her, she had what later proved to be a God-sent inspiration to slip them into one of my stack of folded charts, which lived in a rack above the navigation table.

Hardly following what she had in mind, I was persuaded then to part with some sheets of closely typed instructions from an electronics manual, which she inserted into the document case, re-securing the lock and restoring the adhesive tapes back around the flap.

To my astonishment she began to bite and chew one lower corner of the case until there was a sizeable hole with rough nibbled edges. She then poured some water from the galley tap in through the hole and wringing and scrunching the plastic case around for a minute or so, soon had the paper contents in soggy tatters, the printed typeface running in blotchy smears and entirely illegible.

"A few more hours submerged in seawater and visited by inquisitive and hungry fish and this paperwork will be unidentifiable," she explained.

I stared at Naomi in undisguised admiration. This girl knew

what she was doing.

I drew her attention next to the steel canister in my bookcase, challenging her with a slightly raised eyebrow to think of a clever solution to that as well. I was just beginning to feel a trifle superfluous.

Naomi shook her head. "We don't need to worry about the plutonium can. They have no idea that I got hold of that as well."

So that was all right then. One less bit of incriminating evidence to obliterate—

I sat up so suddenly that the back of my head took a sharp knock on the deckhead. "What did you just say?" I gasped. "A can of PLUTONIUM? What the hell—?"

She gave me a rather tired smile and ran her fingers through her hair. "It's rather a long story, I'm afraid. But don't panic, it's a triple-skin vacuum flask designed for transporting the stuff. We won't be glowing in the dark."

Don't panic, she said. Just as well my earlier curiosity had not extended to unscrewing the lid and poking my nose inside.

I turned to matters more within my comfort zone. "Well, I guess we had better slip away south under cover of darkness and ditch this kayak. Somehow we need to set it up to make it look as though you had a fatal accident."

We both went up into the cockpit. It was a clear starry night sky overhead.

"Here, you had better put these on," I said, pulling a pair of old jeans out of the locker as we went. "You do look a sight."

She struck a comical figure there in the starlight, shirted and jerseyed above but bereft of anything else but a pair of thick hiker's stockings up to the knee. Rather fetching, I have to admit, but refrained from saying so.

Then I spotted the remnants of Naomi's wetsuit and bathing costume lying in a heap on the cockpit sole. I had an idea.

First of all we unscrewed the forward hatch cover on the kayak and pushed the now defaced document case back inside. The hatch cover itself I then slammed down on to a heavy bronze fairlead protruding from the counter deck, causing the fibreglass cover to split along one radius. With some effort, I bent the break until a slither like a modest cake slice snapped off. With my heavy hammer I created another crack and damage to the rim of the hatch itself, and we twisted the circular cover tightly back in place on to the kayak's foredeck. To all intents and purposes the little craft now appeared to have met with a serious collision and sustained a prompt demise. Not at all an unlikely scenario in the Nab Channel shipping lane.

The wetsuit, already neatly carved open with my knife down its spine and backside, proved more difficult to counterfeit as tragedy evidence. Convincingly ripping that thick rubberised fabric was beyond my strength.

Naomi found the answer. Tying the leggings together around *Peggotty*'s boom, and the arms around the gaff, she slowly winched the two gaff halyards upwards, having tightened the main sheet to hold the boom fully down.

The winches objected a little, but with the levers we cautiously wound them up until with a most satisfying release, the wetsuit split diagonally into two sections.

One of these we wedged and trapped on a butterfly clip used for adjusting the kayak seat position, to make it look as though it had caught there after a life-and-death struggle by its occupant to escape.

There was not a lot more we could think of. We just hoped that anyone finding this reconstructed wreckage would conclude that without the protection of a wetsuit the canoeist would long since have perished from exposure and was now drifting submerged, bloated and half eaten by scavenging fish towards the coast of France.

* * * *

We weighed anchor, and slipped away from Freshwater under engine and jib, running due south. I reckoned that the now rising tide would carry us a little south-east to a spot five miles off that which might reasonably have been where the kayak could be expected to have reached of its own accord.

A small fleet of coastal fishing boats crossed our path heading west, their green starboard lamps blinking in the rise and fall of the Channel swell. Otherwise, we were alone on the water, and judging that we had gone far enough we stopped the engine and listened. Nothing but the slosh of the broken sea surface against *Peggotty*'s hull, and the north-westerly singing gently in her rigging. No thump of any approaching ship, no lights but the stars and a weak rising moon.

Between us, Naomi and I untied the kayak from the dinghy davits, and, turning it upside down once more, slid it quietly off *Peggotty*'s counter and into the water. It lay there on the surface for a moment, and then with bubbles of air curving up from either side the little green cigar shape settled into the swell, its back just awash, and we slowly parted company. When it was barely visible any longer, I fired the engine and we retraced our way north again to the Freshwater anchorage.

I was beginning to feel slightly paranoid about being watched by powers and dominions invisible to myself, but at least on dropping anchor once again in Freshwater Bay I could be reasonably confident that no one onshore was likely to have noticed our surreptitious departure and discreet return. Comforted by the thought, I made up a bed in a fo'c'sle bunk, leaving the saloon, shower and heads to my most intriguing passenger, and sank into a sleep that was repeatedly disturbed by vivid and unsettling dreams throughout the remainder of the night. Some of these were dark and disturbing scenarios of a ludicrous nature, no doubt based on snippets of old spy films and television dramas dredged from my subconscious. But another, no less unsettling, was of an ill-defined crisis of some kind, an imminent danger not to myself but to a shadowy companion whose life depended on me, in some dimly understood setting where I knew I had no choice but to remain.

I awoke blearily and saw by my watch that it was four thirty in the morning. I tossed and turned for a bit, but could not settle again. Casting off yesterday's clothing, I crept silently up through the fore hatch and plunged into the water for an energetic swim around the hull of the boat. The night was fading and the glimmer of a backlit pale-blue sky was beginning to throw St Catherine's Point into shadowed relief over in the east.

What adventure was the new day to bring?

CHAPTER SIX

Refreshed by my bathe, and in overdue clean clothes, I soon shook off my restless night's sleep and trod softly through the saloon to the galley stove, to make an early morning cup of tea and search around for the makings of breakfast for two. Naomi was still completely out for the count, curled up on her side under a mound of bedclothes, my sweater, shirt and jeans lying haphazard on the bunk and saloon table where she had discarded them last night.

I stole the luxury of contemplating her small round face in total repose, framed now by shining black locks after a freshwater shower before she had gone to bed. She hardly looked like a warrior, but maybe there was just something barely definable about the set of her chin on the pillow which hinted at the character of this girl behind her outward femininity – a depth of determination and courage of which I had already seen impressive evidence in the space of little more than twelve hours since she had cannoned into my solitary holiday idyll.

I was still no closer to knowing anything about her, who she was, from whom she was escaping, or why.

Yesterday's cold weather had vanished with the atmospheric low as it had moved overnight across the coast of Belgium and the Netherlands. It was a beautiful sunny morning, the wind backing to the south-west in a warm force 3. Our anchorage was now exposed, and *Peggotty* was gently rolling in the choppy wavelets that were developing from the direction of the Needles. We would need to move on, but where were we going next? It was clearly time to awaken my companion and enquire.

The grilling of bacon in a pan only a yard from her nose did the trick; and with prominent discretion on my part to keep my eyes firmly on the stove and grill pan while Naomi slipped from her bunk, she was quickly united once more with my shirt and trousers and I turned to greet her "Good morning" with a welcoming smile.

I sat her down at the table with bacon, eggs and strong ground coffee. Sitting opposite her with resolutely folded arms, I began.

"Now, my enigmatic young lady, a little explanation, if you please. I need to know my next holiday destination. East, west or south? And ought we to call in at a chandlery to buy a gun for the foredeck?" I was being flippant, of course, trying to lighten the mood of yesterday's crisis in the hope that Naomi would relax enough to open up to me. "Maybe we should start with you telling me who you are and what on earth you were doing in a Special Boat Service commando kayak off Spithead."

She looked at me quickly then, with a quizzical raise of her eyebrows. "So you're familiar with specialist naval equipment?"

"Naturally," I replied. "I've spent much of my career signing chits requisitioning that kind of thing. I was posted to the USA as a principal purchasing officer, weighing the competing merits of everything from kayaks to cranes."

"The USA?" she said. "Did you ever have dealings with a government facility in South Carolina?"

I shook my head. "South Carolina? No. Never been there. Why Carolina?"

"Oh, well, nothing. Just wondered." She paused before continuing. "I have to be so careful in what I tell you. It's not that I don't trust you or anything, but I have certain obligations – official ones – that prohibit me from being frank."

"You mean the Official Secrets Act? Why, are you a civil servant?"

"Well, sort of. Something like that. But the other thing is that the less you know, the lower the risks you yourself might face if this all goes horribly wrong." She gathered her thoughts. "Do you remember back in 2006 the case of that Russian, Alexander Litvinenko, who was irradiated by polonium-210, slipped into his drink by God knows who – probably some undercover Russian agent? He had ten micrograms in his body – 200 times the lethal dose. If ingested or breathed in, its alpha emissions depositing on the lining of the lung cause fatal damage. It is not the first time the stuff has been used to bump people off. It's very hard to detect in medical diagnosis, and its radioactivity fades quite fast – to a small fraction of its original after a couple of years. Also it's easy to transport undetected, as it does not trigger screening alarms at airports. Anyway, the finger of suspicion for sourcing this material points to Russian operatives posing as economic émigrés settling in England. London is filling up with those who have made a fortune under the sell-off of Russian state industries some years ago. No one knows whether these operatives are agents of government, or whether they act for criminal organisations quite outside political direction. However, one thing that looks increasingly likely is that the polonium was stolen from one or other of Russia's secret closed nuclear processing or manufacturing bases, such as Sarov.

"Now, the point I'm getting to is that uranium and plutonium are also stored at the sites, and are finding their way into the hands of people who act without scruple in achieving their ends, through blackmail, extortion, threats of mass annihilation, and assassination. Only a few milligrams of plutonium-239, emitting gamma rays and beta particles, is lethal to human tissue on a wide scale."

I glanced nervously at the bookcase on the cabin bulkhead.

"By the way, none of what I am telling you is secret or confidential. You can read all this on Wikipedia.

"I am involved – and I can't say more than that – in tracking three guys who are known to have murdered by irradiation a high-ranking Ukrainian Army officer, who was over here for a specialist operation in a private hospital in Southampton.

Before he even got there, he was dead in his hotel bedroom with minute traces of the dull yellow dust of plutonium oxide inside his pyjamas.

"To cut a long story short, our complete dossier on analysis, identification and associated links for this crime is there in your chart rack," (here she ran the back of her hand across her forehead and grimaced) "and those guys know I've got it. And they saw me."

Impulsively I reached across the table and took hold of her hands. Her large, dark, troubled eyes met mine.

'How can she possibly be so young?' I asked myself.

She continued: "If those men are agents for any foreign government, and not just some terrorist outfit, their influences and resources at every political and security level – yes, even here in the UK – put me in serious danger. I had clearance to the Royal Marines' equipment depot in Gosport, so I chose my moment, took the kayak and put as much Solent water between me and my pursuers as I could. Unfortunately, I was upended by the wash of a Condor twin-hull car ferry, and you know the rest."

Naomi visibly deflated then, and slumped back against the bench cushion, quite exhausted from her harrowing narrative.

Without a second thought I was round by her side, and put an arm around her shoulders. There we sat in silence for a long time, as her internal spring gradually unwound and her taut frame slowly relaxed.

I was certain at that precise moment that I was shortly about to enter with this girl a place of the darkest foreboding.

* * * *

Continued evasion from discovery was obviously our first priority. Naomi might be spotted by someone – anyone – who was working in league with the pursuing miscreants, and not self-evidently people to be avoided. Besides, she had only seen the three men briefly on two occasions and was not confident that she would necessarily recognise them again.

The safest move, for the moment, was to stay at sea and, if

we had to call in somewhere to re-provision, for her to remain below out of sight.

I remembered something my father used to say when we were children. We lived then only five miles from Dartmoor Prison, and back in the 1960s there was a spate of prisoner escapes which became something of a bogeyman to the residents of nearby villages and the local town of Tavistock.

"Don't worry," he used to reassure us, "the closer we live to the prison the safer we are. Jail-breakers are not going to hang around the locality – they will be getting as far away as possible and as quickly as they can."

I suggested to Naomi that we adopt the same principle, but counter-intuitively and as a bluff. The safest place for us would be Spithead and the Solent, and in plain daylight to sail back east and north. Any search party, official or otherwise, would be concentrating miles away mid-Channel for signs of a kayak or a wreck; and the pursuers themselves, assuming that they had discovered her mode of escape by water, would also be focusing their own search on land – either the Isle of Wight or the coast of the mainland.

Whether by coastguard authorities, the MCA, or by the foreign agents, the best immediate outcome would undoubtedly be the discovery of the kayak wreck that we had – rather ingeniously, I thought – planted with false clues. If Naomi were presumed dead, and the incriminating but unrecognisable documents were clearly still on board, surely any pursuer or rescuer with malign motives would conclude that further search was futile, and the heat would then be off.

So, with this plan in mind, we once again left our anchorage at Freshwater and set sail back east. The wind was now steady from west-south-west at force 3 – perfect conditions for old *Peggotty*, who like most gaffers preferred a good broad reach or run to slogging close-hauled into the wind with a sea on her nose.

Naomi soon showed that she was no stranger to a sailing boat, and in a trice we had the main, staysail and jib well out on their sheets, and the mizzen balancing the helm nicely. We gathered way to more than 6 knots under a bare blue sky and a hot sun, and I began to relax back into a state of mind and body with which I was once more familiar and in my element. Now, however, my inner equilibrium had the added exhilaration of companionship with this young person sitting alongside, her presence with me quite relaxed in our mutual recognition that she was less than half my age.

We both wordlessly accepted that while I could offer vigilant shelter from her enemies, in my physical custodianship the reserved and honourable course for me could surely be little more than fatherlike.

* * * *

We had run well south of St Catherine's Point by lunchtime, and were hove-to enjoying the sunshine and eating apples and cheese, sprawled comfortably on the cockpit benches. Naomi had done the best she could to sunbathe in men's clothing. Her arms and legs were as exposed as she could get them, by rolling up her sleeves and trouser legs as far as they would go. We were beginning to feel pleasantly drowsy, and I was having difficulty in keeping my eyes open.

Abruptly, I was awake and alert. Over off our port quarter the tranquillity was broken by the unmistakable sound of a helicopter engine, the noise rapidly increasing in volume.

It was coming towards us from the south, straight out of the sun, a dark object quite low over the water. It certainly wasn't a Westland Sea King. I was well acquainted with the sound of that engine from my days on a base for the Royal Navy Search and Rescue Service. This had a much higher note, and as I shaded my eyes into the sun I could see that it was a small two-seater.

Five hundred yards off, it changed direction to the west and after a couple of minutes turned south again, then east. It was manifestly following a search grid pattern, and I knew what for.

As the helicopter approached us once more, my blood ran a little chilly. I now had a clear view of the machine. This was no reassuring red-and-white air/sea rescue aircraft that saves lives. This was a diminutive dull black beetle-like gizmo of utterly sinister aspect, its spherical windscreen of darkened glass and its identification markings so worn and obscured as to be unreadable.

This time it kept coming, heading in a straight line for *Peggotty*. I whipped round and opened my mouth to yell at Naomi, instantly realising the possible implications of her being spotted by the helicopter pilot.

But the starboard bench was empty. Her wits had been quicker than mine, and she was already down through the companionway and safely out of sight in the cabin.

I retrieved my own wits, such as they were, and with slow deliberate nonchalance lay back again on the bench, grabbed an apple from the lunch box and took a large bite. The machine was now only 100 yards off and about to fly overhead. I turned my face up towards it with an expression that I hoped would approximate to innocent curiosity, and gave it a little wave as it passed above our masts.

The little black beetle shortly made a steeply banked turn with a raucous clatter of engine and rotors, ripping up the surface of the sea in a flurry of spray, and took off eastwards, once again resuming its grid search some two or three miles astern of us.

We stayed as we were for about half an hour, slowly drifting hove-to eastwards. By then the helicopter had become a speck and disappeared into the distance. We resumed our passage, now in this early afternoon accompanied at long range by one or two other yachts, their white sails conspicuous against the blue of sea and sky. A powerful modern white motor cruiser, ugly and ungainly with its un-nautical hogged sheerline, raced westwards, bouncing from one swell peak to the next, leaving a long straight cream wake like a gash across the skin of the English Channel.

Such normality and such repellent menace, all sharing our horizon from *Peggotty* on that summer's day, were hardly my idea of a sailing holiday. Still, there was one saving grace, and she was down in the cabin watching the kettle boil.

CHAPTER SEVEN

I decided to take a broader reach and head south-east for a few hours. The longer we were at sea the better, at least until we had been able somehow to ascertain if Naomi had been reported missing and there was some official conclusion. We would then have a better idea of how a plan of action could be reached, both for her safety and for the completion of her mission, whatever that entailed.

We had Channel 16 on VHF continuously open, to pick up any alert that the kayak had been found by a passing vessel; and we listened to all the regular news reports on Radio Solent and Radio 4. So far there had been nothing at all.

And then, at about half past four in the afternoon, our luck was in.

I was just discussing with my crew member the merits of making a gybe and heading up north towards the Solent, when away to the south we saw and heard once again the appearance of a helicopter. This time there was no mistaking the HM Coastguard markings on what, through my binoculars, I identified as a Bristow Sikorsky S-92 in red-and-white livery. As we strained our eyes to make out at that distance what was going on, the helicopter remained poised in the air, like a kestrel that has sighted its prey, and then slowly lost height vertically until it became partially obscured by blown spray from its rotor downdraught. It then ascended again slightly and out of its side door a helmeted crew member began gradually to be let down on a cable. A minute or two of confused water and vision veiled by surface disturbance, and once more the crewman appeared, rising up on his cable, and dangling below him on a hanging strap a long green cigar-shaped object trailing a piece of black material.

I set down my binoculars, and looked round into the smiling gratified face of my companion in deception. Naomi's blue eyes were dancing with relief, and impulsively she reached out and gave me a bear hug.

Before I could think, speak, or in any way prompt my brain to engage I let go the tiller, wrapped both arms around her and hugged her in consoling response. How far this was merely fatherlike, I cannot honestly say.

In a moment, I had let her go. Here I have to stress that this was not so much an emergency act of conscience, but more the fact that in abandoning the helm I had let *Peggotty* come rapidly round into the wind and all four sails with their sheets were now thrashing to and fro, their heavy old wooden pulley blocks flailing around in a demented dance, at least two of them threatening any second to wallop one or both of us on the side of the head and into oblivion.

With the helm hard down I set the jib to get our bow round and to fall away back on course, the sails full once more and their sheets and tackle back in tight repose.

"Well, I guess all we have to do now is wait for the find to be reported by the coastguard to the police," I said, "and a bit longer for the news to be picked up by the local media. Then with a crumb of good fortune your murderous friends will draw the conclusions we want them to."

"I think they will do more than that," Naomi replied in a sober tone. "I'm pretty sure that with their web of connections they will have little difficulty in getting access to the kayak and taking a very close look. After all, they know – and the authorities have no idea – that their real target of interest will be the document case in the waterlogged forward compartment." She glanced at me, seeking some reassurance from my own expression. "The crunch factor will be whether they believe that the papers inside are the original contents. If so, that gives me a breathing space." Her hand closed over mine in an instinctive search for comfort. "Whether they will believe me drowned is another matter. If they are unconvinced of that, I'm still a marked woman. They've seen me, and they know I've seen them."

She gazed unfocused out to the horizon.

"You see, our government alongside France and the Yanks are allies of the Ukrainian state. They will do all they can to ensure continued independence of Ukraine as a buffer against the growing militarism of Russia. The assassination of their four-star general in England is a major embarrassment.

"Our lot will leave no stone unturned to discover the culprits – I mean, that's what I and a number of other personnel were tasked to do. That's why I'm here. I shouldn't really be telling you all this." Her jubilation over the locating of the kayak was starting to wane.

How was I to offer any sort of consolation or means of reaching safety? What could I do? This whole game was well out of my league. 'There must be a lot more to Naomi than meets the eye,' I reasoned to myself. She was some kind of 'personnel', to use her own word. How does a woman in her early twenties get to be commissioned into this cloak-and-dagger stuff? On behalf of whom? And she had hinted that even the UK authorities might be compromised by infiltration by these malign agents. Who was she answerable to, and were they on the right side? It struck me that this international espionage business was nothing but a nightmare for all concerned, and here was I, truly an 'innocent abroad', sailing right into the thick of it in the company of someone whom I must presume to be an expert. Was my sense of responsibility for her entirely misplaced – merely some paternal response on my part occasioned by nothing more than the chasmal difference in our ages?

I was conflicted in myself as to how I saw my involvement in this extraordinary affair being brought to an end. I could of course make for a convenient harbour or marina this evening or tomorrow morning, and simply wave Naomi goodbye, leaving her ashore with my good wishes, shirt and trousers, and that would be that. I could resume my holiday and make for Chichester as if nothing out of the ordinary had ever occurred. It would just be an amusing anecdote for my nightly phone conversation with Anne at home, although there had been some aspects of this adventure – Royal Navy survival methods in particular – on which I would no doubt have maintained a prudent silence.

These had nothing to do with respecting Naomi's professional confidentiality. I was mentally censoring from my imagined call home certain risks of inevitable misunderstanding. They would have to wait for more opportune explanation on my eventual return to the bosom of my family, where I might justifiably expect much mirth and ridicule from four daughters, and only a little less from my dear wife.

In the event, however, my interior debate as to an exit strategy from this spy story was to be shattered long before the various options had even properly formed in my mind.

The course of action which had the most immediate appeal was to find some prompt refuge in which we might plan a practical resolution to this affair, but maybe also some continued company for both *Peggotty* and me as we cruised the coastline under the summer sun.

This was to be more than fulfilled.

CHAPTER EIGHT

When I had set off the previous day from Newtown, I had imagined that by now *Peggotty* would be on a quiet mooring off the village of Birdham up the estuary from Chichester Harbour, and that I would have walked round into Itchenor or taken the bus to the city with my shopping bags.

In the event, we were now getting very low on provisions. We also, I realised, needed to get poor Naomi some clothes. My shirt and jeans were one thing, but offering her my spare underpants was distinctly beyond the pale.

We discussed together the best choice of immediate destination. I was trying to put myself in the shoes of her pursuers. They had a rather wide field of search, and as they were so few in number it was inevitable that in any one location their hunt would have to be fairly cursory. Time was not on their side to intervene between Naomi and the authorities that she would presumably be trying to reach with the explosive information in her possession.

My 'Dartmoor prisoner' principle held good, but it was also going to be prudent for us to become just another tree in the forest, to take another analogy. We wanted to be inconspicuous, and to go where there were plenty of other boats and plenty of other people.

We set sail for Cowes.

The tide was with us through Spithead and into the Solent, but the wind was on our nose. We had the late afternoon and evening ahead of us in daylight, but I was anxious to make our next berth or mooring before dark. This was not the stage for a dawdling close-hauled beat back around the island shoreline. We furled the foresails, tightened the mainsail sheet and motored at a fair pace westwards, occasionally catching an offshore breeze in the Ryde Roads to fill the mainsail and give us an extra knot of speed.

In good time we reached the entrance to the Medina river. The marinas of Cowes itself were heaving with craft of all shapes and sizes gearing up for the regatta due to kick off in a day or so. Corporate banners, in the ubiquitous vertical Nepalese style, fluttered in profusion from quayside and pontoon; ensigns, courtesy flags and pennants of all colours of the rainbow flapped and snapped in the wind; little launches and RIBs scuttled about in earnest busyness. The great red-and-white Southampton car ferry was just ahead of us, ponderous and imperious, nudging towards her rubber-lined berthing cradle wholly immune from the frenetic activity of glass fibre, Dacron and outboards littering the surface of the water around her hull.

I quickly realised that there would be no hope whatever of obtaining an unbooked mooring that night anywhere in West or East Cowes. We kept going into the Medina, one among a dozen other boats also heading upriver. We had to hold steady into the ebb tide for a minute or so to allow the 'floating bridge', a smart, shiny new version since my last visit, to rattle across our bows on its chains, and I then edged *Peggotty* upstream into the quieter water of the industrial shoreline, almost instantly leaving the razzamataz of Cowes behind us. Another couple of hundred yards, and one would never have known all that excitement aft of us had ever existed.

We dropped the mainsail and motored slowly up towards the Folly Inn on our left bank. This has been a favourite haunt of mine for several years. Lying off the frontage of the pub and operated by the local council is a walkway and pontoon used by a water taxi to take folk down to West Cowes, and down the centre of the Medina river a row of further floating pontoons, some of which are for visiting boats.

I have never found these visitor berths fully taken, and on this occasion my hunch proved to be correct. There were plenty of spaces. We pitched out our starboard fenders and slotted *Peggotty* neatly on to a pontoon, securing her with warps fore and aft and in springs in proper Bristol fashion. We settled the berthing fee with the man in the launch, as the sun began to set behind the gigantic wind-turbine factory on the western bank. I was ravenously hungry.

Naomi was clearly reluctant to go ashore. The risk of being recognised, she believed, was anywhere and everywhere. Even in the Folly Inn, crowded as it was that evening with the crews of visiting boats, families from further inland and a handful of locals, she was afraid.

Here I must explain that, in my estimation, her anxieties were not solely for her own personal safety. She had a keen sense of mission, and, as far as I could judge, her concern was for the safe passage of those key documents in my chart rack, and that alarming capsule of rock-like substance in my bookcase, to ensure they would reach the right authorities as quickly as possible. Discovery of her by her pursuers would very soon be followed by a merciless invasion of *Peggotty*, and who knows what fate for me as well? This I unquestionably understood.

"How about a disguise?" I suggested. "If you cut your hair short, we could kit you out as my teenage son, with a bit of ingenuity."

She looked at me a little doubtfully.

"I suppose it might work," she said eventually. " I can't stay cooped up in the cabin for ever, and sooner or later I'm going to have to make contact again with Thames House – oh, sorry, I shouldn't have mentioned that. Anyway, let's give it a go."

* * * *

Half an hour later, after our combined efforts with the galley scissors and my electric razor, Naomi emerged with quite a decent short haircut; I was pleased with my efforts and we both felt better for finding the process really rather comical. We knew it was not a farce, but the levity was welcome.

My jeans were not exactly figure-hugging on her, but the overlarge Donegal sweater hid the loose waistband and generally obscured her most obvious feminine features. We hoped for the best. The locks of hair we bagged up to take ashore and bin.

Lowering the dinghy from its davits, we rowed ashore, tying up with some difficulty in the jam-packed dinghy area behind the bridge pontoon, and made our way into the Folly Inn. We found a table tucked into a corner by the kitchen door, and Naomi sat with her back to the rest of the dining room.

After an excellent supper and a bottle of Malbec I felt a good deal more cheerful. We agreed that in the morning we would walk into Newport and get Naomi some more convincing young men's clothing, and replenish the poor girl with some underwear and basic essentials. We would restock the boat's stores and then plan our next move.

We rowed back out to *Peggotty*, and, this being the usual hour, I phoned home. This time, I was determined to tell Anne something of the truth, although Naomi cautioned me against saying anything about her mission. In the event, I was saved the difficulty since my wife was out for the evening and so I simply assured my daughter Mary that I was well and on the Isle of Wight, and left it at that.

* * * *

The next morning was dry and bright. We had an early breakfast on board and made our shopping list.

The tide was too low to take *Peggotty* up to the visitor pontoons in Newport, which would be drying out on the mud by now. We could have rowed upriver in the dinghy, but it would be quicker to walk. But what could Naomi walk in? Obviously any shoes or plimsolls of mine would be far too big. I scrounged around in the lockers and eventually found an ancient pair of Anne's canvas slip-ons. The soles were worn, but at least they would survive one way to town.

The footpath along the east bank of the Medina into Newport is excellent, much of it recently resurfaced and widened by the local council. Several steel and timber bridges span the little streams joining the river. After crossing the top of the lock gate at the marina we walked past the crumbling corroded skeleton of the noble old paddle steamer *Ryde*, surely well beyond restoration despite the continued hopes of her preservation society.

The path opens out on to the generous grassy expanses of a town park, and we were then into the scruffy old maritime fringes of the county town. Under the brutalist concrete road flyover, and up the hill into the doubtful attractions of 1960s architecture, we might just as well have been in Basildon. Never mind – our purpose today was not as tourists, but as consumers.

After buying some provisions to keep us independently afloat for a few days, we had some fun kitting Naomi out with a basic wardrobe. She was of course far better informed than I over the current tastes of a boy in his late teens. Any shade of grey, black or dark blue seemed to be the least ostentatious acceptable colour range. I left her to it.

A cheap pair of trainers completed the outfit, and we decided to celebrate with a cup of coffee and a flapjack in one of the many indistinguishable chain cafés in the town centre.

On the way I picked up a copy of *The Times* and, on a sudden whim, the local *County Press*, both of that morning's date.

Two large lattes now before us, I opened the *County Press*. At the bottom of the front page the following headlines stared back up at me.

'MISSING PRESUMED DEAD.
KAYAK WRECK FOUND OFF VENTNOR'

I turned the paper round so that we could both read it together. The article continued:

The coastguard reports that yesterday afternoon a kayak and

the remains of a wetsuit were retrieved from the sea eight miles south of Ventnor. A helicopter and fisheries protection vessel search was made of the area for the rest of the day, but discontinued at nightfall. No survivor or casualty has been found.

The kayak belongs to the Royal Marines, but official sources have confirmed that no service personnel are missing, nor have any such craft been involved in service exercises in the area.

Our reporter understands that the kayak contained no evidence of the canoeist's identity, but that items found have been retained by the police for further examination.

The coastguard operator we spoke to expressed his opinion that without a wetsuit or life jacket the canoeist would after this length of time stand almost no chance of survival. The search is expected to resume today.

We looked up at each other. 'Oh, well – so far so good,' our expressions told one another without words.

I picked up *The Times* and flipped through the first couple of pages to see what had been happening in the world since I had left home five days previously. Not much had changed since I had last read the paper. American politics remained unpredictable, and the trials and tribulations throughout the Middle East entirely predictable.

I was just about to turn to the cricket news when a brief paragraph caught my eye, buried at the bottom of the page:

SECURITY LEAK

The Times has learnt that security at the Atomic Weapons Establishment at Aldermaston was breached ten days ago with the theft of documents and an undisclosed item. No official confirmation has been given, but our source believes that both MI5 and MI6 are jointly investigating, and have dispatched officers to follow and recover the theft in liaison with the police. This would indicate official concern that the incident could have both domestic and international implications.

Possible terrorist involvement could not be excluded.

I passed the paper over to Naomi.

"I suppose this just about completes the picture," I said.

She nodded. "Except that no one but me has yet caught sight of the thieves, and could maybe identify them again. But at least I've got the goods, and some more incriminating evidence added to the pack of documents." She paused. "I wouldn't want to be the person who spilt the beans to *The Times*. Not if they are in the service. They will be in dead trouble if they're found out. I wonder who that could be," she continued, her forehead creasing up into a thoughtful frown.

I thought it prudent not to quiz her further along that line of thought. It would have been unfair. I just reflected, as I sipped my latte, that it is not every retired naval officer who has shared a sleeping bag with a naked officer of MI5, nor then taken them on as boat's crew in the guise of a teenage son. This situation was becoming increasingly bizarre. I had never been entirely convinced that Ian Fleming's books portrayed that life as anything but fanciful.

On the other hand, mine had been a sheltered existence. Maybe I had walked through a doorway into a world of make-believe and intrigue that ran parallel to my own and with no less humdrum a routine. One aspect of this affair that continued to strike me was the air of normality with which Naomi handled this parallel experience. She sat there now, gazing out through the café window at the street scene, coffee mug in both hands, seemingly as casual as any other disinterested observer of daily life in Newport. As I watched, however, I saw her knuckles blanching under a tightening grip of her mug, and she turned her face slowly and deliberately away from the window and caught my full attention with her eyes.

"It's them," she murmured calmly, "two of them. They've just walked past."

CHAPTER NINE

"Are you sure?" I said, rather inanely. "I thought you had only caught a glimpse of your pursuers before now."

"I'm sure. I'm trained to be sure, but I wasn't expecting to be so instantly certain. It's them all right." She had a new alert expression and the set of her jaw took on the resolve that I had seen once before. "Right," she continued, "two priorities: one, to get those items on the boat up to London into safe hands; two, to keep tabs on those guys out there and set a trace. Part of my role was to blow their cover, and thanks to you I guess I now have the upper hand."

Now, faced with a dilemma I am a great one for rushing into doing nothing. If I paused less for cautious rational thought, I could so often have reacted with frenzied energy and had the whole thing sorted instantly. So my usual habit in a crisis is to act much too late, thereby needing to accelerate the frenzy and energy that was inevitable from the outset. Such was my reaction on this occasion. My first inclination was to order another cup of coffee and think this over.

Not Naomi. She was up and had slipped out of the door with a quick "Meet me back at the Folly Inn later," before I had a chance.

I settled the bill, gathered up our purchases and made my slow and bemused way back along the Medina footpath. There was nothing I could do. I had not, of course, noticed the two individuals that Naomi was now following and so could be of no help there. I rowed the dinghy back to *Peggotty* and packed away the stores.

All I could offer was to be prepared as skipper of the boat to leave the berth if necessary at a moment's notice, and in the meantime to act as guardian of the package of documents and the sinister little steel canister lurking in the cabin bookcase. At least they were both still there where we had left them, and there was no sign that anyone else had been aboard in our absence. I sat in the sunshine in the cockpit trying to read the rest of *The Times*, my binoculars on my knees so that I could spot Naomi over on the shore pontoon when she eventually returned. If she eventually returned.

I was suddenly overwhelmed with a warmth of devotion that was not just anxiety for her safe reappearance on the riverbank. I had to admit to myself that my emotions were not limited to a sense of responsibility by one generation for the next. That, after all, had been a familiar kind of relationship in the navy, particularly between officers and ratings of both sexes when under the stress of action. I had not been actively part of the naval presence in the Falklands conflict, but many of my friends had been, and they often record the bond which developed in those conditions, hard to describe or even admit to in the cold light of retrospection after their return.

No, here and now I had an understanding of desolation in loss, a glimpse of what bereavement would be if one of my own daughters and my own wife together had not made it home one day. This was not an imagined grief, a speculation of possible responses should the riverbank not yield up Naomi again. This was more like experiencing a dress rehearsal for the real thing, sitting there with my newspaper and binoculars, pathetically waiting.

I went below just once, for some cheese and an apple, and nodded absently to the few other boat owners and crew who occasionally walked past me on the pontoon during the afternoon.

Once again the sun set westwards behind the turbine factory, and dusk crept across the water. The windows of the Folly Inn blazed with light, the row of lamps out on the veranda swinging gently in the breeze, casting their beams over the smiling happy faces of the diners and drinkers enjoying the summer evening. The path to my right along the bank from Newport was now in darkness. No one walking there would be visible at this hour – not until they reached the frontage of the inn. No one was visible, and no one appeared.

What if she returned in the night, after the inn had closed? There would only be a few dim lights near the shore pontoon. What if she needed to rejoin me urgently and could not give me a loud hail?

I decided to row ashore again and wait for her during the hours of darkness somewhere discreet, where I could spot her easily. On the edge of the grass car park by the sailing-club boat hard was an old shed with some dilapidated garden chairs leaning against it. I positioned one of these in deep shadow between the shed and the trees, with a clear view of where the path emerged into the peripheral lights of the pub, and sat there as patiently as I could.

The last patrons of the inn had long since left, and silence had descended. Sporadic movement and crackling twigs in the woods behind me and the clumsy flap of wings meant nothing more than a cat, a wood pigeon and perhaps a fox.

"Will ye not wait with me one brief hour?"

I began to sympathise with the disciples in the Garden of Gethsemane. Not knowing quite what we were waiting for, but still nervous and afraid, we still tend to fall into an uncomfortable doze, eyelids heavy despite the thumping of hearts and the sick anticipation. It was not long before I succumbed as they had, and was asleep in my damp canvas chair, chin on my chest.

I awoke two or three times, alerted by who knows what? but not to any welcome sight of Naomi. Each time I then ventured around the front of the pub in case she had passed me and was on the shore pontoon. But no such luck.

Each time I then returned to my chair and eventually nodded off. I was cold and stiff, wincing with backache, wanting to be steadfast in my lookout, but to no avail. I slept.

What finally woke me was not the pale dawn breaking

over the steeple of Whippingham Church up on the hill, but the sound of tyres on gravel and the unmistakable sound of a bicycle chain in freewheel.

Down the lane behind me, from quite a different direction than the riverside path that I had been so ineffectually monitoring, came Naomi on an old rusty cycle that had clearly lost its last shreds of brake pad many decades ago.

She saw me as I saw her, and did an impressive if unintended rear-wheel skid to bring her decrepit machine to a halt, scattering road gravel in a graceful arc. She leapt off as I ran to meet her, and our heartfelt reunion might well have puzzled any onlooker (had there been one) as surprisingly effusive for a morning greeting between man and boy.

The relief swept through me like a hot shower on a cold day. Maybe that analogy struck me immediately, because we were standing right outside the twenty-four-hour shower block for boating visitors, which the inn proprietors so thoughtfully provide at the rear of their premises. We both agreed that her report of her adventures could wait until we were back on board *Peggotty* after a sorely needed refreshing shower.

A quarter of an hour later we were home in the cabin with the kettle on the hob.

* * * *

"I caught up with them at the end of the street," Naomi began. "What helped me recognise them was that they were so distinctive together. If it had just been one of them on his own I might not have looked twice. I don't know their names – yet – but one is a great bear of a man with thick hair like a scrubbing brush and a bushy black beard. Immensely strong, I guess, and about six foot three. He wore a rather incongruous shiny blue suit that is too small for him. Almost a caricature of a Russian sailor on shore leave. The other man is a thin, devious-looking guy, pale with washed-out ginger hair and not much of it. He had the same nondescript grey tee shirt and black jeans he had on when I saw him in Portsmouth. I'm pretty sure he's concealing a small handgun under the arm of his denim jacket that he was wearing yesterday. He looks the type who would use it – with me in his sights, I suppose."

She took a gulp of tea and forked the bacon and fried bread I had grilled for breakfast.

"Anyway, I had no difficulty following them. I learnt that art under my training officer. She really knew her stuff – had worked in Belfast in the seventies. I had to be careful in case the third man in Portsmouth was there too and trailing along behind me. But no sign of him anywhere.

"At the end of South Street they turned down across St Thomas Square and the High Street into Quay Street – those lovely old cottages back near the boatyards. I nearly lost them when they ducked in behind there and slipped into a half-derelict old warehouse or chandler's. I'm guessing that is just a temporary shelter for them to discuss their next move. I only hope they've swallowed our false clues and assume I'm dead. They were both forever on their mobiles, so they must have a wider network of friends elsewhere.

"Incidentally, you may be wondering why I don't phone into HQ myself to report the position and tell them I've got the paperwork. I daren't. There has to be a double agent up there – there has to be. I can only hand the stuff over personally, without prior notice. I just hope and pray it's the right person when I do."

She broke off her narrative to finish her cooked breakfast, and I refilled her mug.

"It was easy enough to get close to where they were in the building. Most of the windows have lost their glass, and the interior doors and woodwork have all been pinched. All I had to do was listen in. Mostly they were planning their next theft, but never mentioned the target by name. Could be GCHQ, a nuclear dump, Aldermaston again . . . Who knows?

"The important thing is that I have learnt the whereabouts of what must be their own UK base. This is hot stuff, but I've got to decide now which is the first thing on my list – to get the documents to HQ or follow up my lead to investigate the spy base down in Dorset."

"Dorset!" I exclaimed. "That's home ground for me." But I paused. "I suppose you can't tell me where. None of my business."

"Listen," she replied, "I've already let on to you far more than I should have officially done. If at the end of all this I have to face a formal reprimand, I reckon I could put up a good argument. You saved my life from drowning or hypothermia, and hopefully have saved it again from murder by setting a false trail that I could never have done on my own. You had to know what I've already told you.

"My bosses will want me to stick to my mission, which is to find and tail these agents or whatever they are. To leave that trail and return to London has to be wrong. I still need your help."

She didn't say "and I still want your company", and maybe she had a cooler head than I in that respect. Just as well.

"OK, so where are we heading next?" I asked.

"Somewhere in Poole Harbour called Lang Isle, or Lone Island – some name like that."

I laughed. "I know it well. Many's the time I've anchored nearby. It's the only anchorage in the harbour with shelter from a strong west wind. If you rowed ashore on to the mainland there, it's only about fifteen minutes' drive back to my home.

"Thinking of which, I didn't phone home last night. I'd better give Anne and the girls a ring now to assure them I've not drowned. The other night I tried to say something about you being on board too."

"Best not to, for the moment," Naomi cautioned. "The less said the better on any phone or media network. Surveillance these days is so widespread, and my lot will be monitoring everything in the area where I have apparently disappeared, I'm sure of that. They damn well ought to be, anyway."

I managed to catch Anne at home this time.

"Change of plan, my love. I'm coming back to Poole Harbour with the tide."

"Oh – anything wrong?" she replied in surprise. "That was a short trip."

"Nothing wrong, no. There's something I need to do back there, but may go on again afterwards. I may pop back home anyway." I looked enquiringly at Naomi, who understood and nodded. "We can . . . um, I can give you all my news then.

"The girls OK?" I hastily continued.

"We're all fine, darling, thanks. See you when we see you, then. Go carefully."

And Anne rang off, saving me further explanations.

We fired up the Bukh, recovered our mooring warps and slid away from the pontoon. As we took in the fenders I brought *Peggotty* round in a wide sweep to head downriver, while Naomi released the jib to give us a spanking run back towards Cowes, through the busy activity of race boats, ferries, and RIBs criss-crossing the entrance to the Medina. Off we set westwards down the Solent and clear of the Needles and the Shingles across Christchurch Bay towards home ground and whatever lay in store for us around the islands of Poole Harbour, away up in the isolated corner of that great inland sea off the shore of the Arne peninsula.

CHAPTER TEN

I had taken the Needles channel out, as the quickest straight line back into Poole Bay through Dolphin Sand and well clear of Christchurch Ledge, but we both soon began to regret it. We were with the ebb spring tide, but the south-westerly wind had sprung up fast and was blowing a good 27 knots as we cleared the Fairway buoy. The Shingles bank off to starboard had been boiling ferociously, and head to wind *Peggotty* was constantly being pushed nearer and nearer to that fearsome graveyard for small boats. Only when we could pass the Needles and change tack southwards could I begin to breathe more easily. Even so, the sea state was daunting. The wind was strengthening further, and we were driving the boat's nose into breaking swell, meeting the cross-current coming up from south of the island in flying spumes of white water as the two armies of regimented waves converged on each other in endless collision.

Peggotty being the heavy old gaffer she was disliked beating into that confusion of water, and I was keen to get her on to a broad reach as soon as possible. But we had to head south and out to sea for a fair stretch first.

It wasn't raining, but that was irrelevant to the quantity of water flowing into our faces and constantly obscuring my vision as salt caked the lenses of my glasses. The sun was obscured by high cloud, and the air was chilly.

I soon saw that my companion was in some distress with seasickness. She had gone very still, and was as white in the face as a painted mannequin, shivering despite several layers of clothing. I sent her below to lie flat on a bunk and warm up.

How I wished we had chosen the North Head route into Christchurch Bay, and gone into Mudeford at mid tide to pick up a mooring and get some shelter from the south-west until the wind had eased. That was too late now. We were a couple of miles off Hengistbury Head and there was no way I was going to do battle with the tidal race over the Ledge in that wind.

We would just have to press on.

A few big, powerful fishing boats passed us from time to time, making a beeline for the Poole Harbour entrance, flattening the swell astern of them with their foaming wash and wake. I did slightly envy them their directional ability and warm covered wheelhouses in those conditions, at the same time admitting to myself that I could never have coped with the harsh, exhausting and dangerous life those men lead for a living, for a financial return that year by year grew ever less predictable.

At last, some four miles offshore we came level with Bournemouth, whose pier I could just identify through binoculars, and I brought *Peggotty* about on to a reach, right on her beam. I could almost feel her smile as she settled down on a path that suited her so well. Easing the sheets, I too settled on to my seat with a sense of relief. Our speed picked up to 6 knots or more, and we sliced diagonally along the ridges of swell, foredeck now no longer submerged, the spray on my back and not my face, and I set a course straight for the Swash Channel and the blue-and-white car ferry shuttling to and fro across the harbour entrance.

Late afternoon, and we joined the mixed fleet of yachts, powerboats and line fishermen drawing into the neck of the funnel of Poole Harbour at slack tide, casting a wary eye astern in case the dread Condor cross-Channel ferry was looming up behind, demanding the entire width of navigable water and scaring us lesser mortals perilously close to Stoney Island, that heap of stones which sits incongruously smack in the middle of the open expanse of water, unmarked by cardinal buoy and inviting a grounding for anyone unfamiliar with the area or the chart. I had entered the harbour so frequently that the routine was second nature, and I suddenly realised that, as on most other occasions, I was single-handed and alone in the cockpit. How was my poor seasick first mate getting on down in the cabin?

I gave her a shout. "Naomi," I called out, "are you OK down there? We've nearly arrived and the water's as calm as a millpond."

No response. Fast asleep, I supposed. We really needed to discuss and decide our tactics for investigating the enemy stronghold on the long flat little island up beyond Brownsea. I had given some thought as to whether it would be more effective to take *Peggotty* right up to Shipstal Point, spitting distance from the island, and use her as our base, or whether we should restore the boat to her home mooring in the Frome Estuary and approach from the mainland, perhaps with a small dinghy.

The vital thing was to maintain the impression of normality. I was inclined to anchor up at Shipstal. Messing about in the dinghy from *Peggotty* in the little muddy creeks and inlets of Middlebere and Wych Lakes would be entirely natural, and rowing close to the target island was unlikely to raise suspicion. Landing on it and penetrating its overgrown interior would be another matter altogether.

"Naomi," I yelled a little louder as we motored up Middle Ship Channel off the north shore of Brownsea, "time to get up!"

Still no reply – no appearance of a face at the companionway. I was puzzled.

On an impulse, I gathered a warp from the locker and made for a vacant mooring buoy at the group of moorings in the Wych Channel, usually full of rather sleek forty-footers of much elegance and expense.

Having secured *Peggotty* to the mooring float, I went below. The saloon and Naomi's bunk were empty. I walked forward to the fo'c'sle and heads, where the shower and WC are crammed into their own little compartment.

She was sprawled on the sole boards, her head face down beneath the lavatory bowl and resting on a forearm that was besmirched with vomit and a pale-green mucus that lay in threads over her hands and wrists. She was quite still.

I rushed to her side. Mercifully she was still breathing – a rough and liquid snore rather than breath, but at any rate evidence of life. She was, however, unconscious. How long had she been like this? I kicked myself for having failed to check up on the poor girl long before.

Gently I began mopping up the mess on her and around her. After a great deal of kitchen roll and Dettol had been dispatched into a tightly knotted bag in the garbage bin, I stroked her face and neck with a sponge and warm water; and eventually, as she recovered, I sat her up with glasses of water to flush out her mouth and nose into the lavatory pan. After a while I heaved her up and half carried her up the companionway steps out into the fresh air. There we sat in the cockpit, side by side, my arm around her slim shoulders as I whispered "Sorry" to her several times.

The boat lay still in the sheltered water, and behind us, over the tops of the pines on Brownsea, the sun on its western descent warmed our backs. We sat there for a long time, Naomi's head on my shoulder and her light form gradually relaxing its slight weight against me as she fell into a doze. I had no wish to move. None whatsoever.

At the same time, this uncertain proximity to a young woman held an amplified dimension in these home waters – territory that until now I had, so far as company is concerned, identified only with members of my own all-female family. This new experience was all the more intrusive in this domestic setting, its attraction all the more unsettling for the physical contact being with a girl who was dressed and shorn as a boy. Somehow this did nothing to diminish the sensual frisson of her companionship.

As we sat there, I tried to justify to myself the possibility of giving in to this force of circumstance, which I reasoned to have been hardly of my own engineering. Naomi had landed on my scene through no initiative on my part other than a response to mortal emergency.

On the other hand, had our convergence been any more a free choice on her part? What opportunity had she had to decline it?

She could have walked away in Newport, of course. I had rather expected that she might. But was her decision to stick with me and *Peggotty* solely a strategic one – the best option in her professional duty to uncover enemies of the state? In many ways this girl's character seemed to suit the template of an undercover surveillance officer. She had given away to me almost nothing of herself at all. I had no clue as to her family, her home and friends, nor her background or wider interests. I did not even know her surname.

She had evidently found me a great comfort, both in her recovery from near drowning and now in the aftermath of seasickness. Was this just the warmth of reliance on a trustworthy father figure, in which case this very debate I was holding with myself was desperately unfair?

It was the physicality that she offered that prompted me to doubt this. Our contact, other than that collusion of life-saving body heat wrapped together in the sleeping bag, had been virtuous to a fault in anyone's eyes, but nonetheless more responsive on her part than mere support from a paternal stranger. If she was having a similar internal debate, however, there was no sign of perplexity or doubt on her open face beside me, her dark eyes closed and the regular rise and fall of her breathing transmitted steadily to me, rib to rib.

And then as I gazed along the north-west shoreline of Brownsea and recalled with such familiar pleasure the days I had spent there with Anne and our daughters, larking about with the dogs (contrary to National Trust rules) on the beach that consisted of shards of broken brick, ceramic drainage pipes and over-burnt kiln residues left from the failed nineteenth-century pottery industry there, I overhauled once again in my mind and conscience my first and foremost emotional commitments to my wife and children. I knew well enough from the experience of others, including several naval colleagues, that some people managed to rationalise close attachments to those other than their spouses – relationships that were not necessarily sexual, but usually ended up being so. Indeed I myself, when a good deal younger, had been propositioned by a woman in an unhappy marriage who was convinced that she, Anne and I could have established a congenial threesome without unduly disturbing our *modus vivendi* or even prejudicing the tenets of my Church.

Such arrangements are generally intended to become long-standing ones, although of course not many last more than a brief and painful few months.

Chance encounters naturally arise with no opportunity for forethought or plan. The male mind, in particular, is unsuited to instant wise choice when faced with this situation. The mind of a woman, on the other hand (in my absurdly limited experience), takes a cooler, more objective, view from the very outset of such a meeting. As a result, the outcome is usually determined by female wisdom – in my case, Anne's.

I am sufficiently modern in outlook to recognise that men have a feminine side (that Almighty God is probably feminine), and perhaps that the same applies vice versa, but for the life of me sitting there on our borrowed mooring in the failing sunshine that evening my intuitive skills, if any, evaded me. Any deep discernment on the matter within Naomi's heart and mind must likewise have been truly hidden. Her form resting against me did nothing to promote the intellectual approach.

All I really knew, at that moment beyond dispute, was that my identity lay with the woman I had married – for all that she was now and had been then – and my coterie of daughters too, an awareness brought home to me now by my rooted surroundings in the Purbeck Hills.

And an unfathomable attachment to this mysterious girl beside me rested somewhere in the pending tray of my orderly, filed existence.

CHAPTER ELEVEN

What seemed like hours later, but was probably only about thirty minutes, I roused myself from this introspective reverie and offered Naomi something to drink. A mug of hot sweet tea clearly fitted the bill, and I went below to organise.

I put to her the question of a land-based assault or ship to shore, as the two options for discovering what she had slipped into professional jargon to refer to as her 'target personnel'. Like me, she thought continued use of *Peggotty* as an HQ close to the island presented the least risk. I wondered if I should go and get my car and leave it in the RSPB car park at Arne, just over the hill, in case we had to make an escape on to the mainland beach and overground at a faster pace than was possible by boat.

She saw my point, and we therefore decided that on anchoring off Shipstal I would go ashore and walk to Arne, then get the bus or a lift up to Redclyffe Yacht Club where I had left the car, bring it back to Arne and walk across over the heath to rejoin Naomi on board later that evening. In the meantime she would keep her head well down in the cabin and start a watch on Lone Isle, a few yards across the creek from our anchorage.

This we duly arranged without incident, and it was gone ten o'clock with dusk falling before Naomi spotted me waving on the shoreline, and rowed across in the dinghy to pick me up.

As darkness descended, there was no sign of life or activity on Lone Isle – no light, nor any evidence that there was anybody there at all.

We retired to our bunks equally exhausted, in her case from physical suffering, in my own from mental and emotional exhaustion and a surfeit of what I can only describe as exhilaration. Or rather, that is all she was showing outwardly. Who was I to diagnose her exhaustion so simplistically? Goodness only knows what else was going on in that brave and determined frame that was a closed book to me. I was in no mind for guessing games, and fell quickly asleep.

I awoke, instantly alert, and looked at my watch. It was quarter to five in the morning, and the light from the east was just penetrating the dense trees on Brownsea and Furzey Islands away across the harbour. The surface of the water between us and Lone Isle was still in shade, the outline of the island sharp against the sky.

Equally sharp but a great deal noisier was the silhouette of a familiar black object approaching from the north. I was very experienced in identifying engine sound, and this one we had last heard off the southern shore of the Isle of Wight those few days previously.

It was the anonymous little two-seater helicopter that had roared over us at masthead height in such an inquisitive and sinister manner.

I dashed from my bunk back aft into the saloon to grab the binoculars, but Naomi was ahead of the game. She knelt on her bunk, binoculars in hand, and nose glued to the porthole.

Lone Isle has an open shoreline all round, a bare fringe perhaps fifteen yards deep, rising gently to a slight plateau densely covered with scrub and low trees. At least, to my casual eye on previous occasions I had assumed the cover was complete. No building had ever been visible, nor indeed any man-made structure other than the plethora of 'PRIVATE NO LANDING' signs placed at frequent intervals around the high-tide mark. Only an old houseboat, dragged up the beach on the western side, offered any indication that the island's owner made use of his or her property. Only once have I ever seen people on the houseboat – a couple of years previously, when they had spent a morning carrying a series of cardboard boxes from the vessel and a small launch, up the beach and into the trees.

At any rate, the tree cover was evidently not as it appeared, because the helicopter reached the island, hovered over it for a few seconds, and then slowly sank vertically to land on the plateau, entirely concealed among the trees. Evidently there was a hidden clearing in the centre.

The clattering engine slowly wound down, and after a few minutes all was peace and quiet once again, nothing disturbing the isolated silence but the oystercatchers pecking and pottering along the water's edge cackling to one another, and the terns darting and diving over and under the muddy surface of the ebbing tide.

Naomi and I made breakfast, and over the remains littering the saloon table we held a council of war. Clearly there was nothing we could do in daylight except monitor any comings and goings. Action on our part must await nightfall.

I say 'our part', as I had prematurely assumed that the two of us were now a partnership so far as this adventure was concerned. Naomi soon put me right on that score.

"Listen – I can't possibly let you put yourself in personal danger as a direct accomplice of mine on government business," she insisted, laying her hand on my arm as though I needed physical restraint then and there. "Besides, you haven't been vetted!"

I smiled back and raised an eyebrow. "How do you intend to stop me?" I answered.

"No, seriously, Robert." And I noted that she had used my Christian name for the first time. She was now back on track as a professional, and her self-confidence had reasserted itself. "If anything should go seriously wrong and you came off worst, I would have two reasons to regret it. For one thing, my career would be over as I would certainly be dismissed from the service and probably prosecuted; for another" (and here she looked away, then glanced awkwardly back at me) "I could never forgive myself. You didn't choose to get embroiled in all this, and I hope you don't mind my saying that I've become quite fond of you."

Quite fond of me. I took a deep breath. Maybe I ought to abandon ship right now, run to the car and drive home to Church Knowle and Anne, firmly shutting the door when I got there.

Had I done so, and in light of events as they unfolded, mine would have been the restless, sleepless nights of bitter regret and self-recrimination.

* * * *

There were two or three other boats chugging up Balls Lake to shelter at Shipstal from the west wind – mainly daysailors and elderly couples in their old-fashioned motor boats choosing a calm sunny spot to sit and read the paper or knit. *Peggotty* became just another visitor at anchor, and this suited our purpose admirably.

The day warmed up. Fleets of small white sails out across the harbour signified a busy race programme for the dinghies off Parkstone. Strings of brightly coloured Lasers full of children learning to sail were being towed about behind powered RIBs, steered by fierce young instructors bawling ineffectually at their juvenile charges, who ignored them and were having a great time. Occasionally twin-hulled Hobie Cats would skim through all this activity, barely touching the water, their wetsuited crews stretched far out over the water, feet on gunwale, carving straight lines of white wake and oblivious of the shallows. Around the fringes of this wet expanse sober canoeists doggedly dug their paddles in clockwork unison into the teeth of the wind, or glided with relief into the foreshore to sit on the gravelly beach and recover their breath.

Such utterly normal and happy sights and sounds on a summer morning. No doubt these observed images hid a diversity of the inevitable pains and sorrows, anxieties and sadnesses of lives beneath the gaiety; but none surely was as sinister as that black helicopter lurking in silence behind the trees on

Lone Isle, representing to our acute awareness the horrors of assassination, vengeance and the sabotage of national security. To Naomi and myself, lounging in peace and comfort on a lovely old boat in the sunshine, these two incompatible worlds were separated merely by the narrow silver streak of water partitioning *Peggotty* from that menacing island shoreline.

The rest of the day passed on much the same note. One by one our boating neighbours shipped anchor to wend their way home, until by early evening there was only one other yacht evidently intending to remain overnight, away off to the south by Rand Island and the reed flats of Middlebere Lake.

Well-clad and booted walkers still strolled along the beach below the white cliff at Shipstal, pausing in their perambulation of the Arne wildlife conservatory to admire the boats, identify the bird life or just sit and gaze.

As far as Lone Isle was concerned, nobody came and nobody went. Dusk settled hazily over our outward serenity. Neither of us felt hungry. Too much was at stake.

Naomi had been deep in thought for much of the afternoon, deciding her course of action. She told me that her purpose was to gain as much intelligence as possible on the set-up at Lone Isle – personnel numbers, descriptions, structures and equipment – and then get the hell out (as she put it), finding her way back to London with a memorised report and of course the two recovered items still nestling in the shelves of *Peggotty*'s saloon.

Her night-sight field glasses and camera had long ago been abandoned when she had made her frantic escape by kayak from Gosport. All she had now to rely on were her eyesight and memory. I had a small digital camera with internal lens, but Naomi's own little smartphone, which she had tried to keep dry in the kayak, had been flooded on her capsize and was useless. In any case, a camera dependent on a flash at night-time would be worse than dangerous on the venture that she was planning.

We caught the seven-thirty MCA weather forecast on VHF to gauge the likely state of the night sky. If it remained cloudless, the moon was going to be a problem. Darkness was going to be impaired enough by the aerial glow of light over Poole and Bournemouth, and the last thing we needed was an additional spotlight overhead. To our slight consolation therefore, the promise of a low front emerging from the west, with cloud and drizzle, soon after one o'clock in the morning, meant poor visibility and welcome murk.

"And, Robert," Naomi declared with that familiar set of chin as I switched off the VHF, "you are not coming with me – no way. It would be madness, and also I need you back here on the boat. If things get out of hand, I may have to re-establish contact with you by means that we can't anticipate. You are the only person who knows the situation, and I'll leave with you a secure phone number and scrambler password. If I don't return, you must use it to get the documents and canister into safe hands, or at least into what I only hope are safe hands, at Thames House. Burn or swallow the bit of paper with the numbers on it as soon as you've used it."

Good grief! This sounded like some farcical extract from a James Bond novel.

My intrepid and unlikely espionage agent then put her head down for a few hours' sleep, my alarm clock set for midnight. I stayed awake, trying to read my book and constantly finding that I was still on the same page. It was an old copy of de Bernières' *Captain Corelli's Mandolin*, which like many other old favourites lived in faded, dog-eared mustiness permanently aboard *Peggotty*. I had quite a library of assorted random reading in my bookshelves – P. G. Wodehouse for dull drizzly days when I needed comforting amusement; Bill Bryson when I wanted a really good laugh; A. J. Cronin or Melvyn Bragg for atmospheric shade. Now of course I also had a real-life prop for some of my lighter Hammond Innes thrillers in the form of a shiny can whose contents could, for all I knew, kill off every living being within a five-mile radius.

The alarm buzzer woke us both up with a start. I retrieved Captain Corelli from the foot on which he had fallen, and put my head up out of the main hatch. The night sky was already clouding over. The other boat's riding light merged with the occasional star at masthead level. A dim lamp on Rand Island's landing stage glimmered weakly. As for Lone Isle, nothing. A black outline against the distant glow of Poole lay there ominously, as though waiting for something.

CHAPTER TWELVE

Naomi was now quite hungry, and I made her some thick hot soup with a couple of tiger rolls, with a pot of strong coffee.

Most of her newly acquired fashionable outfit was already black enough for the job in hand. A dark navy fleece hat and a pair of my black socks completed her attire. I then helped her to black up her face and the backs of her hands in traditional style using several old bottle corks scorched over the flame of the spirit stove.

Into her jeans pockets went a miniature torch I kept by the radio, together with my folding bosun's knife with its wicked marlinespike, a small notebook and a pencil.

I had persuaded her to add over her T-shirt my dark sleeveless waterproof mid layer, which was just as well since, as we quietly emerged into the open cockpit, the drizzle was beginning to set in. A few hours out in that, scrambling through dripping undergrowth, and she would have been wet through. At least she would remain warm.

The wooden dinghy was already floating alongside *Peggotty*. I had vaselined the rowlocks the previous day, and now we wrapped strips of old rag around the oars to wedge them into the rowlock crutches to avoid clatter, and to enable Naomi to leave them shipped when she reached the island shore, so as to minimise noise and possibly speed up a hasty departure.

Over the side she went, and I released the painter. Slowly and carefully she pulled away, and with a quick glance back up at me, with an expression I could not fathom, she and the dinghy disappeared into the murk.

I felt in my pocket for the slip of paper with the numbers on it, which Naomi had passed to me earlier. There was nothing more I could do now except to await her return, hopefully undiscovered, and to visualise what other courses of action might be open to me if the outcome of that night's adventure should prove to be one of an alarmingly diverse range of chilling alternatives.

I went back down below, and by the light of a single paraffin lamp resumed my book. My ears I kept tuned to the open companionway. This was letting in the light rain down the steps and on to the sole boards, but I was anxious to avoid blocking any slight sound from outside that might be in any way significant.

'To travel hopefully is a better thing than to arrive,' wrote Robert Louis Stevenson, and I had often agreed with this sentiment. The anticipation of a pleasure, the imagining of the joys to come while on one's way to meeting them, do indeed surpass the event itself in so many circumstances. By this I do not mean the planning or the preparation of a journey or an endeavour. I am not one of those people who relish the poring over timetables and road maps, the booking of tickets and the accumulation of documents. To me these are tedious chores that tend to discourage me from setting out to travel in the first place.

No, what I savour is the foretaste of arrival – the contemplation of future fulfilment on completion of a challenging objective. How often has the actual outcome proved to be more disappointing, the product more boring than the advertisement, the delivery a mere shadow of the manifesto? This has certainly been true of my naval career, despite its outward success of high rank and organisational achievement. Of course there had been exceptions – not least my marriage and family life, which had exceeded all expectations – but so often I have had good cause to affirm the general rule so famously summarised by R. L. Stevenson. The satisfaction, the pleasure, had been achieved. Whatever the cold reality, the antecedent imagining had been a living experience that could not be diminished or gainsaid.

No such warm, comforting thoughts came near me, however, on that long wet night vigil awaiting Naomi's safe return to the boat. I could anticipate the relief that I would feel at the sound of the dinghy's soft bump against *Peggotty*'s side, and at the resumption of a role in the protection and defence of this girl, but on this occasion the hopefulness evaded me. Contemplation of failure is a very different emotional experience to that of expected success. I was not so much scared or alarmed as I sat there, useless book in hand, but rather was I deeply despondent.

From time to time I would extinguish the lamp, and after allowing my eyes to adjust to the dark, cautiously climb into the cockpit and with elbows on the coaming, supporting my chin, fasten my gaze on the even darker mass of the island across the creek. Once I thought I saw the brief glow of a light through the scrub, but it may only have been my imagination. No movement or sound was discernible, except for the sudden affronted squawk of a seabird disturbed at one time by who knows what?

The drizzle remained relentless, falling now in vertical droplets as the wind had died away to nothing. It made a skitter-scatter sound on *Peggotty*'s coach roof like a host of little creatures perpetually running away from something. 'Why running away?' I wondered to myself. I had clearly plummeted into a mood in which I was even implicating the rainfall in the web of intrigue surrounding me.

I might have supposed that the night would drag on interminably for me as I sat and fretted there in helpless anxiety, but the early dawn took me by surprise, despite the low cloud pervading the sky to the east. Quite quickly the shapes of the hills and trees emerged from the gloom, and the liquid of the water began to distinguish itself from solid land by the glittering, puckering effect of the raindrops on its surface. In no time at all, small details started to appear – individual branches of trees, the white forms of gulls poking about on the muddy beach, the blue hull of the old houseboat drawn up on the shore opposite me – and then the distant sounds of early risers starting a new day over in Poole, the slow crescendo of dull traffic roar speared by the occasional racket of an accelerating motorbike on a dual carriageway, all somehow still remote from me both in distance and reality. The nearer birdsong of waders searching for their breakfasts under the beach stones were so much more a part of my immediate world.

Before long, my watch showed 5 a.m. and anything within view could be seen and identified without difficulty.

Of the little wooden dinghy from *Peggotty* there was no sign of any kind.

Surely, I reasoned, Naomi would have rowed across to the island shore over the shortest distance possible, which would naturally have been right opposite *Peggotty*. There would have been no point in searching for a landing place where the dinghy could be hidden, as the shoreline of the island was open and exposed all around its perimeter for several yards.

She might, I supposed, have had reason to row around to the other side of the island, hidden from me, and landed there, in which case the dinghy would be invisible from my vantage point.

The plan had been of course for her to return with the dinghy while it was still dark. If for whatever reason (and my imagination ran to hellish riot) Naomi had become stuck ashore after the night had passed, the obvious presence of *Peggotty*'s dinghy on the island beach, visible to the island's occupants, would spell disaster. The transom of the dinghy held in prominent white lettering the words 't/t Peggotty', and even in an entirely innocent situation it would have been reasonable for the islanders to come across to me and asked what the hell my tender was doing on their private beach.

"Oh, well, my crewmate was doing a spot of espionage during the night. I hope you don't mind." My mind boggled.

I tried to put myself in Naomi's shoes. How might her experience and training have guided her strategy?

She would have considered the prospect, I realised, that

daylight could return before she was able to leave the island. In that case, the dinghy would be a serious problem.

I studied the landscape. Lone Isle ran in a lengthy strip of ground close to Rand Island, which had a good landing stage and a couple of houses. The slip of water between the two islands was very shallow; indeed at low spring tides one could probably wade from one to the other.

Rand Island was quite densely covered with trees and shrubbery, and its shoreline was steeper with more tree cover. What if Naomi had decided, prudent girl that she was, to land the dinghy on Rand Island and swim or wade across to Lone Isle?

This idea raised my spirits considerably. To be sure, there was no sign of the dinghy from my position, with binoculars, on the Rand Island shore facing me. This was mainly the landing stage and several buildings, and so an unlikely choice of landing point for the dinghy. Too much risk of other people being around and asking questions. I would have to investigate further.

It was still only six o'clock in the morning and no one on Rand Island seemed to be stirring. I suddenly knew exactly what I should do.

I scribbled a note and left it on the saloon table. It read, 'Gone for a swim around Rand Island. I'll be straight back.' And I added the time.

Then, quickly changing into bathing trunks, I slipped over the side and swam purposefully up the creek towards Wych Lake and Rand Island.

It was a warm and humid morning, with a feathery light drizzle almost suspended in the windless air. The water was not exactly clean, but its slight soupiness was only honest mud. My swim was rather refreshing after that clammy sleepless night, and I enjoyed the muscular exercise which released the cramped and tensed monotony of my vigil.

The sluggish tide carried me past the windows of the Rand Island house by the private pontoon. I kept quite still in the water in case any casual eyes spotted me from a bedroom, although most of the curtains were still drawn across their glass.

Once clear of the domestic frontage, I resumed my breaststroke, carefully scanning the dark shaded lengths of beach where the old oaks and hazel spread their crowns out over the water's edge, their tips forming a straight horizontal line around the island at precisely the height of peak spring tide.

And there, at the very southernmost tip of land, drawn up to the sandy bank at the top of the stone beach and almost completely hidden under the low dark cover of leafage, lay the dinghy tender, her painter most professionally looped around an exposed oak root with a quick-release half hitch. Her oars had been unshipped and lay fore and aft on the thwarts in proper fashion. Evidently Naomi had concluded that a quick getaway from Lone Isle was unlikely to impinge on the later use of the dinghy, and it seemed that she had been right. But where was she now?

I considered the situation as I trod water just out of my depth off the shore. I smiled to myself as I recognised how appropriate was my precise position that morning – truly out of my depth in more senses than one.

After a few moments' thought in which I tried to put myself in Naomi's position, it became obvious that if she had yet to escape Lone Isle now it was daylight, it would be madness to retrace her steps across the length of Rand Island to retrieve the dinghy. There would be too high a risk of discovery and awkward questions. The main residence – an imposing 1920s summer villa – lay on the east side, with the landing point on the west, and so people might be crossing her path just at the wrong moment.

By the same token, the dinghy might all too easily be discovered as well. I had heard children's voices the previous evening, and could well imagine youthful explorers on that magical island playground coming across her and rushing breathlessly home to report their exciting find to their parents.

My best plan now was to row the dinghy back to *Peggotty*

myself and await developments.

I waded ashore and as quietly as possible slid the boat into the water. Then I made my way nonchalantly back down the creek under oar and secured the boat back alongside *Peggotty*.

A brisk rub-down with a towel, and a hot cup of tea, completed my early morning adventure, and I was beginning to relax when, all of a sudden, my spine ran icy-cold and I stared in disbelief at the saloon table.

The little paper note I had left in case Naomi had returned before me had vanished. I searched frantically around on the bunks and sole boards, but it was nowhere to be found. It could not have blown off. There was no wind, and I had weighed it down with a coffee cup. The mug was still there, but I noticed that it was on the other end of the table from where I had placed it.

Early morning is not my brightest hour as a rule, and it took me a few seconds then to glance across at the bookcase. I had obscured the little steel canister behind *The Observer's Book of Birds* and a tide table. These looked undisturbed and a scramble along the saloon, during which I banged my shin painfully against a seat edge, confirmed that all was in order there.

Breathing heavily, I then flipped through the stacked charts above the navigation station and found the document folder likewise untouched.

While I had been out for my swim, someone had come aboard. Someone who had been a little careless. Perhaps in a hurry.

I stepped, very focused, back up the companionway steps out into the cockpit and searched around me. I soon found what I was looking for. Two or three faint muddy shoe prints were now evident to this scrutiny. They were far too big to have been Naomi's. As for me, I had of course left the boat barefoot. The tread pattern bore no resemblance to my own sailing shoes, which I had left below.

CHAPTER THIRTEEN

So, they had either caught Naomi and were establishing her contacts, or else they'd seen or heard an intruder on their island in the night and were pursuing their own search to find out who he or she might be. I fervently hoped for the latter. I had this nice image of myself as the knight in shining armour saving the helpless princess from the clutches of evil. Or St George slaying the dragon to rescue the terrified maiden from its teeth and claws. A sorry substitute I would ever be in such circumstances. All I knew was that this girl who had literally landed in my boat and life in a wetsuit had become something precious, and I suppose rather exotic, and could now be in very grave danger. This was not a romantic mediaeval fairy tale. This needed practical and sensible action.

I decided to phone Anne. She belonged to my real, sane world. I would tell her where I was and where *Peggotty* was moored; I'd explain that the car was now at Arne and say that I would be home as soon as possible and that I would have someone with me.

With Anne in possession of that basic information I would feel more confident in undertaking whatever search or wait for Naomi proved to be necessary over the next twelve hours or so, during which something surely was bound to happen.

I opened the locker where I had left my mobile phone before my swim that morning. It wasn't there. I looked in the other lockers and in various pockets. Nothing. My phone had gone.

Had I given it to Naomi the night before, as she prepared for her clandestine spying? I knew I had not. It would have been sensible, but I had not thought of it. Besides, whom would she have phoned? And anyway, I had put it in that locker when I undressed only a couple of hours ago. No question.

So my intruder had taken my phone. Had he after all just been a young thief, who had pinched the only item he had recognised as being valuable? I had a good search round. Nothing else was missing as far as I could see.

I wondered whether I should get to the car, drive home and tell Anne what was going on. But the plan had been for me to be on hand in the boat, so that Naomi could reach me and know where I was. What if she turned up in dire straits, maybe only a few minutes ahead of some pursuers, and I was not there? It did not bear thinking about.

And then I remembered that I kept an old mobile phone in the car, in case of breakdown. I always tried to keep it charged up, though I seldom used it. It would only take me twenty minutes, fast walk, from Shipstal Beach to the RSPB car park. I could phone Anne as intended, and hasten back to the boat in the hope that Naomi had not reappeared in the three-quarters of an hour this would take me.

Checking that I had the car keys, I scrambled into the dinghy. I then hastily climbed out again and left another note on the saloon table, this one reading 'Back in 45 minutes' with the time, which was ten o'clock.

The sky had apparently shed all the water it had held for so long, for the mizzle had broken up into definable cloud, and a light blue appeared in patches. The rain had gone, and a light southerly wind had sprung up, warm on the face. It promised to be a fine day ahead. Somehow my spirit rose a little, in line with the barometer.

I hauled the dinghy up the sandy shingle beach on Shipstal Point and wedged the painter with a large stone. I left it just above high-tide mark, a fringe of seaweed, sodden twigs and bits of wooden flotsam, although I was hardly going to be away long enough to bother.

I set out at a good pace over the cliff dunes and on to the

gravelly track that led inland to the car park. No other walkers were in evidence except a couple of obvious birdwatchers with their cumbersome cameras, tripods and long lenses, heading north to the timber hide overlooking Arne Bay.

Then, as I turned on to the main farm track leading up to St Nicholas Church and the tarmac road, I met two unlikely hikers coming towards me through the trees which closely overshadowed the path at this point. They were unlikely because they were so inappropriately dressed, in dark jackets and ties over thin-soled town shoes. I gave them a cheery "Good morning" as they approached me, which was acknowledged non-committally with a nod, and they passed on.

Maybe five or ten seconds later I felt a searing pain in the back of my neck. My legs were kicked out from under me and I crumpled to the ground. As I tried to turn I received a severe blow to the side of my head and the raw sting of scraped skin as I was dragged over the gravel.

As I met the bramble and the nettles at the side of the track, my head bounced on a protruding stone, and all went black.

That was the last I knew of the flora and fauna of the Arne peninsula that day. It would be many hours before I was again in a position to register my surroundings, and it would be nowhere that I was familiar with.

* * * *

I woke up aching all over. My shoulder and leg muscles were cramped, and my left wrist gave a sharp twinge when I tried to move it. I say 'woke up', but it was more a case of my brain and eyesight emerging in slow motion through a thick fog into an unnecessarily bright daylight and a state of confused semi-consciousness. I blinked rapidly to try and clear my vision, and otherwise I thought it prudent to remain as immobile as I could.

I was evidently indoors. The room was small with a low ceiling and a wooden sash window, through which from my prone position on the floor I could only see a tiled roof and chimney of an adjacent property. The floor was not uncomfortable. Exploring with my right hand I could feel a deep pile carpet, and a couple of cushions which had been thoughtfully placed under my head and the small of my back. Well, at least I had not been dumped in a cellar or an empty warehouse. My captors clearly departed from the script of those frightful doom-laden television thrillers with which viewers were nightly entertained.

In fact the room was positively chintzy. There was a floral three-piece suite, and a pale wooden sideboard draped in a rather overdone lacy cotton cloth. The whole ambience to me spelt 'furnished holiday letting'.

Presumably someone was going to come in before long and start some kind of interrogation. Despite my gross discomfort and queasiness I made up my mind to play the outraged guileless boat owner who had become the victim of wholly unprovoked grievous bodily harm. The more manoeuvring space I could give Naomi, whatever her current predicament, the better.

Sure enough, twenty minutes later the door opened and a tall, rather distinguished-looking man came in and sat down on the sofa facing me. He was well dressed in a lovat suit that was clearly by a bespoke tailor. Rather leonine in appearance, his severe face held piercing grey eyes under a fine head of salt-and-pepper hair swept back over his head. Not a man one would easily forget.

He studied me for a moment, and then reached into his jacket pocket and extracted a small piece of paper.

"Gone for a swim around Rand Island," he read out to me. "I'll be straight back."

Whatever his expected reaction from me, this revelation suffused me with genuine anger. I raised myself with difficulty on to one elbow.

"This is a confounded outrage. What the devil are you doing with my note – stolen from my boat? And you have the effrontery to sit there without a word of apology after causing me serious injury – assault – and now bloody kidnap . . ." I could hardly get my words out coherently, I was so worked up.

I collapsed back on to the floor.

The man gazed at me, entirely unmoved by my outburst. He then reached into another pocket and calmly withdrew a mobile phone – my phone – which he leant over and placed on the floor by my hand.

"Mr Penrose," he said slowly, "I have one or two questions to ask you and would be grateful for your cooperation."

So he knew my name, I imagine as a result of hacking into the memory of my phone. I was not going to let him off so lightly.

"Commodore, RN, if you wish to address me, sir," I responded stuffily with a frown.

I could see from his eyes that this information threw him for a second or two. Just for a moment his authority seemed to flicker, and then his severe features restored themselves and he continued.

"Commodore Penrose, I wish to know for whom you left that note on your cabin table this morning when you decided to go for a swim."

"And what business is that of yours, I'd like to know? What the hell is going on, and who might you be?" was my riposte.

The man sighed and crossed his elegantly trousered legs. "You are here for a reason. I will say no more than that. If you have ever worked at the Admiralty you may understand what I am saying."

"I have had nothing to do with the Admiralty in my life, I am happy to say," I assured him. "My career has been about ships, equipment and stores, not all that cloak-and-dagger nonsense. Why, are you from the Admiralty?"

He seemed to find that rather amusing. His mouth twitched into a smile and he raised his dark bushy eyebrows.

"Can we come back to my question, please, and then we can get you up into a bit more comfort?"

That was certainly an appealing prospect. I was getting very stiff there on the floor. I had prepared my story hours ago, back on the boat.

"I left the note for my wife, of course. She went home last night and was going to rejoin me this morning. We only live a few miles from Arne and she had to get back for something or other."

I had hoped this would more or less fit the bill. The presence or absence of the dinghy at various times was a bit tricky, but otherwise the scenario might be convincing enough.

My answer was apparently not what he was expecting. I decided to press on with my version of events.

"When I found the note missing, I wanted to phone my wife, but then discovered of course that my own mobile had been pinched. I was attacked on my way back to Arne or Ridge to find a phone and get hold of Anne to tell her to come back to the boat, so we could discuss what to do about the theft and so on."

I thought it unnecessary to mention that I had the car still sitting in the Arne car park.

I consolidated my bluff: "If you are unconvinced, I will phone my wife here and now, and she can confirm everything I have told you. We were having a nice quiet day or two pottering around Poole Harbour in our boat together, and now all this. I haven't a clue what is going on here."

Please, God, if he called my bluff, Anne would be out.

The man on the sofa looked thoughtful. I began to suspect that his assumptions had been very different.

"I will be straight with you," he eventually said in a rather more resigned tone of voice. "We are looking for a young man who was snooping around last night in a place where he had no business to be. My men caught a glimpse of him, but he has evaded a subsequent search of the isl— of the private location. They had reason to suspect an association with your boat."

"I see." And I pressed home my advantage: "Well, I don't keep a young man on board my boat, if that's what you had in mind. My crew tends to be exclusively female, and I can assure you that this has been the case for several days." This at least was undeniably the truth, and was the cause of my considerable emotional upheaval, but I was not about to divulge all that.

"Now, if you've quite finished," I risked in a glimmer of confidence, "I wish to go home immediately, and on arrival it is my intention to phone the police and report my assault and unlawful restraint."

Had I gone too far? Without any change of expression my jailer rose to his feet and simply walked out of the room, shutting the door quietly behind him and leaving me still on the carpet.

I put my phone back in my own pocket.

CHAPTER FOURTEEN

After a couple of minutes he reappeared in the doorway, a hand on the doorknob.

"By the way, Commodore," he asked rather casually, "did you ever have a naval posting to South Carolina?"

I looked at him blankly. What an odd question! But it rang a faint bell in my mind. Somebody else had asked me that quite recently – but I couldn't place it.

"My naval postings are my own business, but the answer is no. I have never been near the place," I retorted.

He contemplated me for a moment, and then nodded. With that he withdrew once again and closed the door.

South Carolina – what did I know about that? A state down on the south-east coast of the USA with some quite well-known landmarks – Charleston, Columbia, three or four big lakes – what of it?

I had been to several parts of America years ago requisitioning orders for naval equipment, dockyard machinery, routine stuff except for some weapons systems including those designated for Polaris on one occasion. But never that far south.

Where had I heard that enquiry before? And then it came to me – Naomi, of course. She had asked me the same thing.

An odd thought struck me: was that question, and a particular response, some kind of coded password exchange that would identify both parties as belonging, in common with one another, to some secret organisation?

Evidently I had given the wrong answer on both occasions.

But what could Naomi have in common with this suave, rather chilling gentleman interrogator? Surely he could not be 'on her side'. He revealed himself all too obviously to me, knowing what I know, as a representative of whatever was going on at Lone Isle. And what about the behaviour of his henchmen in attacking and kidnapping me in that violent manner? I could not for a moment suppose that this was standard practice by employees of Her Majesty's secret service. Perhaps I was being hopelessly naive.

One agonising thought went round and round in my head as I sat there on that holiday-cottage floor recovering my wits and my physical equilibrium. An icy nagging doubt had sprung from this incident and that curious Carolina query, and that was the possibility that, after all, Naomi herself was not what she had so convincingly presented to me over the last few days. Espionage was a closed book to me. I knew nothing of double agents, double counter-bluff, nor indeed of the rights and wrongs of whoever ultimately acted in the interests of the state. All that was a topsy-turvy world.

Hadn't Harold Wilson even when prime minister been the subject of MI5 surveillance as a potential subversive element? In the end, who was the state? After excavating through all the topsoil and subsoil of national paraphernalia, digging around the roots of plants, both roses and nettles, who would identify finally the buried rock, the bedrock, that was truly the state? And even then, did anything even more fundamental lurk beneath the bedrock?

I got carefully to my knees, and then hauled myself on to the sofa. That was a great improvement. I was feeling quite human again.

As if on cue, the door opened and a nondescript man I had not seen before, certainly not in Newport, came in with a mug of strong tea. He handed it to me without a word and left the room. The tea was sweet and milky, and most welcome. I sipped it slowly and meditatively as I contemplated my likely immediate future. I fervently hoped they had finished with me, evidently disappointed. They could hardly just let me go, walking free out through the front door. I would be straight round to the police station with the cottage's name and street, demanding charges. I had no idea what town or village I was in, but imagined that I was still somewhere in South Dorset – Wareham, perhaps, or Dorchester. I knew both very well and would instantly recognise my location.

What a fool! Even as I mulled these things over in my mind, and drained that timely mug of tea, the lights went out in my head; the room darkened as in a total solar eclipse; the mug slipped from my fingers and all went rather peacefully black. In the seconds before I lost consciousness I recognised that my kidnappers had, of course, prepared the obvious solution to any risk of identity or discovery.

Night and day, sleeping and awake, form such a natural pattern in our life story – the unconscious state heralding a fresh new chapter – or maybe just a paragraph – commencing each morning as regularly as breathing. Sleepless nights will disturb this routine, and perhaps it is this break in pattern rather than the absence of sleep, as such, which accounts for our feeling out of sorts on the morning after.

Afternoon naps, to which I was increasingly prone, can have a similar disruptive influence on this rhythm of our storyline if they descend into proper sleep.

Either way, it is as though a page, or half a page, has been interfered with, crowded with tedious footnotes on the one hand, or clumsily torn out on the other hand, leaving us unsettled and insecure.

Deep sleep will always have this tendency towards closure of one scene in our play, or one act, denoted by the dimming of the footlights or the falling of the proscenium curtain. The theatre audience (our own introspection) assumes that this anticipates a new scene or act, resuming the story of the play, perhaps after the interval.

My own play was certainly about to develop a new and surprising relationship of characters and cast members after the unforeseen intermission in which I had been served refreshments not of ice cream or indifferent house red, but of hot tea spiced with a Mickey Finn.

$$* * * *$$

What brought me back to consciousness, long before I opened my eyes, was the rising and falling 'pink-a-pink-a-pink' trill of oystercatchers. Such a familiar sound to me on the shorelines of Poole Harbour, alongside the darting antics of little black-headed gulls and the piercing dives of terns.

I was exceedingly uncomfortable. I was lying on something hard and wooden, my lower back unsupported across a void, giving me a severe backache. One leg seemed to be dangling over a prominent edge, causing a stab of pain behind the knee.

I opened an eye. Immediately framed in my vision, fortunately still in focus through my glasses, stood a white egret, poised elegantly like a ballet dancer, as stock-still as a statue, on a muddy water's edge.

I doubted whether it was yet prudent to open the other eye. I left it for a bit, and reclosed the first one.

Well, fact number one was that I was alive. So far, so good. Secondly, I was by the sea, or tidal water at any rate. Thirdly, I appeared to be alone. Fourthly, I was damn annoyed.

Suddenly another noise broke into the background music of the oystercatchers. From behind me came the evidence of running feet, crunching over sandy gravel, accompanied by a shout still some way off. I knew that shout. Indeed, I had played tennis very frequently with the owner of it, who was inclined to use it loudly, despite my remonstrations, on the regular occasion of my losing straight sets. It was the voice of happy triumph.

It belonged to my daughter Sarah.

I opened both eyes wide, and regretted it. The Mickey Finn effect was still boring holes in my temples. I tried to raise my head to look round, but instantly decided against. I let go, and lay there like a stranded haddock.

In a moment, the footsteps were with me. Several pairs of arms were reaching under me. The relief from that pain of dead weight was blissful.

The next voice above me was my wife Anne's.

"Robert, my poor dear, whatever has happened to you? You look all in. We thought we would find you on board. What on earth are you doing lying in the dinghy like that? Let's have a look at you."

She gently straightened my aching limbs and I lay on my back gazing up at her from the muddy pebbles, mutely saturated with thankfulness and release.

"Well," I managed to croak, "I didn't actually know I was here. I've only just come to. I've been otherwise engaged."

Anne looked at me in bewilderment.

"Give me a moment and I'll tell you all about it."

My sight now restored, I scanned the view from where I lay. There was *Peggotty*, quietly sitting at anchor a few yards off. I had evidently been dumped unceremoniously into her dinghy, just where I had left her on the beach. Full circle. How long had I been away?

Then I heard another voice behind me: "I think we should all get out to *Peggotty* and move well away from here. We don't know who might have their binoculars trained on us."

I swivelled round, and winced with the effort. There was Naomi, my comrade-in-arms, smiling down at me, hands on hips. But Naomi with a difference. No longer the teenage boy, but very definitely restored to female form, dressed in what I recognised to be a skirt and shirt belonging to one of my daughters, a rather stylish band of cloth around her head hippy-fashion, hiding her short-cropped hair.

"Naomi!" I exclaimed. "So you got away!"

"I got away, Robert, only just. I saw enough, but unfortunately they saw me."

"I know," I acknowledged grimly. "They told me so in no uncertain terms."

She looked quickly at me, her smile vanishing.

"Come on," with new urgency in her voice, "the sooner we are gone the better."

And so the three of them slid the dinghy to the water, and Anne shipped the oars ready to row.

Sarah and Naomi escorted me gingerly to the stern thwart and pushed off, jumping in over the gunwale as the boat cleared the ground.

Clambering aboard *Peggotty* was a struggle, but with six hands helping me I was soon in the cockpit getting my breath back.

"Knockout pill in a cup of tea," I muttered to Naomi. "Then they bundled me back into the dinghy."

"Thought as much," she replied. "Too groggy to have been just whisky."

I smiled back. Thank goodness we could have the luxury of a quip. I had more than doubted that I would ever see her again.

Rowing back in the dinghy we had decided to motor back down Balls Lake and Upper Wych to anchor round at Russel Quay for a council of war. As we pottered slowly along, one eye on the depth sounder as the tide was on the ebb, Anne and Sarah filled me in on their side of the story.

To my astonishment, this early evening was still the same day that I had been assaulted and kidnapped in the morning. It seemed like a week ago.

At about ten o'clock that morning, Sarah had opened the door of our home in Church Knowle to an insistent knock from a complete stranger – a very bedraggled, muddy and thoroughly unkempt young man – asking to speak urgently to a Mrs Anne Penrose.

Anne is a resourceful woman, and as competent as any in a crisis. She recognised a crisis immediately in the form of this slim figure standing dripping on the doormat. Sarah was simply intrigued. As soon as the crew-cut youth opened his mouth to explain, it was of course evident that this was no male voice box. Here was a girl in disguise, out of breath and bearing an extraordinary story.

She told them, they said, that she had been rescued off Spithead by Anne's husband a few days previously, having been trying to flee a group of men who wished her harm. She was an investigative officer for a government department trying to follow a lead which had now brought her to Dorset, having hitched a lift with me, Robert, back to Poole Harbour. (Anne looked quizzically at me at this part of her story, with a sceptical expression and a slight grin, possibly recalling the content of my first telephone report home on that first evening).

Naomi, continued Sarah, who took on the narrative, said that she had made her investigation but had been spotted by her suspects and had made a run for it. She had deliberately avoided returning to *Peggotty*, as this would have drawn her pursuers straight there (I resisted the temptation to make a cynical comment at that); and as I had told her where I lived, she had made a beeline to Church Knowle by swimming the creek, jogging to Arne and hiding in the church, then tagging on to a group of twitchers walking to Ridge. She had later thumbed a lift and walked the rest of the way. She was confident that she had shaken off her pursuers in Arne.

So, this young woman had said to my bemused family in the kitchen of our home, she was there seeking refuge and safety and could they please be very careful not to answer the door to any more strange men?

In the meantime, she had assumed that I was still aboard *Peggotty*, biting my nails in frustration and anxiety, wondering where on earth she could have got to, and thinking the worst. (I nodded my head in complete agreement at that suggestion.)

Sarah, bless her, had then volunteered to drive to Arne and walk down to Shipstal to hail me and bring me up to date. On arrival, of course, all Sarah had found was the empty dinghy and no sign of Dad whatever.

All three (my other daughters being away) had then set out again in the afternoon, checked that my car was still in the Arne car park, and found me at last, slumped over the thwarts of the dinghy tender, totally out for the count.

"And here we all are," I rather fatuously commented as the anchor chain rattled out into the mud of the old quarry wharf at Russel Quay.

CHAPTER FIFTEEN

It was perfectly evident that Anne and my daughter had taken quite a shine to Naomi during the course of the day. I think this gained added lustre in their growing confidence in her story, from what I was able to fill in later by way of detail. I kept glancing at Naomi as I related our adventures, but she gave no indication that I should be more circumspect in revealing her identity and purpose than she had been with me.

She must have concluded that her breaches in professional secrets, arguably inescapable in her predicament so far as I had been concerned, could land her in no deeper water now; although she had more than once impressed on Anne and Sarah an obligation never to reveal the information to anyone else. Readers may already have wondered, in this respect, why I am now broadcasting these secrets and Naomi's role in them by the publication of this book. My excuse is that there is nothing written here that could possibly now link even the most assiduous enquirer to her present identity, occupation or environment. Her organisation has long been a past master in obliterating all such traces. As for the national-security element, readers must form their own judgement, should they be generous enough to read the book to its finish.

As for our personal relationship, whatever that really comprised, I hardly know to this day the extent to which Anne's intuition had formed an accurate interpretation of the rapport between Naomi and myself. Certainly I have never succeeded in translating it with the remotest degree of articulation. Restoration of her company on board the boat that evening only confirmed that my feelings for Naomi were not just paternal, avuncular or strictly concerned with protection. It was a devotion of some depth, but it was not love in any conventional sense.

Words from my current reading – *Captain Corelli's Mandolin* – came back to me as I pondered this question that night.

'We who truly love,' wrote Louis de Bernières, 'had roots that grew towards each other underground, and when all the pretty blossom had fallen from our branches we found that we were one tree and not two'.[1]

By this I wish to cast no aspersion on the continuing attractiveness of Anne at that time, as she held a fair degree of blossom still, and on a tree of a most appealing profile. No, the point was that this link of abiding strength lay largely underground, hidden from easy view.

Articulation of feeling for Anne lay with these buried roots, largely inaccessible. Somewhere, scarcely below the surface of the soil, lay also my inability to express the magnetism of Naomi, which itself in its attraction pole to pole ran all too exposed in the open air above. That is all I can say.

Now it was Naomi's turn to report on her clandestine exploration of Lone Isle the previous night. As I had surmised, while rowing away from *Peggotty* in the small hours she had realised the implications of a delayed escape in daylight, and so had taken the dinghy round to the far side of Rand Island nearby, where I had found it. She had then walked carefully across to the north shore, using a well-worn path which considerably eased the task. With the torch and notebook held above her head she waded the short distance over on to the isle, up to her waist in water, and crawled flat (as she had been taught on a course by the Royal Marines) up the exposed beach and into the low undergrowth.

As soundlessly as possible in her canvas sneakers she crept around to the western side by the old houseboat, which appeared deserted, to find the gap in the trees which gave unobstructed passage to the hidden interior.

1. Louis de Bernières *Corelli's Mandolin*, (Vintage International, 1999)

Inside the ring of scrub right around the island was an inner belt of pine trees of some height, the combined effect being that of a crown. However, in place of the dome of the monarch's head inside the crown lay quite the inverse – a surprisingly deep hollow possibly blown into an even deeper crater by a Second World War bomb, jettisoned by a Heinkel after an air raid over Poole or Southampton.

In spite of the high wire-netting fence around the rim of this hole in the ground, Naomi could see right down to its base from her vantage point in the shadow of the pines. There sat the black helicopter, illuminated only by shaded ground lights that cast no beam higher than knee level. It squatted toad-like on a circular pad of concrete. Nearby, on the edge of the crater base, stood a rough timber hut with small windows, pitched corrugated roof and a single door. A dull glow penetrated the closed blinds in the windows.

The ridge of the hut's roof, and the pivot of the helicopter's rotor blades, rose no higher than the rim of the crater. Viewed horizontally from ground level, where Naomi stood, the clearing in the centre of the island would have revealed nothing at all within its perimeter fence.

The fence itself, although some eight feet in height, was not ostensibly of high-security design. It consisted of wooden posts, seemingly cut from pine-tree trunks, with sheep netting on strained wires. Immediately opposite where Naomi was standing was a timber-and-netting gate of the same design, with a closed padlock.

It was too dark to tell whether CCTV cameras were installed anywhere. There appeared to be no tripwires close to the fence, nor indeed anything of any sophistication whatever. No signs except a tatty board on the gate reading 'Private. Keep Out'. Except for the hut and the concrete pad far below, the general ensemble looked to the casual eye to be much like a pheasant-rearing enclosure.

Maybe that was the intention. The presence of the helicopter, of course, gave the lie to that impression, but its visits were perhaps few and far between.

The sloping sides of the crater were steep, but negotiable. They were thick with brambles, low mountain ash and coarse grass. A flight of steps had simply been carved out of the surface in an easy diagonal down the slope from the gate to the flat base, some but not all of the treads laid with pieces of paving slab.

Naomi crept on her hands and knees to the foot of the fence, and slowly began to work her way along it, from post to post, looking carefully for the slightest gap between fence and turf that could be eased up enough for her to slip through.

It was not long before she found what she was looking for. The straining wire running just above ground level reached a narrow dip in the terrain – probably an old badger run. It was full of nettles and the fencer had clearly omitted to net into the gap. With a little more excavation with her bare hands, she soon had a hole big enough for her to snake through. She also knew about nettles – grasp them firmly between finger and thumb at the very base of their stem and they will pull out easily without stinging.

Keeping to a reptile manoeuvre, crawling on thighs and elbows, she pushed her way down the slope towards the hut, pausing every so often to listen acutely for any sign of danger. By now, thanks to the endless drizzle and the wade across the muddy tide, she was soaked through. It was a warm night though, and she felt fine – except that by the time she reached the bottom she was scratched on hands, arms and face from brambles and now well and truly throbbing from nettle stings on all exposed skin.

Once she had reached the back wall of the hut, on the windowless side facing the crater slope, she sat on the ground, leant her back against the planking and took stock of the situation.

'No heroics', she said to herself. If the occupants of the hut were who she thought they were, she had a score to settle. Her recovery of the document case and the plutonium canister from their rented flat in Portsmouth the previous week had not been without incident. They had almost caught her before she had smashed a window and fled down the fire escape. One man had grabbed her sleeve and hit her hard on the cheek, only letting go because his colleague had barged into the room and sent him flying with the edge of the door. That man had then landed a kick on her shin before she managed to leap through the window, attracting some nasty cuts from the breaking glass on the way.

But no, this was not the time or place for retribution. All she had to do was identify the occupants to establish their link with Lone Isle, and note any useful additional information. Her job was to report to her superiors, and they would take the necessary practical steps. She just hoped this would include a bit of strong-arm stuff by special forces when they came to arrest these jokers.

Naomi took some deep breaths and calmed herself down. "Concentrate, girl," she whispered to her own shadow.

She crawled around to the end of the hut, to a position beneath the window, and listened. A murmur of low voices was all she could discern. The window was shut and old-fashioned metal venetian blinds were drawn, the slats angled down so that she could not see in.

She made a similar inspection of the other three windows of the hut, with much the same results. Then she noticed that the window in the far end, the last she came to, had a window stay that was not properly secured on to its pins. The traditional latch, however, was firmly in place.

Extracting my bosun's knife from her pocket, she unfolded the blade, slid it into the slit between casement and frame, and gingerly levered sideways. The window budged not an inch. She dared not lever it lower down, as the last thing she wanted was the splintering of wood and the cracking of glass. She turned the blade the other way below the latch, and gently pressed it with a sawing action into the gap. The window was just ill-fitting enough to permit the blade to rise slowly until it engaged the bar of the latch. Cautiously she pushed upwards, and the latch lifted. A little leverage, and she could get her fingers around the edge of the casement.

She distinctly heard the hinge squeak. She froze, and waited. Voices were now much louder, but did not pause in their conversation. Naomi breathed again.

The window was now just open sufficiently widely for her to get her hand and wrist through the gap. There was a very narrow internal cill, and beyond that the venetian blind. Did she dare insert a finger between two slats to distort them enough to see into the room? What if that particular blind was in the direct sight of one of the men inside?

She thought the bottom slat was the one to try – perhaps the least risky. Would they notice the sudden increase in volume of sound from outdoors, now the window was ajar? Happily there was no wind, just the relentless soggy mist.

Slowly does it.

The first thing she could discern through the warp in the slats was the back of a head. Pale ginger hair in a long fringe over a collar, a freckled bald dome above it. Sticking-out ears and a thin scraggy neck. Hmm. Familiar. This was the character with the handgun in his denim jacket that she had spotted in Newport, and indeed one of her two adversaries in the Portsmouth flat.

She looked past his shoulder. Hidden from her line of sight was a large person, the only parts of him she could see being one arm and a knee dressed in a shiny blue suit. She remembered that suit. It had been worn by the ginger-haired man's colleague in Newport – a bruiser of a fellow with a dark beard.

'Bullseye again,' she thought to herself.

There was a third person in the hut, and Naomi could see him clearly in profile, seated in a comfortable-looking armchair. His was the authoritative voice that dominated their discussion. An elegant man, patently educated at one of the older public schools, judging from his tone and from the blue, red and gold striped tie in his impeccable collar. He wore a classic worsted suit with turn-ups in a tasteful lovat green.

This gentleman she had never seen before.

In retrospect, Naomi admitted to us, she should have left it at that and crept away. With the knowledge that she now had, a report to base could have led quickly to a raid on Lone Isle and some prompt arrests. She was on the point of withdrawing, however, when she spotted on the end of the window ledge the corner of a folded piece of typewritten paper. The ginger-haired man had evidently lodged it there behind his shoulder for convenience, and it was very likely the notes or report that was the subject of the present discussion in the room. He had just stood up, presumably needing his hands free for some other purpose, and indeed at that moment interrupted the conversation with an enquiry as to whether his colleagues would like a cup of coffee. Murmurs of assent were followed by his leaving that end of the room, no doubt to organise kettle and milk in whatever cubby hole in the hut served as a kitchen.

CHAPTER SIXTEEN

Naomi then made her fateful and impetuous move. She reached in to full arm's length and closed two fingers over the corner of the paper. In the slowest motion she slid her arm back again along the cill, drawing the rest of the paper sheet from beneath the drop of the venetian blind.

As the glow of the room's light lit up the face of the paper through the slit in the blind's slats, she immediately recognised what it represented. She had seen these before, on her very first mission two years previously. It was a commercial bill of lading for a shipping line – the kind of thing that schedules the authorised cargo for a particular passage of one of its merchant ships and carries the import/export registration and Customs and Excise stamp.

This one, legible now on the window cill and its vanishing act apparently unnoticed by those indoors, Naomi now had the opportunity for a few seconds to scrutinise. Unlike lading schedules she had seen in the past, this one had 'RESTRICTED' stamped in large capital letters across the top right-hand corner. This was a rather poor photocopy, obtained in a rush or perhaps reproduced from a Minox camera shot.

The list was not long. It did not deal in large quantities of bulk goods, but in racks of hazardous waste recycling and pharmaceutical products with technical names that meant nothing to Naomi. The products were described as being in cartons of the usual plastic and metal containers familiar to anyone queuing at the pharmacy counter in Boots.

Her frantic glance was immediately drawn, however, to an entry helpfully made prominent by a yellow highlighter. It simply read, '165 number canisters contents 330 kg each plutonium-239 as solid oxide'.

The destination of this cargo ship (from Liverpool) Naomi noted with some satisfaction and a nod of her head as if it confirmed what she already suspected. It read, 'Commercial harbour entry, Charleston, South Carolina, USA, State Ports Authority clearance'.

The departure date from Liverpool was stated to be 31 August.

'Jackpot,' she said to herself. 'Box 500 are going to be over the moon with this.'

The vital thing now was to restore the paper to the end of the ledge, push the window to and make her escape. Capture and detention of these people, now 'hostile personnel' in her jargon, depended on their carrying through their plans until the right moment of surprise by special forces. She must not sabotage this inadvertently by raising the alarm precipitately.

She folded the lading bill and slipped it back along the window cill behind the blind, concentrating hard on avoiding inadvertent movement of the blind or window. Her aim was to shove a corner of the paper back under the base of the blind approximate to the position in which she had found it, so that Gingerhead would find nothing amiss when he returned to his seat.

Absorbed as she was in this task with every ounce of single-mindedness, Naomi had failed to notice that Blackbeard had also risen from his chair.

He had chosen that moment to gain a breath of fresh air.

At the very instant that Naomi's fingers were inserting the paper under the blind, he flung open the outside door beside which she was standing. The rattle of the latch made her start involuntarily, causing her hand to jerk against the heavy metal blind, sending it swinging, its slats riffling with a clatter.

The man in the lovat suit snapped his head round to the noise, in time to see the lading bill float gently to the floor.

Naomi wrenched her arm back out from the window opening, her elbow nudging the casement open with a slam against the timber cladding.

Simultaneously the door was opened by the unsuspecting Blackbeard, and the light from the room streamed out, casting its full beam directly on to Naomi from head to foot as though she were the class act at the climax of a theatre revue on a London stage. All that was missing was the drum roll and clash of cymbals.

They stared at one another for a second and a half. Then a yell from Lovat-suit inside galvanised them both synchronously into activity.

Naomi turned and sprinted into the blackness of the night, blinded by the sudden light, and scrambled on to the bottom of the crater slope, unable to discern what undergrowth she was running into. This immediately proved to be the edge of a thick bramble, but her searching arms found the stem of a small tree, which she gripped; and she was about to haul herself up by it on to the higher ground when Blackbeard's stertorous breathing closed in at her shoulder, and he, equally blinded, barged into her from behind, knocking them both to the ground.

At this point, Gingerhead, who had abandoned his coffee preparation and emerged to see what all the fuss was about, reached the doorway at the same microsecond as Lovat-suit. The door opening was of inadequate width to permit a tandem exodus, and the consequent logjam prevented immediate reinforcements for Blackbeard, providing precious extra moments for Naomi to get the better of the collision.

With a vicious backward kick that caught Blackbeard with an oath in the groin, she again found her little mountain-ash stem and, night vision improving, made her way quickly up the slope to the foot of the fence.

She knew that she had to go right, along the line of the fence, to find her original point of entry, and so pushed away as quickly as possible through the undergrowth, which grew thick and thorny against the wire netting. In places she needed to make a detour as the obstruction was too dense to penetrate.

It was slow going, and to her alarm she realised that the chase was still on. The men below had found torches, and had spread out around the base of the slope. Two torch beams were already halfway up, the third (no doubt Lovat-suit's) remaining at base level.

One approaching torchbearer was behind her and one in front – this one quite likely to cut her off from her hole in the fence if he made it to the top before she had reached it.

A diversionary tactic was called for. Naomi felt around the ground until her hands found a couple of large stones, big enough to make a noise but light enough to throw some distance. These she lobbed in quick succession diagonally back down the slope between her and the man in front. Both stones made a satisfactory rustle and thud in the bushes, prompting a shout of hopeful triumph from the man with a torch, who changed direction and began to descend the slope again in the direction from which the sounds had come.

* * * *

From there, Naomi's escape was uneventful so far as violent action was concerned. The retreat across the creek to Shipstal and her trek to my home in Church Knowle was as already described. The birdwatchers whose group she had tagged on to along the road had unsurprisingly made comment on her (or rather his) disreputable appearance, but she had muttered in as low and gravelly a voice as possible that she had regrettably fallen into one of the marshy standing ponds which litter the northern part of the woodland on the Arne peninsula. This was all too believable, as another of the party was squelching in one boot and sodden trouser leg from precisely the same predicament.

They all thought him a rather silent, morose young man and hardly a congenial walking companion.

On the conclusion of Naomi's tale of adventure, my principal reaction was one of relief and self-reproach. The South Carolina business I now knew to have nothing to do with codes and passwords, and I was ashamed of myself that I had raised doubt in my own mind over Naomi's integrity or allegiance. I was still puzzled.

"So what goes on in Charleston, South Carolina, then?" was my first question as we sat there over mugs of tea, anchored off Russel Quay.

She seemed reluctant to respond, no doubt wondering how much to say.

"Well," she eventually began, "there is a US government facility there which processes, for purposes I don't need to go into, the residues of certain radioactive material acquired from nuclear industry around the world. It comes in by land, sea and air. It is commercial hazardous waste from power stations and so on, but obviously its export and import are closely controlled by government agencies. Terrorist theft en route, or in fact theft by certain nation states, is always a risk.

"That is what these jokers on Lone Isle have been planning for months, but it is only now we have documentary evidence that we understand what is going on. They have already broken into the Atomic Weapons Establishment, as you know from what we recovered, but they have also infiltrated UK government agencies – and that is the nightmare. I don't know who to trust."

The three Penroses present digested all this in silence for a few minutes, gazing across Wareham Channel to Ham Common and the lights of Rockley in the gathering dusk.

"Does this mean you are a spy?" Sarah broke the silence.

Anne looked alarmed.

"Well, as I said to your father when we first met," Naomi replied with a slightly mischievous smile in my direction, "I am a sort of civil servant. I ought not to say more than that, Sarah, but I expect you can read between the lines. I work for a government agency."

"And now", I chipped in, "our job is to help you get safely back to that agency with the vital information you have, and the items recovered, in time for interception of the planned theft to be organised well before the ship leaves Liverpool in about three weeks' time. What's going to be the best plan? We don't know", I continued, "if they have dismissed me as an irrelevance. Thank goodness we decided on that sex change at Newport! I think that has put them off their stroke completely. Even so, they can hardly imagine that I am going to simply shrug off an assault and kidnap. If I had been what I made out to be – an entirely innocuous boat owner caught up mistakenly in some nefarious crime that I knew nothing about – surely they would expect me to have gone to the police by now, even though I could tell the cops nothing about my captors or where I was held, except for personal descriptions.

"We must assume that these people have no infiltration into the Dorset Constabulary, so are unlikely to follow up that train of thought.

"Of course, they will know where we live, and our Church Knowle address, simply by looking up my name in the phone directory. They might just keep an eye on our house for a while to see if I do anything out of the ordinary. Certainly they will think it a bit odd if I just resume my pottering in the harbour on *Peggotty*. I guess that we should now get *Peggotty* back on her mooring in the river, and all go home to work out a plan of action."

And so it was agreed. There was still just sufficient light to motor *Peggotty* up Wareham Channel and spot the spindly withies marking the upper reaches of the navigable stream. Before long the boat was securely moored, back home after the most extraordinary few days' passage no doubt in her entire long life.

We took the dinghy up the river to Redclyffe Yacht Club, and by half past ten were back in the house.

It was strange being back home. For the evening and following day, my life resumed its routine pattern of familiarities – the chores, the family banter, catching up with the emails. Sarah had adopted Naomi as a rather exotic elder sister and Naomi rose to the challenge. I had no idea at all of her own family, whether she had brothers and sisters or cousins. Her private life was the proverbial closed book, and I knew that this was deliberate on her part. I guess that anyone working in the profession in which she was engaged has very good reason to keep occupation and personal matters resolutely separate. I imagine that this is not merely an emotional commitment. No doubt there is a real and pressing necessity on grounds of personal safety – one's own and that of one's family and friends.

I suppose this was, in a way, part of her attraction to me. Private lives involve roots, and mine were deep enough – and, I hoped, strong enough. This girl was like some gold coin, or valuable brooch, that I had spotted on the ground and picked up out of a curiosity that grew instantly to excitement on close examination and touch, its history, ownership and provenance a complete mystery. And like the precious brooch or coin, Naomi would have to be handed in to the authorities to re-establish where and to whom she belonged. The brooch is not mine, however beautiful it is to me. It is a temporary joy, and having enfolded it in my hands, bare and entirely unwrapped, letting it go will probably give me a painful scratch with the end of its pin. This I knew and foresaw at home back there with my family and was at once discomforted and relieved.

CHAPTER SEVENTEEN

The following morning, Anne, Naomi and I sat down after breakfast to consider our position. The canister and documents (the former hidden in a small canvas bag – revealing its contents to my family would have diverted us from urgent concentration) had of course come with us from the boat, and Naomi had written up her Lone Isle discoveries in a notebook, which joined the file.

"Surely the simplest and safest answer", I suggested, "is for me to drive you straight up to London today in the car, and you can just walk in on your boss and hand it all over. Job done. No need to telephone in advance if there is a risk of his office phone being tapped."

"What if our Lone Isle friends are still keeping tabs on you though?" she replied. "They could follow the car, and when they see it pulling up outside Thames House things could get suddenly nasty for both of us – blood on the pavement."

"What's Thames House?" asked Anne.

"The headquarters of the security service in Britain," Naomi replied. "That's where I am based. But the trouble is I'm pretty sure that someone in Thames House, or maybe more than one, is working for the other side. There have been too many security leaks to be coincidence. It may be someone I know – one of my colleagues – but my own immediate boss I would trust with my life. I've got to let him know, somehow, that I have all the information we need to pin these people for the data thefts and the burglary at AWE, and most importantly to nab them at

Liverpool at the end of next month. If I just turn up at Thames House with the goods in a bag, and try to clear security to reach the boss, the chances are that *someone* will have infiltrated security and would prevent my reaching him safely.

"It's a big building. Too many systems; too many potential route diversions," she added rather ominously. "Too many unused storage rooms."

We nursed our coffee mugs in silence for a minute or two.

"Do you think" – I voiced a sudden thought that had that moment struck me – "we could get your boss to meet up somewhere other than Thames House or any other MI5 office? And need it be you, in the first instance? Listen – I've had an idea. You remember I told you that my kidnapper asked me whether I had ever worked in the Admiralty? Of course, what he was inferring was that I might have been involved in naval intelligence – in other words, espionage, which is one of the things that go on in that hothouse range of buildings. A lot of underhand wheeling and dealing, if you ask me, but I'm only a plain sailor.

"However, I think I could get myself into the Admiralty buildings. Possibly fix up a small meeting room. I know one or two former navy colleagues who could arrange that. The offices and rooms there will be squeaky-clean so far as security and confidentiality are concerned. Your boss would, I guess, be quite relaxed about a meeting there.

"The Lone islanders would be making no connections with the Admiralty, so would not be alerted if your boss was seen heading there for a meeting. In fact, I reckon he probably goes there a fair bit anyway, to compare notes with his fellow snoopers. Sorry, Naomi – I don't mean to cast aspersions on your profession. I think."

Naomi smiled at me. "Now who's being devious?" she asked. "You have the makings of a good spy yourself."

I continued my train of thought. "Why don't I get my Navy Department contact to get in touch himself with your man at MI5, and find a pretext to set up a meeting with him? And then I'll turn up by prior arrangement with my pal and give your boss the story?"

"What about me?" Naomi objected. "I ought to be there as well."

"As I see it," I replied, "better not. If I set the scene at that meeting, your man will know the best way to fix a handover with you in a secure environment afterwards."

She nodded. "You phone your Admiralty man, then, and I can tell him who to contact at Thames House. If you don't mind, I ought to give him my boss's name and security link with no one else in the room. Sorry, but I've broken too many rules already."

"Just a minute," Anne interposed. "Is it safe to phone her from here? What if Lovat-suit has tapped our own telephone?"

"That's a possibility," I agreed. "I know – we can do the phoning from the office in the lifeboat station. I sometimes help out down there. I doubt if anyone is using the office this morning."

Now that we had a firm plan of action, we set to with enthusiasm. I gathered the necessary contact numbers and drove Naomi down to the smart new RNLI station in Swanage, which had recently been rebuilt to accommodate the new class of lifeboat that had been delivered the previous season.

Fortunately no 'shout' had been raised so far that morning, and the Deputy Launching Authority was only too happy to relinquish the office for a while. We had the room and phone to ourselves, and quickly made the calls we had arranged. My old friend Bill Thomas, captain RN, was quite willing to oblige. He had been in the Admiralty for years, and was by now completely immune to curious and incomprehensible requests for clandestine meetings.

He had, as it happens, met Naomi's boss himself on one occasion during some obscure joint liaison probe between MI5 and the navy.

He promised to phone me at home when he had fixed a meeting date. His call would be suitably coded. He was good at that.

* * * *

"Bit of a snag, old man." Bill Thomas was on the phone very soon that afternoon. "The 'golf club' is members only, and you're not a member. I've gone right to the secretary, but he says you can't hold your little party there without joining and paying the subs. Your principal guest you mentioned is very happy to come, though, and he and I provisionally booked for twelve noon tomorrow. Somehow we've got to get past the club secretary."

Typical, I thought. Trust the Ministry of Defence to be difficult. Too many damn Sea Lords and politicos and not enough common sense.

I thought quickly. "Bill, if I just turn up and you are there to meet me, maybe it won't be too much of a problem." I instantly had an idea that made me smile. I said laughingly, "If I'm in full golfing clothes – you know, plus twos with fancy socks and a colourful jersey and flat cap – I can bluff my way in."

There was a pause at the other end of the line. Then an amused response from Bill. "You mean, you've still got your old ones? You haven't played for several years."

"Of course I kept the old bags, Bill, and I might even be able to forage around a bit and unearth my membership card. Different club, of course, but perhaps they have reciprocal arrangements and won't look too closely at the expiry date. I'll see you there tomorrow."

With a chuckle, Bill hung up and I went upstairs to see what I could find in my wardrobe and desk drawers. They might need some attention with a stiff clothes brush.

I went to find Naomi to report my phone conversation, and eventually discovered her in Sarah's room, where they were both engrossed in rewriting Sarah's CV.

"It's no good being modest with these things," Naomi was saying as Sarah responded to my knock at the door. "It may go against the grain – I expect it does – but these days you've really got to blow your own trumpet with the CV, and boast of your achievements and talents for all they're worth."

Sarah turned and made a face. "Dad, you've always taught me to do the exact opposite."

"I know, darling, but I'm well out of date and look where it's got me."

She smiled.

I then compared notes with Anne about arrangements for the following day. She and the girls would remain at home and be ready to field any phone call I might have to make. I would catch the early train from Wareham and get to London by mid morning, and take the Tube to Horse Guards Parade, or a taxi if the train was delayed. The days were passing, and 31 August approaching with alarming speed. This meeting with Naomi's boss had to work. Lovat-suit and whoever he worked with, or for, had received a fright and would be on their guard at every turn. Time was truly of the essence.

Anne was studying me with a critical expression. "Have you tried the shirt?" she asked. "And what about the collar? Your neck has not got any thinner over the last six years, you know. Golly – that's a thought. Whatever did we do with those stiff collars? They'll have gone all yellow round the edges."

She dashed upstairs and shortly emerged with two of my old white collars, size 15½. These days I took size 16. One of them was tolerably presentable, if a little limp. My old Dartmouth instructor would have had something trenchant to say if I had turned up on parade in that. However, no time to get it re-starched at the laundry. It would have to do.

We decided that it would be a mistake to pre-empt the formal, official meeting between Naomi and her MI5 superior by my presenting him the next day with any of the tangible evidence in her possession. My job would be, as an objective observer of events, to describe to him verbally all that had occurred from my perspective, and everything which Naomi had herself described to us of her adventure on Lone Isle.

Naomi did, however, ask me to include in my conversation her conviction of internal infiltration in Thames House and other state authorities, to alert her boss to the importance of an appropriate secure arrangement for her eventual meeting with him.

The rest of the day passed without incident. We all tried to act naturally, in case binoculars were trained on the house. Sarah went shopping in Dorchester, and Anne and I walked up to the church laden with rags, brushes and buckets as it was our turn on the rota to do the church cleaning that week. We spent a happy hour or so with a couple of other members of the congregation, brushing and dusting. As a navy man I had been given responsibility years before to keep the brasswork gleaming. There was rather a lot of it.

It had always amused me that the cleaner-in-chief, a formidable lady of impressive girth and bust who was a JP and still tended to wear a hat in church, had allocated me this duty on the assumption that I had spent my early naval career sharing brass rags with my fellow matelots and presumably for the rest of the time on my knees scouring wooden decks with soap and sand.

In reality, I struggle to remember ever setting eyes on solid brass, except for the engraved nameplate on Admiral Keys' office door when I was a nervous young ensign. I used to give it a rub with my sleeve while standing there waiting for his barked order to "Come in and straighten up, lad." By the time I had my own nameplate on the door in Devonport, it was laminated plastic. *O tempora! O mores!*

As Anne and I strolled through the village I kept looking surreptitiously for signs of any stranger hovering in the vicinity of our home, or watching out for me, but there was nothing. A couple of young families, obviously summer visitors, passed us on their way to the pub, and a car or two went by, but life in Church Knowle continued with its usual predictable normality. Perhaps we were being just a little paranoid.

I had even adopted a stern expression when we were out of the house, trying to give anyone who might be particularly interested the impression that, yes, I was the victim of a disgraceful attack and false imprisonment; had reported this to the police; and was expecting a personal report very soon from at least the Chief Superintendent. How I thought I might be conveying all this information simply through my pursed lips and furrowed brow I cannot now imagine. Was I secretly rather enjoying myself?

CHAPTER EIGHTEEN

After a quick breakfast with Anne, both Naomi and Sarah being still fast asleep, I drove up through Wareham to collect a morning paper, and boarded the train.

I was wearing a fairly nondescript dark-grey suit over my white shirt and ancient stiff collar, which was adorned with my green-and-pink Billings & Edmunds prep-school tie (now a rarity so many years after the sad demise of that neo-Edwardian establishment of fond memory). This enabled me to wear my black navy-patterned socks and lace-ups without drawing attention to them.

In my overnight valise were my carefully pressed uniform jacket, trousers and cap. I carried no notes or papers of any kind, relying on my rehearsed memory alone to report what I had to say when I reached the Navy Department building. The less tangible evidence of any kind of involvement in this incredible rigmarole the better.

Other than my wallet and diary, the only document I had was my personal security pass from the office at Devonport Naval Base, complete with a little photograph of me with thicker and blacker hair, but otherwise recognisable. I had kept it as one of my private career mementos, little imagining that one day I might be dusting it off for a little sleight of hand to gain entry into, of all places, that fearsome building which I had always regarded as the British equivalent of the Kremlin.

To my surprise, I realised that although the card displayed an issue date (fourteen years previously), there was nothing to indicate its expiry. This might make things easier, I thought, when being scrutinised by gimlet eyes at reception.

At any rate, my service cap would hide most of my hair. I just hoped that the thickness and weight of gold braid on jacket and peak would do the rest. I could always hold my own when eye to eye with a subordinate in the old days. Reception would be the first to blink, I felt sure.

On my arrival at Waterloo the public address system was warning of delays on the Tube following some glitch in the signalling software, and so I hailed a taxi. I thought I would, for old times' sake, head for Brown's Hotel to effect my change of costume. I had not been there for very many years – unsurprisingly, in view of the room charges in that august institution – but had always regarded it fondly, as it had been where I had first given Anne dinner when we started to go out together, more than thirty years ago now. I had of course been trying to impress her with my man-about-town suavity and (non-existent) wealth. I am not sure what she thought about it, but the place had certainly impressed me.

I took an armchair in the spacious vestibule and ordered coffee and toast. I was in plenty of time. I had read my *Times* on the train and opened one of the hotel's copies of *The Telegraph* to compare their opinions on some of the pressing issues of the day. Musing on one of the articles, I lowered my paper and gazed up into the middle distance across the foyer to digest what I had just read.

A liveried porter was carrying a suitcase and escorting its owner to the entrance doors. I caught the back view of this hotel guest just as he was turning to tip the porter and accompany him out to a waiting taxi. Something vaguely familiar came to me. The same back view of a well-cut suit and dark swept-back hair worn long on to the collar that I had seen from my position on the floor of that holiday let – not much lower indeed than my present angle of vision from the old-fashioned depths of the Brown's Hotel armchair.

My momentary glimpse of his profile as he left the building confirmed my recognition: Lovat-suit, today more formally dressed in grey chalk stripe. Well, well. Clearly a man of taste and, judging by the size of suitcase, a person of considerable substance if he had been staying at Brown's.

I resisted the temptation to get up and follow him. I have always wanted to be in a position to hail a cab and cry, "Follow that taxi, wherever it goes!" as though being filmed in black and white in the glory days of Ealing Studios, of which I am an avid fan.

But I had a more important task ahead of me that morning. I finished the elegant silver jug of exquisite coffee and strolled into the gentlemanly Gentleman's Cloakroom, emerging minutes later as an immaculate Royal Navy commodore (save for a slightly off-white and decidedly tight collar). I tipped the waiter, acknowledged the respectful farewell of the head porter and walked briskly back up Albemarle Street with my valise.

At ten to twelve I approached the frontage of the Admiralty citadel and psyched myself up as best I could to summon the old air of effortless authority that used to come so naturally with Senior Service seniority back in the days when I was actually entitled to it. I squared my shoulders and marched in purposefully.

"Captain Bill Thomas, please. He is expecting me," I launched in clipped tones to the uniformed sub-lieutenant at the desk. "Robert Penrose here to see him in a reserved meeting room."

The junior officer gave me "Good morning, sir. Just one moment," and lifted the internal telephone.

"Captain Thomas? Commodore Penrose has arrived. Will you come down? Thank you, sir."

So far, so good. I maintained my brusque manner and said nothing while I waited. I had no wish to engage the man in conversation, in case I raised suspicions by saying something obviously out of date. With hands behind my back I turned aside to survey my surroundings.

Mercifully for my nervous system, Bill Thomas quickly appeared, bounding up with all his old energy and shaking my arm wrenchingly by the hand.

"Bob, my dear chap, good to see you. The meeting room is all arranged. Now," he turned to the officer at the desk, "formalities complete?"

"Um, well, sir," he responded with some diffidence, "I have not actually seen the Commodore's pass just yet, and I regret he is not familiar to me personally. Do you regularly visit the Admiralty, sir?" He looked round to address me with polite respect.

Bill answered for me. "Lord, no. The Commodore has been across the Pond in the States for years. You've got an ID, Bob, I suppose? Merely a formality." His eyes held a fleeting look of anxiety.

I dug my hand in my pocket and extracted my dog-eared old card, handing it across with as much assurance as I could muster.

"My word, sir! Haven't seen one of these for a year or three," the Sub-Lieutenant smilingly exclaimed as he briefly checked the photograph. "You have been out in the sticks," he ventured, handing it back to me and making out a visitor slip to insert into a ribbon card, and noting my name and rank in his desk book.

Bill promptly led me away by the elbow before anything more might be said, and whisked me into the lift. We looked at each other with relief and I ran a dramatic back of the hand across my brow.

I was in.

Bill showed me into a small windowless room on the first floor, furnished with a table and a few chairs. There he left me, to await the arrival of MI5 downstairs. I had not long to myself.

Naomi's boss was a small, neat man with the quick, precise manner and movement reminiscent of the famous television representation of Monsieur Poirot, albeit of a lineage closer to Wales than Agatha Christie's Belgian character. Bill introduced me, notably omitting to tell me the name of this gentleman in return, for which the Welshman gave a regretful apology on grounds of unavoidable security. The Captain then left us to it, promising to arrange coffee and to be on hand to see me out of the building in due course.

Little need be recorded here of our meeting. I gave a full and detailed account of all that had occurred. The MI5 man was a good listener, and rarely interrupted with any query. He took no notes. His first response was of genuine heartfelt thanks to me for rescuing his young colleague from almost certain death. He had been very anxious over the last few days, knowing full well that the debris of the upturned kayak found off Spithead could only have accounted for Naomi's disappearance. Bill Thomas's phone call the previous day had been received in Thames House with huge relief. She was evidently a popular member of staff, which naturally came as no surprise to me.

We broke off at a knock on the door, and a young man in civvies set down a tray of coffee mugs and a small plate of biscuits. I noticed with chagrin that public-sector budget cuts had reduced navy hospitality to instant coffee. Our repast was a sad comedown from my elevenses in Brown's Hotel, and indeed from the standard fare I had enjoyed each morning in Devonport and Faslane in the 'good old days'.

My listener took due mental note of the imminent incident planned at Liverpool, and was very anxious to retrieve from Naomi's own hands the documentary evidence she had purloined that identified the connections at very high level linked to the plots to acquire nuclear material.

He nodded glumly when I passed on Naomi's conviction that Thames House, or at least a regional office or two, contained a small network of double-crossers working for this outfit. He admitted to me that he had originally asked her to delve into this possibility as part of her mission.

I was keen to give him a description of the man who had been central to both Naomi's and my own recent experience, Lovat-suit, evidently a figure of authority, at any rate locally.

Disappointingly, his physical appearance and general manner appeared to ring no bells with my listener at all – or if they did, he did not want me to gain any such impression.

He was able to put my mind at rest to some extent over the risk of our home telephone being tapped by the suspect organisation.

"These days, sir," he assured me, "it is really very difficult for groups or individuals with no established authority to tap phones. There are so many more productive methods of hacking data than listening in to landlines. Smartphones and any other communication devices connected to the Internet are a much easier target, and of course carry the bulk of information these days. In fact, the security services are returning to the use of good old BT landlines in many situations for that very reason.

"Of course," he added, glancing at me a little cryptically, "that's not to say your phone isn't being tapped – by us!" I took this to be a quip, and responded with a smile – a slightly uncertain smile.

He confirmed that he would personally handle all communication direct with Naomi to arrange a debriefing with her, and I assumed that this would take place somewhere other than at Thames House.

I gave him my home telephone number and postal address. He stood up and shook my hand, and with that he was gone.

I rang the internal number Bill had given me, and he escorted me back to the reception desk to pick up my valise and be signed out. There he left me as he needed to return to a meeting my call had interrupted.

The Admiralty citadel foyer was busy with staff leaving or returning from their lunch break and pausing to chat with colleagues beforehand. Virtually all were in civilian clothes, and I did rather stand out in my blue and gold. A man had reached the foyer from the stairs at the same time as I got out of the lift. It seemed to me that he had immediately spotted me in uniform, and had paused deliberately, hovering at the foot of the stairs to fumble unnecessarily with his mobile phone.

My friendly sub-lieutenant at the desk signed me out and went to retrieve my case from a locker. Another official was standing behind him and came forward.

"I have been asked, sir," he said, "to recommend that you

change back into civilian clothes before leaving here, in your own interests. I can show you to a private cloakroom. Captain Thomas has given certain instructions in connection with your meeting this morning, and the Admiralty will be providing ongoing discreet protection. You need not concern yourself with these measures, which will not inconvenience you in any way."

I followed him, decidedly bemused, and did what he had suggested. Just as he was wishing me farewell from the cloakroom doorway, he gave me a knowing grin and this departing shot: "I do hope you are enjoying your retirement, Commodore, after so many years out of uniform."

I was spared acute embarrassment over their easy recognition of my subterfuge by the prompt and tactful absence of either official as I walked the length of the foyer and out into the sunshine of Horse Guards Parade.

My emotions were mixed as I made my way home to Dorset that afternoon. I had achieved my objectives all as planned, and was content with the reception I had been given by Naomi's superior. Her side of the business was now all in hand, as best it could be in the circumstances. I could have done no more.

But it was a chilling reflection to acknowledge that the Admiralty, almost certainly in liaison with MI5, considered that I was in sufficient danger myself to require their 'protection', whatever that was intended to mean.

Equally, it was heart-warming to know that I was still regarded as part of the naval family and that they would keep an eye out for me. Whatever that might involve would take resources and much expense at a time when public finances were under such pressure in the economic conditions that prevailed.

As I left the train in Wareham Station and plodded across to the car, quite exhausted from the day's excitement, I spotted fleetingly out of the corner of my eye the young chap who had been so engrossed in his smartphone at the Admiralty stairwell while I was changing back out of my uniform. He too had emerged from the train and was resolutely studying a large railway advertisement for holiday discount tickets.

Good old navy!

CHAPTER NINETEEN

After returning the old uniform with some relief to its place at the back of the wardrobe, I found Anne and we joined Naomi in the sitting room. I recounted my visit to the 'Kremlin', and spared myself no ridicule in amusing the two of them with my feeble attempts at sartorial subterfuge. Naomi was very taken with my analogy of her boss as Monsieur Poirot, which gave her a good laugh.

I had assumed that her troubles were now nearly over. All she had to do was await his call and arrange a handover venue with Poirot (as I now decided to call him in the absence of his real name) and her mission would be complete. She would then no doubt be taken under the wing of MI5 and whisked off to an appropriate obscurity in preparation for her next assignment.

I would have expected Naomi therefore to hear me out in an increasingly relaxed frame of mind. But as I finished my report her expression was anxious. She gave me that Mona Lisa smile that I had learnt to interpret as a sign of courage combined with scepticism and uncertainty. There was something emotionally appealing about it, in more senses than one. This was not the time to dwell on Naomi's attractions, however.

"What are you thinking?" I prompted. "You don't look happy."

"Something you said just now," she replied. "Captain Thomas's phone call to my boss revealing that I had survived the kayak incident. It sounded as though that news was released to other staff in Thames House. If that reached the wrong ears, the hunt for me could be back on."

I digested this for a moment. "But if they know that your boss has all your information, it would be pointless continuing to chase you down."

Anne broke in. "Don't you believe it. What about vengeance – revenge? We don't know what they're capable of."

Naomi glanced at her with grateful eyes. I had to admit that having made the acquaintance of Lovat-suit myself, we should not underestimate the potential for violence in one form or another.

Perhaps he was answerable to other, higher influence, presumably of a powerful and sophisticated political nature. In the turmoil of recent events I had forgotten the Ukrainian brigadier general whose poisoning by irradiation had launched Naomi on this professional quest in the first place. Access to such substances, and the network trained and positioned to dispense them at the right place at the right time, surely required organisation at nation-state level, not least to bypass customs and passport control through sanctioned abuse of diplomatic immunity.

To a layman like myself, a casual but reasonably intelligent reader of what used to be called the serious broadsheet newspapers, the finger would point at Russia if the target was the Ukraine. Threats of invasion and subversive revolutionary support were currently in the headlines.

But this world of international intrigue was never what it seemed. The Brigadier General may have been obliterated by his own nation as a Russian sympathiser. Or he may have been silenced by any one of a number of former USSR satellite countries with long-standing grudges and suspicions. All this lay beyond the scope even of Thames House. That line of enquiry would doubtless be high on the agenda of their sister organisation south of the Thames at Vauxhall Cross, the Secret Intelligence Service, MI6.

That was a book that would remain closed so far as my own story is concerned. I have never read any newspaper report to indicate that anyone has ever been charged with the murder of the General, let alone convicted; nor any (published) attribution of the crime to any organisation, political or otherwise.

"All right." I readjusted my thoughts to the matter in hand. "Firstly, we must fix the handover meeting for Naomi urgently. What she possesses is red-hot. I'm not having her travel too far for this. It must be local to here, and, Naomi, you must not be seen out of doors. Keep clear of the windows of the house too. There is no particular reason why Lovat-suit and Co. should associate you with me at all, but we can't be too careful.

"Secondly, I think you should disguise yourself from the image they will have of you from your contretemps in the Portsmouth flat. Different hair colour? I know – what about glasses? We could pick up one of those specs in the chemist's with general-purpose reading lenses. I guess they are weak enough for you to see out of without falling over."

"Thanks, Robert," came a doubtful small voice from Naomi's direction.

Anne got up. "I'll see what I can find in the girls' rooms. One way or another we can transform you beyond recognition."

"Don't overdo it," I cautioned. "I wish Poirot would phone. We need to get on with this."

Sure enough, shortly after nine o'clock that evening the phone went. Anne picked it up, listened for a second or two and handed the phone to me without comment, nodding her head.

"Hello. Robert Penrose here," I said, and recognised Poirot's Welsh lilt in acknowledgement. "We've been worried about the risks to Naomi now it is known she survived. Can we arrange handover near here?"

A pause. "Anywhere particular in mind? It does need to be a safe place and well away from public access."

"Yes," I replied, "we can meet in the Rectory in Corfe Castle. I know the rector well, and have asked him if I can borrow his dining room for a confidential meeting. It's a large U-shaped house, lovely actually – local stone, in a huge garden well out of earshot. The village rec is next to it, and the primary school and playschool on one boundary to the west can be relied on to make covering noise at break time. The rest of the garden runs down to the valley and the steam railway. There's a long winding gravel driveway with good visibility of anyone approaching. Can we do this tomorrow morning? We are getting a bit nervous down here," I added.

"Certainly, sir. That all sounds excellent. Can you collect me from the station?"

We made the necessary arrangements and fixed on eleven o'clock for the meeting in Corfe Castle. The rector would be out, but his wife would be pleased to welcome us.

* * * *

"Good morning, miss." I looked up from the breakfast table as the door opened and Naomi appeared. "Have we met before? I don't think I have had the pleasure." And I made to stand up, with a broad grin.

Before me stood a very self-conscious figure hovering sheepishly on one foot. From one ear only hung a small silver ring, under a slightly too obvious deep-chestnut topknot, her coloured hair swept up all round, the hairpiece held on to the crown of her head like a shaving brush with a glittering hairband of some sort. Her eyebrows were made up in a dark tone, while her lips shone with an unlikely gloss. Below this she wore a thin cream top like a singlet, alluringly low-cut, over a pair of hugging white jeans and white trainers without socks. Around her shoulders was slung a pale-pink cardigan.

Closely behind Naomi, a triumphant Sarah appeared and spread her arms out with a loud "Ta-da!" like an old-time music-hall compère introducing a new act on stage.

Following up behind came Anne with a tray of cups. She looked across at me and cast her eyes heavenwards.

"Glory be!" I muttered. "Who is responsible for this vision of loveliness?"

"Oh, come on, Dad," pleaded Sarah, "this is very carefully thought out. Haven't you ever sat on the quayside in Swanage in summer and watched the world go by? Naomi would be completely anonymous in this get-up. Couldn't be better. No one would give her a second glance."

"Thank goodness!" I think I heard Naomi whisper under her breath.

"Yes," I acknowledged, "I can absolutely see your point, Sarah, but we're not going to the seaside in Swanage; we're going to the Rectory in Corfe Castle. The rector's wife will wonder who on earth I've picked up."

A pause.

"Sorry, Naomi – I didn't mean it quite like that. Apologies."

"But you did pick me up, Robert," she came back at me quietly. "And I thank God for it."

I swallowed suddenly and felt my eyes beginning to water, most annoyingly. Anne looked quizzically at each of us in turn, no doubt trying to assess the invisible electric charge that had flashed across her view. She later told me that this was the moment when she had truly understood for the first time the tumultuous effect this quite involuntary relationship was having on my inner condition.

Sarah, of course, was oblivious. "Well, OK, mebbe if we use that blue buttoned blouse, Naomi, and add the second earring. Then if Dad can pick up a pair of dark-rimmed specs, you'll look more like the PCC secretary or something."

Anne and I burst out laughing, simultaneously visualising dear old Joyce, our local church secretary for at least forty years, alongside this frankly sexy spectacle now sitting down to breakfast with a determined expression and an arm across the table reaching firmly for the packet of cereal.

Afterwards, with the slight adjustments in her attire disconcertingly in mind, I drove down into Swanage to choose a suitable pair of glasses, and a few other things Anne had requested from the deli there.

Naomi and I then left the house for Wareham Station to collect Poirot and drive back to our meeting place in Corfe Castle. The battered documents and sinister can of plutonium that had accompanied us on our travels were safely locked in the boot, down with the spare wheel under the floorboards. I was taking no chances.

Give him his due, Poirot did not turn a hair on first sight of Naomi sitting in the back of the car. I guess he was well used to colleagues in disguise. Settled in the front passenger seat, he stretched a hand back on to Naomi's arm, shook her warmly by the hand and said how delighted and relieved he was to see her again in good health and being so well looked after.

She smiled back, equally relieved at re-establishing contact at last with her fellow professional.

The rector's wife gave us a friendly welcome and led us down into the dining room, where she had already laid out plates of home-made cake. Having plied us with tea and coffee, she returned to the kitchen at the other end of the house.

Naomi emptied the document folder on to the table, and at that point I thought it tactful to go for a stroll in the garden. I left them to it.

On leaving the front door, I walked down the slope towards the valley and watched the white smoke plume of the approaching steam train coming up from Swanage with its array of 1950s coaches trundling along behind. It made an attractive sight and was evidently popular, judging by the number of passengers and the enthusiastic waves I received in response to my own as they all passed by. It was the week of Swanage Carnival – a marvellous event run by stalwart local volunteers all in their bright-red sweatshirts. The town, and especially the quayside, would be thronged with holiday-making families enjoying the old tried-and-tested amusements, such as Punch and Judy, crab-catching competitions, wacky children's races, and more serious swimming races for grown-ups across the bay. Purveyors of temporary tattoos, pedalos off the beach and the stringing of children's hair with bright and glittery threads and ribbons would all be doing a roaring trade. Little underpowered miniature speedboats ("Come in, number 9, your time is up") pootled around the moored fishing and diving catamarans that lived off the shore. It always amazed me that this seaside throwback to the scenes and pleasures of Enid Blyton sixty years ago still survived the competition for holiday happiness in the face of modern sophistication and electronic virtual reality that today's youth is assumed to prefer.

I resumed my perambulation of the garden perimeter. Trudging back up the slope towards the driveway entrance, I was amused but reassured to spot a figure on the pavement outside, leaning against the gatepost and ostensibly immersed in his newspaper. My young Admiralty minder.

'What a tedious time he must be having, poor fellow! Long may it remain so,' I thought.

Some hope.

He was not alone as a pedestrian along the road frontage. I had forgotten that of course it was the school holidays, and so the noise and activity I normally associated with the adjoining primary school was entirely absent. Other than the relentless road traffic through the village, there were few people in sight. On the far side of the road two men were standing together closely, having just shared a cigarette lighter, and were gazing up and exhaling nicotine vapour in feeble parody of the steam engine that had just vanished from view down below.

One was a great bear of a man with a thick black beard. At his chest level I could just see the head of his shorter colleague, a weedy-looking individual with skimpy ginger hair and his hand in his right pocket.

CHAPTER TWENTY

I turned away instantly, my insides plunging to ice. Naomi's description of her assailants and pursuers in Portsmouth and Newport had been too accurate for me to mistake this pair for anyone but them.

I strolled along the drive back to the house, desperately trying not to rush too obviously. Once indoors, I ran down the passage, knocked once on the door and barged into the dining room. Poirot and Naomi looked up in surprise. They were just shuffling the papers together back into the folder, having more or less completed the debriefing.

"Blackbeard and Gingerhead," I explained breathlessly, "out on the pavement."

Poirot looked to and fro at Naomi and me with a mystified expression, and scratched his head.

"My pursuers, and two of the men in the hut on Lone Isle," she explained.

"The young chap shadowing me from the Admiralty is also out near the gate, by the way. But I imagine he would attach no significance to the two men on the pavement," I added.

At that point, Poirot whipped out of his pocket a bulky black device with a telescopic antenna that he extended to full length.

As he pressed some numbers he corrected me. "Actually, he's not Admiralty. He's one of mine. I thought it prudent. Seems I was right." He made crackly contact. "Zebra, this is Delta. Don't move or look around. Two males near you on the roadside. Suspected target personnel, presumably aware of November or Delta presence in this house. Imperative keep track. Description: one, large with black beard; second, slight with ginger hair. Acknowledge once you have cover. Out."

He switched the device to 'receive', and laid it on the table.

"Damn and blast!" His face was grim. "You and I have been right, Naomi, ever since Aldermaston. Infiltration in our office. Someone at Thames House who knew I was coming here, or at any rate had me followed here on the train, and then in the Commodore's car. Now, let me think. It may be that they are keeping track of me alone, and have made no connection at all with you in your present disguise, Naomi. That would be something. On the other hand, they will now have seen a link between me and the Commodore here, having ridden in his car with him here this morning. They will have seen you, Naomi, as well, of course, but may not have identified you, with a bit of luck. Goodness knows what they make of you in that get-up." He smiled and tried to inject a bit of humour into the situation. "Perhaps the Commodore's rebellious daughter? Let's hope so.

"My man outside has a tiny earpiece, but will need to find somewhere out of sight to return my call with his satphone. The antenna is rather a giveaway.

"Now, my priority, I'm afraid, is going to have to be getting these documents and the canister back to London. Naomi, you are formally released from this mission, which you have achieved with distinction, and the organisation will recognise that in due course. Thank you. You can go on leave now for a month, and I will expect to see you at Thames House the first week in September, when no doubt I will have something else to exercise your considerable talents.

"In the meantime, I remain concerned for your safety until we have rounded up this little nest of vipers, hopefully in Liverpool. The same goes for you too, Commodore, I'm afraid. Somehow, you've both got to keep your heads down below the parapet for the next month. You and your family, sir, will continue to have monitoring protection from us. Risk to you and yours will be much diminished once Naomi has left this area completely.

"Naomi, rule 6 at-risk staff monitoring protection and privileges will apply at least till I see you again. You know how to access all that. And good luck."

Poirot's satphone vibrated on the tabletop. He put it to his ear. He grunted an acknowledgement and put the device back in his pocket.

"By the time my man was alerted by my call, those two jokers had gone. He walked along the pavement both ways for a bit, but saw no sign of them. So that's that."

We all three digested the position in silence. I took a large slice of the Rectory cake. The whole outlook had altered radically since breakfast, which now seemed rather a long time ago.

"But hang on." I broke the silence. "How are you going to get back to base safely with the evidence in your briefcase? If I drive you into Wareham and you catch a train to London, you are bound now to be followed and, more than likely, intercepted. Their entire set-up is blown apart by the documents you are carrying, and they would go to any lengths to ensure that you and the papers never reach Thames House today."

Naomi's boss smiled. "Don't you worry about me, sir. I have ways and means. Your spotting those two men has been a bit of a silver lining. If you hadn't, I could have walked straight into a trap by going back on a train. Now I can make alternative arrangements. I wonder if the good lady of the house would permit me to use her telephone."

He hastened off to find the rector's wife, and returned shortly, accompanied by the rector himself.

"Robert, I do hope we have provided all that was necessary. Successful meeting?"

I assured him that his wife had made us very comfortable and that the arrangement had been just what we had needed. Poirot had already introduced himself, in I know not what terms, and I followed suit with Naomi, explaining simply that she had been staying with us for a few days. The rector, who was renowned locally for his rather risqué sense of humour, shook her by the hand in an appreciative manner, looked around at me with wide eyes and raised eyebrows and mouthed the words "lucky old you" before ushering us both out to the car.

Her boss remained behind, no doubt awaiting whatever mode of transport for himself he had just organised.

I turned the car and drove slowly down the drive. My minder was still at the gateway, but, glancing to right and left, I could see no sign of Blackbeard or Gingerhead. I signalled left, and as we drew out on to the road I saw in my rear-view mirror a powerful BMW police 4 × 4 also signalling left as it prepared to turn into the Rectory driveway we had just vacated.

I marvelled silently to myself at the influence and authority held by those entrusted to protect the stability of a vulnerable democracy in the intelligence and security services at senior level. A rarefied world in which I was astonished to have become embroiled.

* * * *

Naomi and I returned home without saying a great deal to one another. I think we were both ruminating along similar lines. Huge relief, of course, and a sense of fulfilment – job done. But on the other hand, what next? Presumably she would return home, wherever that might be, or maybe take a holiday well away from danger; go abroad, perhaps. I would resume the retired but busy life with family and neighbours that I enjoyed on the Isle of Purbeck – keeping my head down somehow, as the MI5 man had suggested. It might not be a bad idea to whisk the family off for a week or two on holiday in another part of the country. Then forget the whole thing. Shrug off this emotionally charged experience, this dice with danger and intrigue, as part of life's rich tapestry. Move on.

But first I had to surrender the old gold coin, the beautiful brooch. Re-discipline my single focus on to the blossom tree; reassert the comfort and innocence of its deep roots so bound around and fused with my own.

'Come on, old son, at your age how hard is that?'

We drew up at the gate, and Naomi jumped out to open it. She held it wide for me to drive the car into the yard, her déclassé disguise doing nothing to diminish my image of her as I had struggled to resuscitate her on board *Peggotty* in those dreary and risky waters off the east coast of the Isle of Wight – how many aeons ago?

She gave me a warm, broad smile as I passed her and parked the car. I swallowed hard.

* * * *

After we had all finished a late salad lunch, Naomi wanted a rest and disappeared upstairs. Anne, Sarah and I mulled over our account of the morning's developments. I was impressed by the relaxed attitude of my wife and daughter to the reappearance on the scene of Blackbeard and Gingerhead.

"They're not interested in us, Dad," Sarah said, "and anyway we have that young guy with the satphone trailing us wherever we go, so at the slightest problem the police would be here instantly."

I forebore to cast doubt on the speed of a police response in deepest Dorset after the savage cuts in officer numbers and resources imposed recently by a cluelessly out-of-touch Home Secretary – unless of course one was a high-ranking MI5 official.

Anne and I compared diaries for the next two or three weeks. She had commitments, and after the forthcoming week, when I had expected to be still on my sailing holiday, so had I. Sarah too had planned several engagements, including going to stay with two of her sisters, who now shared a flat in Exeter. Mary was a lecturer at the university, and Caroline a student there in her final year. Our eldest daughter, Diana, was married and lived in Windsor, where her husband, John, was a partner in a firm of surveyors.

A spontaneous holiday away from home together was, all things considered, out of the question.

"I wonder what Naomi will do now," I pondered aloud. "We know so little about her – where her family are, whether she has a settled home of her own, a nice group of friends – you know. Literally all I know about her is her first name. She is a complete mystery."

"Oh, she's told me a fair bit, Dad," said Sarah. "What do you think we've been yakking about for hours up in my room while you've been putting the world to rights? She's an only child. Her parents split up when she was about fourteen. Her dad is now in South Africa and her mum's somewhere up north – Doncaster, I think. They've never got on and her mum hasn't kept in touch. Naomi lived with her granny in Suffolk when her dad did a flit, until she moved into her own flat in London after leaving uni, Cambridge, where she read modern languages and got a 2:1. Hey, Mum, Dad, that sounded a great course and a brilliant place; I think I might change my preferences and put that at the top of the list before Exeter. What do you reckon? It's Oxbridge, of course, but if I really go for it I'm in with a chance, aren't I? Sally Beamish got into Cambridge and she's as thick as two short thingies. Of course they do interviews, don't they? That's how Sally managed to mesmerise the doddery old tutors – by flashing her eyes at them, I 'spect. Anyway, can we go up sometime and have a look round? You'll enjoy the city and its architecture and stuff and . . ."

"Sarah, dear," Anne interposed when at last Sarah paused for breath, "we'll talk about that another time, shall we? It sounds an interesting idea and it's lovely that you are so enthusiastic. Coming back to Naomi's situation, though, did she say whether she still has her flat in London? If so, I guess that's where she'll go now. Pity it's London, though. That's all a bit close to her work and possibly to being recognised by this horrid gang or whatever they are. It might be sensible if we had her address," Anne continued. "At least we could get in touch occasionally to check she's OK. I just don't like to think of that poor girl all on her own in London with these people still on the lookout for her."

"London's a big place," I countered; "much easier to be anonymous and hidden up there than in a small town or village. She'll be all right."

I wished I felt as confident as I sounded. How would I feel if Sarah, or Caroline, suddenly left us for a rented flat in London on her own, fleeing some vindictive relationship or other? Very worried is the answer. I felt worried now.

* * * *

Much refreshed, our young guest reappeared downstairs later that afternoon. She would be leaving the following morning and, if we could give her a lift to the station, take the London train. Was it all right if she kept the odd assortment of clothing that made up her disguise until she got home?

Her boss had handed her a company credit card that morning, so that she could buy her ticket and other necessities.

This was Anne's cue.

"Sarah says you have a London flat. Are you going to go straight back there tomorrow? You won't have your door key, dear, will you? It must be on the seabed off Spithead with your other stuff, surely."

"That's OK, thanks," Naomi responded. "Yes, I'll get back home and then decide what to do for the next few weeks. I can't just sit in the flat all day – I'd go crazy. Just long enough to let my hair grow back to the right length, and colour, and start being 'me' again. I can get in with the key from the key safe at my front door." She sounded rather downcast.

Sarah said, "Stay here with us for a bit longer. It's been great having you around – someone sort of my own age. If you go, I'm left with these two oldies."

Naomi smiled. "I can't tell you how much I have appreciated being here, and all your kindness. You've been so good to me." Her eyes suddenly welled up and she blinked rapidly. "More than that, I've owed you my life on more than one occasion these last few days. I won't ever forget. I've . . . become so very fond of you," she faltered, addressing the room in general, and then as a spark across two shorting terminals striking me with a direct look from her large, dark, tear-filled eyes that hit me dead centre. A millisecond and it was gone. "But I mustn't stay. As my boss underlined this morning, it wouldn't be fair to you. We must get you out of the spotlight beam so that you will all be left alone and can carry on your normal life together."

She paused, and recovered her equilibrium. "I choose to play this game. I'm trained for it and it will take me to other places and crises again before long. It's what I do. But it's a dangerous business, and I must take it well away from you dear people."

Sarah got up and wrapped her arms around Naomi, burying her head in her shoulder and saying nothing.

Anne, bless her, rallied first with her firm common sense. I don't think I could have coped for much longer before making a complete fool of myself.

"You must give me your address and a phone number at home, dear. I'm going to ring you tomorrow, early evening, to know that you have got back to your flat safely. I don't want you delayed by having to shop for food first, so I shall make up a couple of strong shopping bags with enough to see you through for a day or two. Now, come into the kitchen with me and we'll see what you might like. Robert, I'm sure you will nip into Wareham and get anything from Sainsbury's that we need. They're open all evening."

Anne disengaged Naomi from Sarah and led her by the hand out of the room.

I let out a long, deep sigh. Of course I would go to Sainsbury's. I would go anywhere.

CHAPTER TWENTY-ONE

And so, the following morning saw me driving Naomi slowly on to the Swanage-to-Wareham road, after a heartfelt farewell from Anne and Sarah on the doorstep. It was Saturday, and the queues of traffic were already beginning to build up in both directions with locals and holidaymakers. We made hesitant progress through the chain of roundabouts en route around the edge of Wareham town, and turned left into the dreary area of small industrial units and cheap furniture stores that adjoined the railway station.

We said almost nothing to one another in the car. What more was there to say? Our thoughts probably ran along parallel tracks, each of us too conscious of the ties of partnership, of allegiance and indebtedness, to form any meaningful words. Unlike those of Network Rail that we could now see through the windscreen, these tracks were broad gauge because that's what they had to be. Standard or narrow gauge and we would have been in serious danger of derailment. As for tracks of thought that might merge, we both knew that to be a catastrophe of imagination and unreality. Deep roots – deep roots of the blossom tree – they were my blessed and precious reality, and no less the four luscious fruit of that tree that together made up the structure of my existence, my family, my known life.

Such roots and such a framework for living were as yet foreign to Naomi's life experience, but sharing my home for a day or two had been more than enough for her to be grateful to see that, ultimately, they were impregnable. That knowledge – a certainty common to both of us – served as a benign endorsement of what had happened between us. The consequence of our being thrown together so involuntarily was not something engineered or prompted by either of us. It was a function of humanity, an instinct of mutual dependence. That it could never, finally, eclipse or disrupt her pre-existing settled state or mine gave this unlikely brief encounter between two generations a passivity which, sitting side by side in the car, we both found calming, almost relaxing.

The one act of communication which, for a moment, caused this glow of innocence to flicker was as we turned into the approach road to the station forecourt. Naomi put her arm lightly across my back and her head softly against my shoulder.

I drew to a halt at the station entrance, and for a second or two neither of us moved. Then, suddenly, she was out, the rear door open and her groaning shopping bags hauled from the footwell. The doors were shut and she was gone. She did not look back.

I sat there in a bit of a trance for goodness knows how long, probably mere moments, until wrenched back to an awareness of my surroundings by an impatient car horn hooting behind me.

I pulled out of the way and paused by the side of the road, the engine still running, until my hands on the steering wheel were white-knuckled.

I drove slowly home, scarcely aware that I was driving at all.

* * * *

And there one might have expected my tale to end. It had been a personal experience worth recording, if only for its great contrast with my life preceding it, and indeed ultimately with the life that I resumed thereafter. But real life does not fit so neatly into the orchestral score of a romantic fiction with its crescendos of gathering tension, a slow movement of high emotion and the elegant diminishing cadence to a pianissimo finish on a single heart-wrenching note of the oboe.

Using that analogy, actual life as lived rather tends to emulate a symphony performance in which the players are repeatedly required at short notice to move their chairs around the stage and swap instruments at the whim of their conductor, aka Fate.

No, that was far from the end of the story.

* * * *

It was about a week later, and I was in my study at home when I received a phone call from my old friend Bill Thomas in the Navy Department.

"Something's cropped up, old man," he said without any preamble, "that I thought you might like to know. We had a visit yesterday from one of the chaps from intelligence at Vauxhall Cross – you know, MI6 – who called in by arrangement to see one of my colleagues here on some scheme or other involving naval intelligence. No idea what – doesn't matter. Anyhow, afterwards I joined them for a cup of tea and a natter.

"This chap asked me casually if I knew Commodore Penrose. He's apparently bumped into you somewhere – he was very vague – and he seemed to be interested to learn whether you had recently got in touch with the Admiralty or been making any enquiries. It was a slightly odd conversation. I don't know whether he was speaking professionally or just looking to make personal contact at a social level.

"My colleague didn't know you at all, and in view of your own visit here the other day with MI5 the Thomas alarm bells began to ring a bit, so I just told him that I used to know you well and understood you had gone to live in deepest Dorset. I left it at that.

"This MI6 bloke was a suave character, difficult to read. I don't know his name, of course – we never do – but I thought I ought to tip you the wink in case there's something going on that you should know about."

My mind raced over the events of the past few weeks. Why should MI6 be interested in me? All my dealings had been with representatives of the home security service MI5. How could any of this tie me up with our overseas spymasters? Maybe the enquiry was entirely a social one.

"Give me a description, Bill," I responded. "I might recognise an old school chum or something."

"Well," he replied thoughtfully, "so far as school chums are concerned I can tell you that he was wearing an Old Shirburnian tie. Very well dressed, suit and shirt clearly Savile Row and Jermyn Street, you know. Rather elegant fellow – distinguished. Prominent long nose, bushy eyebrows, swept back longish hair, greying a bit. Air of authority – quite senior, I should think, unless it's all for show. Never can tell with those secret-agent chappies – they're good at disguise."

Instantly I knew who this was, of course. I was about to blurt out to Bill Thomas that I knew this rogue only too well, but kept my counsel. There was no point in muddying the waters with the Admiralty. I thanked Bill warmly for the information and hopefully left him with the impression that it meant nothing to me, but that I would give it further thought.

So Lovat-suit was MI6. Perplexing. And he was still worried that I was on his tail. Well, I wasn't, and the sooner all that side of the affair passed under the bridge the happier I would be. Nothing would please me more than to wash my hands of the whole episode, as far as Naomi's mission was concerned.

As for Naomi herself, my mind was resistant to my will. I kept thinking about her, anxious for her safety lying low in that lonely flat, and certainly missing the warmth of her company. She had reached home without mishap and had answered Anne's phone call that evening cheerfully enough. I had not offered to speak to her myself, nor she to me.

I was now faced with a conundrum. I surely had an obligation to get in touch with Naomi's dapper little boss and alert him to the revelation that Lovat-suit appeared to be a senior MI6 official, and presumably therefore a double agent for whatever outfit ran the Lone Isle operation. As a commissioned former officer of Her Majesty, I was under a plain duty.

Would this mean re-entering the fray? That was my difficulty.

I went in search of Anne. This needed a cool no-nonsense approach from a level-headed influence, and that was my wife.

Anne was in the scullery, surrounded by buckets of cut flowers and greenery of all descriptions, both from our garden and from those of several neighbours. She was almost literally immersed in undergrowth and water as she prepared displays for the forthcoming village flower festival. Over this sea of blooms and leafage I reported my conversation with Bill and put to her the question. What now?

Anne pronged a few more stems into the blocks of green Oasis wedged into the assortment of pots and vases on the scrubbed tabletop. I could tell that she wanted to say something, perhaps obliquely in answer to my query, but was being cautious in how she formulated her words. A careful and perceptive woman, my wife, belying the rather stately figurehead front asserted by the archetypal senior naval officer's spouse.

She repositioned one or two stalks of greenery in a tall blue vase and stood back to gauge the effect.

"Robert, dear," she began, having decided her line of approach, "it's no good trying to skate around the real issue. Of course you must inform the authorities about this double agent. That goes without saying. But that's not the difficulty, is it? You talk about 're-entering the fray'– engaging with this shadowy outfit in Poole Harbour and outwitting them with your clever schemes to meet that Poirot chap at the Admiralty and Corfe Rectory – you know you relished that really. Even your kidnapping adventure gave you a new spring in your step. You've actually been rather enjoying yourself."

Anne paused, and concentrated on another vase of blooms, snipping the stems to obtain just the right layered lengths to display each one to perfection.

"No, the fray you are nervous about entering again is the inner battle you have fought over your fondness for that dear girl Naomi. You two have been through an extraordinary experience together, and I don't underestimate the effect it has had on you."

I sat down heavily on one of the hard scullery chairs – the

only one not occupied by flora or pots.

"Nor", she continued, "have I underestimated the dangers. But listen – you know as well as I do that the sensible thing now is to pass this new information to Naomi. You don't need to get embroiled again with MI5 directly, or any other MI. She is the best channel for all that. Naomi is the professional; you are simply giving her personal information as a layman, an observer of events. That way you can steer clear of the official side of the business altogether. You and I and the girls are best kept well out of all that."

Yes, Anne was certainly perceptive. Had she been able to fathom the true depth of that inner struggle, her discernment would have been no surprise to me. How often in the past had she seen through the expression in my eyes or the silences and understood, responding to a predicament with wise words of resolution.

I suddenly had this picture in my mind of an old-fashioned water well. I was somehow part of that well – or in it, at any rate. It was very deep. Looking down into its depths, I could see in the dark shadows the glitter of life-enhancing water for the parched earth up on the surface. The same water also represented danger – the risk of drowning in its unknowable profundity, but with the alarming allure then of immersion into a new existence of some kind, reminding me of the words of the baptismal rite.

The sides of the well are unclimbable, smooth worked stone walling from bottom to top. The upward view from water level, the water unexpectedly comforting, is of bright blue sky in a small disc framed in the golden, sunlit rim of the well head far above. Which state – top or bottom – is the most attractive at that moment? I am where I am, with no detectable means of gaining the surface if that is to be my choice. Of course it has to be my choice – how could it not be? No one wants to spend their time floating in water at the base of a well.

But the whole point of a well is to collect water from below and raise it to the land above. My mind's eye then focuses on the heavy barrel-stave bucket slowly being lowered towards me on its thick hemp rope. Who is turning the handle up there I know not, but I can guess.

When the bucket hits the water, I clamber into it, and someone with immense physical presence is hauling me steadily up towards the surface.

It is not as simple as that, though. Coming up with me in the bucket is a large quantity of that wonderful water. Indeed, having been immersed in it for quite a while I am altogether saturated.

When I reach the top, and hug that dear person who has restored me to normality, I am none the less dripping still with the crystal-clear, delicious, cool and cleansing suffusion that has so nearly overwhelmed me. Despite the warm sunshine overhead, it will take a long time for me to dry off thoroughly, and the present sensation remains so appealing.

* * * *

On my hard scullery chair I shifted uncomfortably and blinked my way back to reality. For goodness' sake, get a grip. Self-psychoanalysis by metaphor can only be taken so far.

I gave out a long sigh. "You're right as usual, my love. I've been out of my depth. I do realise that. I'm relieved that you understand. So, what do I do next? Give her a ring, or go and see her? I don't need to say very much, only that Lovat-suit works in MI6 and is still interested in me. Naomi's boss cautioned against using email or texting, but the ordinary phone should be safe enough, I suppose."

Anne agreed and I tried to phone Naomi then and there at her London flat, but there was no answer. She wasn't using an answering machine or voicemail. I would try again later in the day, when she was perhaps more likely to be at home.

I tried again at teatime and twice more that evening, my second call at about 10 p.m. Nothing doing. It would have to wait till morning.

* * * *

I awoke at six. I had not slept well, worrying about Lovat-suit and the explosive revelation that I had a duty to pass on. I was glad at least that Naomi seemed to be getting out and about, and was not sitting at home drumming her heels.

I reached for the bedside phone on an impulse at six twenty and dialled her number. Still no reply.

It immediately occurred to me that I had no means of contacting her boss at MI5 to give him the message direct, as I did not know his name. I dared not tell anyone else there; either I would be ignored as a crank caller, or I might reveal what I knew to someone working for the other side, as Naomi had warned.

Of course – I would phone Bill Thomas at the Admiralty citadel. He knew Poirot's identity and would put me in touch somehow.

I phoned the Navy Department at half past nine and asked to be put through to Captain Thomas. After an age of clicks and internal transfers I eventually heard a voice, female and clearly efficient.

"Commodore Penrose?" she enquired. "I apologise for the delay. I was not at my desk. I understand you were hoping to speak to Captain Thomas, but I'm afraid he is away on leave. I know he has gone overseas, and he left instructions not to be contacted by email. He is not due back here for another ten days."

I thanked the lady and hung up. I seemed to be spending a great deal of my time recently tapping my teeth and wondering 'What now?' This moment was no exception.

I knew I had only one option. I packed a small valise, checked with Anne that I was doing the only thing possible, and set off in the car in search of Naomi.

CHAPTER TWENTY-TWO

Fortunately, she had left her address with us, and so I knew where she lived. This was a block of flats just off Bermondsey Street, a few hundred yards from Southwark Cathedral. I found it without difficulty – a building of nondescript architecture behind the impressive modernist White Cube exhibition centre. This area seemed a thriving and lively community with plenty of young professional people. Naomi would fit in here rather well, I imagined.

The brick building was well maintained with an imposing single entrance, lined with intercom panels down one side of the doorway. Most buttons identified the flat number and the tenant's name. Some, like Naomi's, held a blank slip opposite the number.

I rang her bell. Having reached London in the middle of the day, I was not surprised to receive no answer. I would just have to sit it out. I wandered round into Bermondsey Street and had a pensive cup of coffee in one of the authentic little Italian cafés, for which I was spoilt for choice.

I was feeling rather self-conscious and nervous. What would Naomi make of my turning up alone and unannounced on her doorstep? Before I would have the chance to explain, she might assume that I had succumbed to immature weakness and abandoned my home and family in desperation at our parting, expecting to shack up (I thought that was the current expression) with her in her flat.

The sense of embarrassment that I anticipated from this

scenario being reflected back in Naomi's eyes, as she stood in the doorway in surprise, was not at all ameliorated by the underlying irresponsible quickening of my heartbeat at the very thought of such an outcome.

I drained my cup, paid the bill and walked back to the flats to try again. No response. This could go on for rather a long time, I thought.

Then, while I was hesitating on the entrance steps, the door opened and a smartly dressed woman dashed out. We both did the involuntary start and simultaneous "Sorry!" that is built into the British psyche, followed by the warm smile and the backwards step.

Unfortunately, this last manoeuvre in my case was a mistake, because I stepped backward on to the nothingness inherent in a flight of steps, lost my footing, and ended up on one knee clinging to the iron railing with my fist.

Commiserations and sympathy over, this lady and I had the usual polite conversation about the dangers of slippery Portland stone, and were about to resume our respective lives when I had a thought.

"I wonder" – I addressed her retreating back – "if you are able to help me. I have called here hoping to speak to a young friend of my family – Naomi, in flat 3. She is proving elusive, and I thought I would look in on the off chance."

The woman paused before replying. I could see that she was trying to gauge from my appearance whether the degree of shadiness in my character was sufficiently muted to allow her to say anything. Happily – indeed vitally, as it turned out – she gave me the benefit of the doubt.

"Oh yes," she responded, "I know Naomi. She lives on the same landing as I do. Such a nice girl. She's been away for quite some time."

'Tell me about it,' I said silently to myself.

"But she was back again last Saturday evening. I helped her in with her shopping. Actually, it's a bit odd: we agreed to meet up on the Sunday in my flat for a cup of tea – we used to do that regularly – but she didn't show. I banged on the door, but no reply, so I assumed she had forgotten. She had said that she planned to be based here at home for a couple of weeks, so I knocked on her door several times over the next few days, to no avail. She certainly hasn't been home since Sunday morning because her mail is piling up on the hall table down here. I'm afraid you're going to be out of luck, unless she happens to get back today. These young people, they do gad about, don't they?"

And with that she was off, leaving me completely nonplussed on the pavement. I began to think that my last recourse might be to go straight to Thames House and ask to speak to the chap who is the spitting image of Monsieur Poirot, but Welsh. A moment's reflection on the likely reaction from their man on the door, however, confirmed that I was entering the realms of fantasy.

In retrospect now, I am astonished that it took me till that moment to transfer my anxious concentration away from Lovat-suit and the national interest to a cold realisation that something might be seriously amiss here in Bermondsey. What had happened to Naomi? For heaven's sake, man, she might have been abducted and that very instant be in some sort of mortal danger. My imagination began to run riot. I half turned to see if the well-dressed neighbour was still in sight, in case I could hail her and share my concern, but she had disappeared.

Then I ran back up the steps with the intention of ringing as many doorbells as might be necessary to get me into the building. This proved superfluous. The lady, in her hurry and diverted by our near collision, had failed to latch the door properly. I was into the hallway like a shot.

Flat 3 was on the first floor. I ran up the communal stairs two at a time and banged on the shiny blue door identified by a dignified '3' in brass. Obviously, no response.

I seemed to be spending the day hovering outside locked doors wondering what to do next. I rattled the door handle. I even shouted "Naomi" at the Yale lock. Silence.

At this point I think I must have been losing my cool a little. I glanced furtively around. The only other flat on this landing was number 4, and that was presumably rented by the lady who had now departed the building. I looked over the banister rail to the hallway below. Empty.

I took a run at the blue door and threw my shoulder at the leading edge. The impact slammed me to the floor in agony. I sat there gripping my traumatised upper arm, my eyes watering. With a taut grimace I let several waves of pain pass through me and gingerly tried the door handle again. Firmly shut, but did I detect a fraction more movement than before between lock and frame?

I staggered to my feet, mentally picturing those Chinese experts in kung fu who could have chopped the door down with the edge of one hand, or cracked it open with a bare foot in one of those high-kicking backflips. Well, I had good heavy shoes on with steel heel reinforcements. Why not?

With my back to the door I tried a horse kick with all my strength. This connected just below the lock, jarring my ankle and knee joints into brief spasm. Again I found myself sitting on the landing carpet.

But the door to the flat was ajar.

I rose carefully to my knees and debated with myself the prospect of standing upright. After a minute I hauled myself up by gripping the door frame and tentatively took a step forward across the threshold.

Before me was a corridor with rooms off to right and left, all evidently with their doors open, judging by the daylight streaming out. At the end of the corridor was the doorway to another room, presumably the sitting room, also with its door wide open.

In that doorway a small side table lay on its side, one slender leg snapped in two. Shards of porcelain littered the carpet around it, seemingly the remains of a vase or ornament that had previously sat on its surface.

By the time I was halfway along the passage I could see well into the room at the end, and it was a horrific sight. Every piece of furniture had been smashed or ripped open; desk drawers hung from the openings like parched tongues lolling from their gaping mouths. Upholstery, curtain linings and carpet underlay all lay strewn about with frayed edges. Pictures had been torn from their frames, slashed in long wounds with a knife. A bookcase was flat on its front, it's literary contents splurged out of it in an orgy of disembowelment, each book and magazine split down its spine, pages torn and discarded like overgrown confetti around the room. Even the wallpaper had been attacked and prised from the plaster.

I went back along the corridor and stuck my head around the door of each room on the way. The same story – the same vile frenzy of destruction had stretched into the very corners of cupboards, wardrobes and kitchen units. The electric stove and refrigerator had been toppled forward on to the floor to expose the wall behind, their power cords ripped from their sockets.

But of the rightful occupier of the flat there was, thank God, no sign. A dead body would have completed the picture all too appropriately.

I sat down on the arm of a sofa that was effervescing with burst foam stuffing. Now I was shaking with more than mere joint pain.

It was abundantly obvious that someone (and I knew perfectly well who that was) had been searching the flat with an intensity that revealed all too clearly the value placed on the items being hunted. Reading between the lines, I now had to acknowledge the fact that Naomi had been recognised – and, being alive, might therefore still be thought to be in possession of the incriminating documents that we had rescued from the kayak in the English Channel. If this was an accurate interpretation of the shambles that surrounded me in that flat, then the pride that Naomi and I had felt in our elaborate disguises of both the kayak and its erstwhile crew had been sadly misplaced.

The only redeeming feature of the present scenario was that those vital documents had been safely in the hands of MI5 for more than a week, and all this frenetic mayhem in Naomi's home would have been to no avail. There was at least that satisfaction.

But the fundamental burning question for me remained unanswered. Where was Naomi?

Having recovered my wits a little, I dug out my mobile phone and rang home. Anne answered and I put her in the picture. We debated whether I should call the police to report the break-in and trashing of Naomi's flat, but we concluded that Naomi might still be in the game, and that she would want to take that decision for herself. She might not, of course, be aware of it.

We left it that I should stay around for a while, keeping a low profile, and await any leads that might point me towards Naomi's present location. I had not forgotten the purpose of my journey, which was to alert her and her organisation to the identity of Lovat-suit, but I was increasingly concerned for her own safety.

I had just rung off when I heard a sound that made me stand stock-still and my blood run cold. The familiar wail of a police-car siren grew to a crescendo along the street outside. I glanced out of the window and saw the car approaching, its blue lights flashing earnestly as it drew up alongside the pavement. I realised my predicament. Here was I, having broken into the flat of someone whom I was not supposed ever to have met, surrounded by abundant evidence of a burglary, and with no explanation for my presence that I was in a position to give to anyone in authority.

Furthermore, in my foolishness I had left the front door of the flat wide open, its lock hanging by one screw from its door frame. At least I had possessed the presence of mind to slam the main front door of the building closed after I had slipped in, which might buy me a little time. But to do what?

I stood back from the window and waited. Perhaps the police car had stopped outside for some quite unrelated purpose. There was silence for a couple of minutes, and then the all too obvious sound of someone climbing the communal stairs to the landing beyond the door.

I held my breath, standing with my back glued to the wall of the sitting room away from the open door.

The footsteps paused on the landing beyond. A sound of

clinking keys and something heavy being dumped on to the carpet. A Yale lock turning.

Then another pause, followed by a slight exclamation of surprise, and the footsteps resumed, but this time into the flat and down the corridor towards the sitting room, where I was lurking.

A head appeared hesitantly around the door, peering aghast into the room. The face was that of the neighbour from flat 4 – the elegant woman I had collided with on the doorstep, now presumably returned with her shopping.

We looked at each other for several seconds, both equally speechless.

CHAPTER TWENTY-THREE

Now despite my rather humdrum life experience there had been moments during my naval career when it had been necessary for me to think fast on my feet. Indeed, on one such occasion, as a junior officer off the coast of Libya, an instant and rather imaginative inspiration had probably saved the lives of three of my shipmates – but we don't need to go into that now.

Some remaining wisp of that talent must have survived into retirement to meet the awkward situation in which I found myself that day in Naomi's flat.

I still carried, in my inside jacket pocket, the old Royal Navy ID card which I had used to doubtful good effect at my Admiralty meeting with Poirot from MI5.

I adopted a stern expression and broke the silence. "Good afternoon again, madam," I said severely. "I think I must take you into my confidence and explain the real reason I am here."

I flashed my ID card at her in its dark-blue leather covers. "Inspector Jameson from the Metropolitan Police. The reason for my investigation is all too obvious, is it not? We had a tip-off on this break-in earlier this morning. I am sorry for my subterfuge on the doorstep as you were leaving just now to do your shopping, but I did not then know that you were who you said you were. You will understand that we have to be careful."

The woman looked at me uncertainly. The discovery of the destroyed flat and of my sudden appearance had, not surprisingly, unsettled her to a considerable extent. I was not convinced that my ruse was working.

I had a brainwave. "My colleagues have just arrived outside to take over the detailed detective work here. You may have heard or seen their vehicle as you arrived home."

To my inward relief, she nodded. I just prayed that the police outside had indeed stopped in the street for some reason entirely unconnected with this block of flats.

I extracted from a pocket the notebook I always carried with me for jotting things down and used for my gradually diminishing memory.

"Now, ma'am, is there anything at all you can tell me that you haven't mentioned before, which might help with our enquiries into this incident? Have you heard anything unusual? This damage around us can't have been caused without a certain amount of noise."

"Well, no, Inspector," she replied, to my gratified satisfaction, "I can't think of anything which might help beyond what I told you on the doorstep. These flats are well built and the sound insulation is good. I can never hear anything from the flat above or below me, and certainly not from across the landing. This is just all so terrible," she continued, looking around the room in dismay. "How can people be so callous and cruel? Poor Naomi – she'll be devastated."

"Quite so," I followed up. "In the meantime, we have reason to believe that the gang responsible for this is likely to return to this block, and others, having sussed out the accommodation. I strongly advise you to stay behind your locked door, and telephone 999 if you hear or see anything untoward. Now, if you will excuse me, I must make a few notes and return to the office."

The woman took my hint and hurried back into her own flat, casting appalled glances into the other rooms of Naomi's apartment as she returned along the corridor. She firmly shut her front door and I heard the sound of two locks and a door chain being resolutely fastened.

I tiptoed out in her wake, quietly closing Naomi's damaged door, and hurried down the carpeted staircase into the entrance hall.

In two minutes I was back in Bermondsey Street among the teeming pedestrians, and thanking my lucky stars. I badly needed another cup of coffee. This knife-edge life I seemed to be leading was hardly improving my nervous system. I sat in the front window of a small Greek café nursing their genuine brew, half liquid and half solid grounds, accompanied by the traditional glass of water. I calmed down a little.

The police car that had stopped outside the flat drove slowly past, a glum-looking individual in the back seat with an officer each side of him, quite definitely not the type likely to be associated with a classy residential block in this area. I lifted my coffee cup to him in a silent toast, grateful that it was him and not me being transported to a cell somewhere in Scotland Yard.

One thing was abundantly clear. I could not now return to Naomi's flat, nor anywhere near it, for fear of being revealed as an imposter. My search for this elusive girl would have to follow different lines. In any case, her flat was now uninhabitable and even if she did come back she would not stay for long. Her organisation would probably find her other accommodation quite quickly, or send her into hiding for her own safety. That could be anywhere – not necessarily in London. I had come to the end of this particular trail.

However, I was in London now and might as well make the most of it. If I could no longer mooch about outside Naomi's home waiting to intercept her, perhaps I could try my luck and do the same in Millbank, keeping an eye out for Monsieur Poirot entering or leaving Thames House. The chances were slim, and success would be entirely circumstantial, but it was worth a try.

I remember Bill Thomas telling me that several unconnected organisations and businesses occupied this Millbank block, all using the same main entrance out on to the thoroughfare. Perhaps this was why it had been chosen as the base for an undercover service, but undoubtedly it would further diminish my chances of bumping into the one man in London whom it was so vital for me to find. But nothing ventured, nothing gained.

I walked back up to London Bridge Station and took the Tube westwards. Rain had spread in from the west during the day. I had come without an umbrella or hat, and was beginning to regret it. I turned up the collar of my jacket as I re-emerged into the open air and made my way along to Thames House, that dreary, featureless edifice that looked so unlikely as a government building. I would be in a position to admire this view for several hours through the accelerating drizzle.

I wandered up and down, and waited in hope for a short dapper figure to appear at the entrance. I felt rather ridiculous.

* * * *

Big Ben had struck 5 p.m. and I was hungry and damp. Soon people began to emerge from Thames House in greater numbers, struggling into raincoats and hoisting umbrellas, hailing taxis or starting to walk briskly in either direction along Millbank. This was the time for me to concentrate, as a single figure would be easy to miss.

I was standing on the opposite pavement, and had been doing so in a rather obvious manner for a couple of hours, making no attempt to disguise the fact that I was keeping a keen eye on the entrance doors at Thames House. I suppose that what happened next was inevitable.

Suddenly I sensed the proximity of someone close behind me at my shoulder. I turned, and there stood a uniformed police officer.

"Excuse me, sir," he said in a quiet, respectful voice, "but I wonder if I can help you? I have noticed that you've been standing here for some time, and would be pleased to give you directions if you are unsure of where you are going."

Goodness, how diplomatic our police constables are in England! A sharp contrast with the attitude that would prevail, for example, in New York, in my experience. Quite evidently this policeman had been instructed to engage with me by someone in authority behind one of those blank plate-glass windows opposite. They must become quite sensitive to the risk of nefarious persons like me tracking the comings and goings of secret-service agents with whom they have a bone or two to pick.

But what was it safe to say to him in response? I opted for the partial truth. "Um, well, officer," I began unpromisingly, "the fact is that I am on the lookout for an acquaintance of mine who works in the building opposite. I have rather urgent information to give him, but am handicapped by the fact that I have no direct contact details with me; and I'm hoping to catch him this afternoon entering or leaving Thames House. So far without success."

A slightly sceptical pause followed.

"Perhaps they could help you at the reception desk, sir. They could point you to the right organisation or department."

"Oh, I know the department. Domestic security service – MI5 – but the trouble is I only know this gentleman by sight."

"You mean you don't know his name?" The policeman looked thoughtful. "I see your difficulty."

My brain clicked into gear, and I blessed my good sense in wearing my suit that day. Out came once again my old Royal Navy ID card, this time in order to reveal its true content. I handed it without comment to the Constable, who examined it carefully.

He returned it to me with what I hoped was a sign of deference, and spoke into the walkie-talkie on his chest. What he said was unintelligible to me – all jargon and acronyms – but I did hear the phrase "staff call to meet Commodore Robert Penrose", so I assumed that I was not about to be led off in handcuffs.

"If you will follow me, sir," continued this excellent officer, whose hand I now wished to shake vigorously, "we will see what we can do."

With that, he ushered me across the road during a lull in the traffic, and we entered the building.

Readers will be interested to know that at this point in the first draft of my narrative I described in some detail the parts of Thames House to which I was taken next, and the process

I had to undergo in order to reach the innermost sanctum. However, my publishers prudently made enquiries, and we were subsequently obliged to edit all that out of this book. I can therefore only tell you that I was eventually taken to a small interview room by one of the staff who had taken over from the police constable downstairs (but not before I had shaken him by the hand).

I was told that a call had gone out for a staff response from anyone familiar with my name and rank. So I sat and waited.

By now it was a quarter to six in the evening. Not a good moment to trawl the staff of an office, many of whom would by now have left the building to return home. The sound of doors banging, footsteps and voices in the passage outside all grew less as I perched on the edge of my chair, willing the door to open and Poirot to appear. Then at six fifteen even the lights were dimmed. I was glad to note that the government took the saving of electricity seriously, but on the other hand it was yet another signal that the building was closing down for the night, and that in all likelihood I would soon be asked to leave, my mission unaccomplished.

The door did indeed suddenly open, just as I was beginning to doze off. A young lady appeared in the doorway.

"Commodore Penrose?" she asked briskly. "If you will come with me, please? I'm sorry that you have had to wait for such a long time."

She led me at a smart pace in a sharp suit and clickety heels along the passage and knocked on a door marked 'PRINCIPAL (LIAISON)'. She showed me in and immediately left the room.

Standing at the window in silhouette, the evening light behind him, a youngish man turned towards me and offered me a seat in front of his desk.

"Now, sir, I understand that you are looking for a colleague of mine, whom you have met before but cannot identify. The name you have given the police officer is not recognised by anyone here, but of course the colleague concerned may not be in the office this evening. Robert Penrose, I understand?"

I nodded. This person was clearly paid to be suspicious.

"Perhaps I could see the identification which you showed to the officer."

I handed it over, and he inspected it carefully, particularly the photograph.

"Lines of enquiry in this department are always confidential," he continued, handing the card back to me. "I know better than to ask you to give me full details; but if we are to help you, I shall need to have a few clues as to your meeting with this official so that I can steer the search in the right direction."

This was naturally a very sensible request, but I was acutely conscious of the realisation by Naomi and Poirot at Corfe Castle Rectory that someone here in their own office was in league with Lovat-suit. I was all the more cagey now that I knew Lovat-suit to be working under the cover of MI6, on the other side of the Thames.

"The meeting was arranged", I began carefully, "by a former colleague of mine in the Navy Department and took place out of London about three weeks ago. I had information, purely as a private individual, which this naval friend thought would be of interest to the home security service." Not quite true, but it would serve.

"Can you give me a physical description?" I was then asked.

"Well, your colleague is quite short in stature, a little on the plump side, very neatly dressed – dapper, I would describe him as – and has traces of a Welsh accent."

The man scratched his head with his pen.

"Of course, you understand that the service is a large organisation, and not all its officers are based in London. He could be a regional official."

"No, he definitely referred during our meeting to his base here at Thames House," I countered.

And then suddenly I remembered Poirot's conversation with his stooge out in the street in Corfe Castle, on his satellite telephone. It came back to me as clear as a bell.

"I've just recalled something he said on his phone before

he left," I blurted out in relief. "How stupid! I should have thought of this before. Your colleague referred to himself as Delta."

On the other side of the desk the man stared at me for a long moment, abruptly stood up and returned to the window, gazing out in silence for a discomforting length of time.

He then stretched an arm back to his desk and pressed a buzzer button that I had failed to notice before.

CHAPTER TWENTY-FOUR

The starchy young lady in power heels promptly entered the room.

"Kindly take Commodore Penrose to a teleconference room with a secure phone, and put a direct link through to Delta as quickly as possible. Tell him the Commodore needs to speak to him urgently, then put him on."

As I rose to accompany the girl, my host thrust out his hand, which I shook with a grateful smile.

"I believe I am aware of the business on which you are engaged, Commodore, and I wish you the best of luck. The gentleman you seek is in Liverpool, but I'm sure we can get you connected."

Liverpool. Of course. He would be tightening the net around those in Lovat-suit's outfit who were planning to steal the plutonium bound for South Carolina by ship in a few days' time.

I sat in a little room like a phone booth, the walls of which were lined with acoustic tiles. After a quarter of an hour the receiver on the worktop buzzed, and I picked it up.

"My dear Commodore, this is a surprise," came the familiar Welsh lilt. "I had hoped we had relieved you and your family of this tedious business."

I thought fleetingly of Naomi's face and form alongside me for all those hours in *Peggotty*. 'Tedious business' was hardly the expression uppermost in my mind.

"I understand you have gone to great lengths today to contact me," continued Delta (as I should now refer to him), "but here I am, sir. What may I do for you?"

I took no time in reporting in some detail Bill Thomas's message and the revelation that Lovat-suit was evidently an MI6 official. I gave as full a description of the man as I could recall.

Delta heard me out, and when I had finished I half wondered if our phone connection had failed, as there was a prolonged silence. He then broke through the ether.

"This is extremely disturbing news. The mission that Naomi and I have been pursuing comes to a head in a few days' time. I must identify that individual straight away. I'll phone your Captain Thomas at the Admiralty and he can establish from his colleague who it was that came to see him from Vauxhall Cross. I am much obliged."

I interrupted. "I'm afraid Bill Thomas is away on leave. I've already tried him. And he never told me the name of his colleague."

"Sod it, if you'll pardon the expression," he replied, the Welsh tone hardening into a definable Cardiff timbre.

"There's another thing I haven't yet told you." I pressed on: "In fact this was the reason I came to London. Naomi has gone missing, and her flat has been completely trashed." I gave a vivid account of what I had seen and heard a few hours ago in Bermondsey, omitting my criminal offence of impersonating a police officer. "I am extremely worried," I concluded lamely.

"Hmm, she is supposed to be on leave, so could be anywhere," Delta mused. "But I don't like the fact that her neighbour was expecting her, and I don't like the sound of that burglary. That was not a casual break-in. It was a targeted search, and I suspect that you and I have a good idea who was behind it."

Another long pause.

"Commodore, I hesitate to ask you this, but I have a feeling that your interests and ours are rapidly converging. I wonder if you would be prepared to join forces with me, in your case to find Naomi?"

My long-dormant adventurous spirit once again rose to the surface. With the resources of MI5 behind me I would feel a great deal more confident; and there was no way that I could simply walk away from Naomi's absence, dismissing it as someone else's problem – she was my problem, and in more ways than one.

"You're on," I replied after a moment's thought. "One thing before we go any further though: it's mighty awkward not knowing what to call you."

He chuckled. "Just call me D, and I shall call you Robert, if you don't mind. Now, I am fully engaged up here in Liverpool. I will put a man on the street where Naomi's flat is, to cover her possible return there. I think the best plan would be for you to join me up here. This is where the action will be, and hopefully the principal parties in this game will be assembling here shortly, with a bit of luck including our friend from MI6. If they are holding Naomi, or if she is on their tail too, then you need to be here. Naturally, my department will meet your travel and accommodation expenses."

We arranged when and where to meet the following day, and before long I was back outside in Millbank in the gathering dusk. In some trepidation I phoned Anne at home and reported my day's latter success, ending casually with the news that I seemed to have been engaged by MI5 in an honorary capacity.

"Oh really, Robert, you are the absolute limit!" was my dear wife's reaction.

I noted a complete absence of concern for my welfare, Anne herself being someone perfectly capable of meeting any challenge with sangfroid and giving no second thought to my own ability to cope.

"Do find that dear girl and make sure she is safe and sound."

I said I would, and we rang off.

Now to find somewhere for the night before departing for Liverpool. I was tempted to return to Brown's Hotel, but felt that would be stretching Delta's offer of expenses beyond what might be tactful. I found a small private hotel in Earls Court and made my way to a nearby Italian for dinner.

Only then did I realise that the shadowy but reassuring stooge from MI5 had never followed me from home when I took the train that morning to Waterloo. He had become a familiar sight during our routine comings and goings in Church Knowle. Presumably he had stayed down there today to keep an eye on my family. I thought ruefully how much simpler my day would have been had he kept pace with me to Bermondsey and Millbank. He could have contacted Delta on my behalf at a moment's notice if I had just been able to attract his attention and have a word.

'Spies are never there when you want one,' I reflected glumly.

I let out a long deep sigh as I sat in the restaurant waiting for my risotto. I was completely drained and utterly exhausted. Whatever next?

I had never been to Liverpool.

* * * *

The following day found me in Bootle. It did not strike me as a place where anyone would particularly wish to be found. A dreary fifty minutes by train north from Liverpool itself, up the shore of the Mersey, and I alighted at the little station in Seaforth Road. I had booked at a promising hotel in Linacre Road, which proved to be smart and comfortable – in sad contradistinction to much of its surroundings.

The secretive Delta had explained to me that the imminent excitement from his point of view could be pinpointed on the Royal Seaforth Dock at the north end of the port of Liverpool. This was where the ship transporting chemical products would slip her mooring for Charleston, South Carolina, the next afternoon.

From my hotel room it was only a short walk across the main road into the sprawling acres of warehouses, heavy plant and noise presided over by the Mersey Docks & Harbour Company. Somewhere in among all this frenetic activity the plot to snatch a large quantity of nuclear material would play out – or not, as the case might be. Almost 200 canisters of plutonium-239 in solid form and in the wrong hands had the potential for transformation into the most horrific scale of weaponry, mass pollution or bargaining power against civilised nations by rogue states or international criminal organisations. I had read this up over the last month, and it was an alarming prospect.

All this, however, was a bit of a sideline so far as I was concerned. The powers that be must deal with that aspect of the emergency as best they could. My personal emergency, my focus of alarm and concentration, centred single-mindedly on a small, slight figure with large wide blue eyes, snub nose and determined chin framed by dark hair, whose immediate safety had somehow become my official responsibility as well as my dearest wish, my motivation for tramping an oily industrial concrete jungle 270 miles from the peaceful southern Purbeck Hills of home.

I crossed the railway branch line from Canada Dock where it arrived at Seaforth, and wandered around a little aimlessly, trying to get the measure of the task I had set myself. Delta had promised to telephone me that evening in case he had by then received some intelligence on the nuclear-cargo theft that might point towards Naomi's location or situation, so that I could be ready to take her under my wing the moment I was able to do so, presumably sometime on the following day.

My horizon westwards was blocked by two of the most gigantic container ships I had ever seen. On the tidal Mersey adjoining Seaforth Dock a new terminal had recently been constructed to take the largest commercial vessels in the world, called Liverpool 2. Even these vast craft were dwarfed by the five giant red Megamax gantries that soared 300 feet overhead above the roofs of the enormous steel warehouses and stacks of multicoloured container blocks. When set against the normal townscape behind me, these ships transformed the domestic scale of Bootle into a miniature doll's-house world of tiny houses, shops and church steeples that suddenly appeared to shrink to the size of one of those open-air toy villages that families love to visit in places like the Cotswolds, where one can tramp carefully down the streets one foot at a time like a latter-day Gulliver or Cyclops.

Somewhere in front of this backdrop wall of painted steel, in the old dock, lay moored the good ship *Seagate Trader*, which was to depart for the USA on the morrow with its unusual cargo. All eyes would be on her and her loading schedule at this very moment, the sealed crates of plutonium waste under watch in a warehouse or railway wagon awaiting shipment.

If there were Special Services personnel, armed police or commercial security officers in place around Seaforth Dock, they were well hidden. No sign of the noose tightening around Lovat-suit and his friends was visible to my anxious eyes as I strolled through this soulless expanse of maritime industrial wealth littered before me in steel, concrete, timber, oil and all-subsuming purposeful grime.

Articulated seven-axle lorries revved and roared in and out with their monstrous loads, while trucks and electric red forklifts buzzed about, intermittently sounding their chorus of reversing beepers in all directions as the yellow flashing lamps on their cab roofs played their ever changing syncopated rhythms with each other, duplicated by the reflections in the greasy puddles through which they to'd and fro'd in their busyness.

I retreated to the streets of Bootle, and found a rather basic café to sit in and have a cup of tea and watch the world go by. Once again from sheer habit I tried Naomi's mobile phone number, which she had given me on that last painful farewell drive to Wareham Station. How often had I tapped in that sequence of numbers over the last few days, each time willing a response, as though by sheer effort of thought I could reconnect some communication through the ether. But, as always, after a few rings my phone would give up the unequal struggle and flash on to its screen that depressing message 'No answer. Call cancelled.' Today was no different.

I could picture her mobile phone, sitting despondently on some tabletop somewhere, out of reach of its owner. Sarah had given Naomi an old but serviceable model that she had used until progressing to a smartphone a few months previously. I was no expert, but I assumed that it was still functioning and with a live phone number, in order for the phone system to generate the message 'No answer.' But where was it, and why was there no response?

The clientele in the café just off Regent Road was a mixed bunch. Most customers looked like dock workers off shift, or maybe ships' crews ashore. Several were of Far Eastern origin and there was a rich variety of languages being spoken, incomprehensible to me – from which I do not exclude the local Liverpudlian. When jotting down my order, the friendly buxom waitress had given me a second involuntary glance of surprise at hearing a customer speak in naval officers' received English, clearly out of place in Regent Road.

Mine was not, however, the only plain English accent discernible in the café. From a table behind a cheap laminate partition towards the rear of the room, low-lit and largely in shadow, I could hear a steady murmur of conversation between three voices. Suddenly I caught a name spoken and then repeated, which put me instantly on the alert. I strained to pick up more of what was being said.

The name was that of the ship *Seagate Trader*.

CHAPTER TWENTY-FIVE

I nonchalantly reopened my copy of the *Daily Express*. (The local newsagent had not stocked *The Times* or *Telegraph*). Having caught the eye of the cheerful waitress, I busied myself with another pot of tea and a slice of sponge cake and settled down to listen in as best I could to the muted discussion going on behind the screen. The voices were all from the south of England, but I could not discern more than that. They could, of course, have been those of the ship's crew members, but there was something more focused and intense in the timbre of the conversation than mere gossip between sailors. Or was I imagining things, inserting my wishful thinking into entirely innocuous talk among mates?

I simply could not make out their words, which was most frustrating. Occasionally I thought I heard the word 'Gladstone', but it meant nothing to me. After about twenty minutes there was a general movement of chairs and clearing of throats and it appeared that the party in the gloomy rear corner was preparing to leave the café.

I immediately decided that the best thing to do was to follow them and see where they led.

Now, like most people I had seen a great many films in which just such a scenario took place. The detective or private sleuth who was the hero of the story would pull down the brim of his hat, turn up his coat collar and saunter after his prey down the rainswept street, staring into shop windows whenever his victims turned around, and leaning on lamp posts reading his newspaper whenever the action stalled, dodging around the corners of buildings as the gap between follower and followed gradually diminished, until the final denouement, the confrontation and challenge, the quick draw of the automatic pistol and the abject surrender of the wicked miscreants before 'The End' and the credits rolled.

Well, the reality is a little different. For a start, I had no hat. Although it was raining in time-honoured fashion, I had left my mackintosh in the hotel, so I had no collar to turn up. The waitress took an age to bring my bill, and another aeon to find some change for my £10 note, and so by the time I had reached the pavement my three suspects had long since gone. I had noted that they had gone west, towards the docks, and I followed in that direction. As I crossed Regent Road I thought I could spot three figures on the far side, walking towards Seaforth. I could not be certain that they were the same men at all, but for want of a better alternative I kept them in view and followed.

They soon vanished behind some buildings, and by the time I reached the same place there was not a soul in sight.

I tried the lamp post and newspaper trick, in case they should reappear and I could resume the procession. In the films, they must use fake newspapers printed on waterproof material, but in real life and a continuous drizzle my *Express* was very quickly a dripping and disintegrating mass of saturated wood pulp.

I wrung it out and squeezed the remnants into an already overflowing refuse bin, wiping my newsprint-stained hands on my dark-grey trousers. I was just about to retrace my steps with the intention of returning eastwards to my hotel in Linacre Road when, bang on cue, two of the three men reappeared and set off at a fast pace to the south around the edge of Seaforth Dock. A rapid change of plan, and I followed at a distance. They were definitely a couple of the party from the café, but otherwise complete strangers to me. I had to admit that they did not look nautical types at all, which only served to raise my suspicions. They were both pale indoor types with unhealthy complexions and short of breath. One was a chain smoker, leaving a trail of half-smoked cigarettes on the ground behind him in the manner of Hansel and Gretel. I walked purposefully along as though on official business, but they in their incongruous cheap town suits and thin shoes were not dawdling, and maintained the gap between us.

In this way we hastened along the greasy concrete passages and service roads for at least half an hour. Sometimes I took a short diversion around a building to offer verisimilitude to my independent purpose, but only enough to ensure that I regained sight of my quarry in good time. We were not alone. Men in boiler suits and yellow hard hats, or jeans and high-vis jackets, criss-crossed our path carrying tool bags or paraphernalia of one kind and another.

My two 'target personnel' (to use Naomi's professional jargon) were deep in conversation and clearly unconcerned about any risk of being followed. They never turned around. Soon we reached what appeared to be a boundary dam or quay wharf of the main dock, at right angles to the perimeter we had been walking down thus far. With a wide opening of water and a similar wharf beyond, this seemed to be the entrance or exit of the main dock into a smaller and older dock surrounded by rather more decrepit and underused old warehouse buildings, many with broken glass windows. A dark-green tanker was steaming slowly through this dock across to what was evidently a huge lock at the far end, beyond which was the tidal River Mersey itself.

This older dock must have been some kind of intermediate passage for ships passing between the Royal Seaforth Dock and the open tidal water, via a canal-like steel lock system complete with traffic lights and elevated control box.

As I followed my two men towards this forbidding fringe of dereliction, I passed a faded cast-iron sign bolted to the corner of the first building. It read 'Gladstone Dock 1927'.

The two men turned into the inner yard of one of these dilapidated buildings and without a backward glance pushed open an old, heavy door that grated loudly on its hinges, clearly needing considerable effort to open and close. It had long since lost its latch and lock, staying put in the whistling wind that blasted around the corners and eaves merely by its drooping weight on half-seized corroded hinges. This was not a building habitually occupied; nor had it been in regular service for many decades. Remnants of old packing cases were stacked against its walls, their faded labels dog-eared and flapping in the draughty drizzle that ripped about these cold passages and forlorn abandoned structures edging on to Gladstone Dock. The atmosphere was positively Dickensian.

I stood for a moment in shadow, and then without formulating any plan sidled around the dark side of the courtyard and cautiously pushed open the same heavy door widely enough to slip inside the building. Once inside I could initially make out nothing. It was pitch-dark except for the weak sliver of grey daylight from the entrance doorway. The broken windows at ground level had been boarded over and revealed not a glimmer. Black pools of water lay on the floor, a steady drip, drip from the brick vault above, indicating a leaking slate roof somewhere above the upper storeys.

Of course, looking back now, I realise what a fool I was. The sensible, responsible course of action would have been to retreat around the corner and to contact Delta on my mobile phone, pinpoint the building and report my suspicions, and then leave it to him to send in the SAS or whatever he had planned for such an eventuality.

But oh no, I had to blunder in myself in this impetuous fashion that I had begun to assume in recent days, quite contrary to my lifelong nature. I knew why, obviously. I was the shepherd who had lost one of his lambs, and true to biblical inspiration had abandoned the rest of my flock to seek the one that was lost, leaving no stone unturned until I had found her and carried her back to safety on my shoulders.

Well, anyway, that is how I try to justify my impetuosity at that moment. The nature of my devotion to this particular lamb, and her own attitude towards this particular shepherd, do not perhaps bear close scriptural analysis beyond simple degree.

I stood stock-still and waited for my eyes to adjust to the gloom. Soon I could make out a flight of concrete steps running up alongside the far wall to the floor above. Presumably the two men had gone upstairs. I tiptoed across the floor through the greasy puddles, and gripping the rusty cast-iron balustrade climbed the steps very slowly, my face peering upwards into the stairwell for the slightest sight or sound. Nothing. I could hear nothing except the steady drip, drip of the sooty rainwater dropping from high overhead and splashing on the floor below.

The first-floor level was better lit, as the windows were not boarded up – another large, single space designed no doubt as a warehouse store or stockroom. Cobwebs hung like tarred fishing nets from the iron beams and columns, laden with the coal dust of ages that had been blowing in through the gaping shattered windows downwind of the coaling yards that still formed the principal operation of the dock. The black dust lay everywhere. Having steadied my cautious climb up the stairs with a hand on the handrail, and then brushed away cobwebs from my face with the same hand, I must have looked like a Victorian chimney sweep. My erstwhile white handkerchief had gone the same way in my efforts to suppress several loud sneezes in that loaded atmosphere.

At the far end of the space was a steel door of sturdy riveted construction, no doubt designed to bear considerable lateral weight from stacked goods, such as laden sacks. It was slightly ajar. I took it that the two men had gone through that way a few minutes earlier, and so I crept towards it. On the concrete floor I made no sound. No light showed in the doorway. I stood (as they do in those films) with my back pressed to the wall alongside the doorway, and slowly moved my head around to poke my nose through the gap between door and frame.

It opened into a long passage, off which on one side was a row of about six similar metal doors extending into the distance at least fifty yards. Presumably each one served a separate stockroom or store. All were closed except for one, towards the far end. That door was half open, and a dull yellow light released from the room behind it shed a beam across the corridor that picked out the suspended coal dust. Trapped moths fluttered hopelessly in its pale cast.

Forty yards separated me from that door – a straight tunnel devoid of useful corners, shadows or hiding places. If I committed myself to begin the long walk towards it I was truly burning my boats. Should one of the men appear before I reached it, my number would be up.

I took a deep breath and moved stealthily forward, concentrating on my feet to avoid stumbling over any extraneous object or greasy puddle on the floor. The cobwebs were catching in my face and hair, and I held my handkerchief ready to stifle any incipient sneeze or cough in the thick dusty air.

I was about halfway down the passage when I heard a sound that made my blood run cold and my heart race. It came from the lit room ahead. It was a sudden raised voice – a voice of both anger and fear, but also of determination and argument. In response another, deeper voice started to compete briefly until the shouting match dwindled again to a low murmur of dispute.

Both voices were well known to me. One was in the polished public-school tones of Lovat-suit. The other belonged to Naomi.

I froze where I stood. I started to shake, and leant against the brick wall for support. It would still have been possible – no, sensible – to retreat to the open air and phone Delta. My mobile was in my pocket. All I had to do was summon the authorities to deal with this in a professional manner.

But somehow, at that moment, I never thought of it. My phone might be in my pocket, but my metaphorical shepherd's crook was firmly in my fist. I had a lamb to rescue, and in my conceit I began to inch forward once again.

I had almost reached the shaft of dim light from the open store and door when my heart gave another great lurch. Into the tense atmosphere of that place came the startling crescendo of a ship's siren, very close by. Five short blasts buzzed my ears and reverberated to and fro across the brick building, their echo dancing in the distance somewhere off another range of buildings.

Five blasts, under the maritime rules of the road, mean 'Your intentions are not understood. Keep clear.' The actual message intended, well known to us in the sailing fraternity, is 'Wot the flippin' 'eck d'yer fink yer doin'? Clear orf!" Or fruitier words to that effect.

Some red-faced skipper of a small craft had no doubt risked a tangle with a container ship and the fact was now being broadcast for public ridicule out in the dock. But I felt that those five siren blasts had been directed at me. What indeed did I think I was doing?

The thick steel door on its parliament hinges offered a good view of the interior of the room through the gap between edge and frame. In the light of a hissing propane gas lamp standing on a packing case in the centre of the space I could make out a rough circle of people. The two men I had followed stood in shadows in the rear, while on a motley collection of seats – old wooden chairs, a stool and another packing case – sat my old combatants Blackbeard, Gingerhead and Lovat-suit. A selection of breaking-and-entering tools and a couple of weapons lay between them on the floor.

Standing before them all, her back to me and the door, was the figure of Naomi, resolute but pale and shaken, in her hands a short-barrelled automatic rifle, its business end hovering over the assembled group of men before her.

CHAPTER TWENTY-SIX

This was not the scenario I had visualised as I crept up the dusty passageway. The boot appeared at present to be on the other foot. My anxiety for Naomi's welfare – I had carried this mental picture of her tied to a chair and in fear for her life, a foul image of interrogation and torture – was transformed into a wave of admiration.

But her present advantage (however had she achieved it?) was all too marginal. She was hugely outnumbered; weapons and heavy tools now lay within easy reach of the men in front of her. A fraction of a second in diverted attention was all it needed for them to seize the upper hand again and disarm her. And how ready would she be in any case to pull the trigger?

I recognised my dilemma. Barging into the room would be a recipe for disaster, the surprise offering just the opportunity for turning the tables – especially for Gingerhead, whom I judged to be the most quick-witted of the three men already familiar to me.

Poised behind the open door in the shadow of the passage, I then noticed something rather interesting. The heavy steel door had an old-fashioned latch bar under my hand, which would secure the door shut on my side, the outside, when slid into its socket in the iron door frame. What was significant, however, was that as far as I could make out the latch bar could not be operated from inside the storeroom. Anyone inside that room would be incapable of getting out once the door was bolted closed.

My tactic then became obvious. On the other hand, there was no way that I was going to bolt the door shut with Naomi still inside. The very thought sent shivers down my spine. Tactically too that would be a grave error as the men would probably manage to disarm her eventually and then hold her hostage against armed authorities re-entering the room later on.

Somehow I had to extract Naomi and slam the door shut in one quick motion, before the men could react. But how quickly would the door close? It was heavy, on rusty hinges that had not been greased for decades. Would the latch bar slide easily into its socket, or jam just at the wrong moment?

My mind raced. I needed to allow sufficient time for one or other of these delays without the risk of those nearest the door also managing to get out of the room. My scheme would only be a success if Naomi and I ended up in the passage with the latched door firmly separating us from everyone else inside.

I had to create a diversion.

In the meantime, a conversation of sorts had resumed beyond my hiding place.

"My dear young lady," drawled Lovat-suit, almost but not quite giving his accustomed air of superiority, "you can't hold us up for ever, you know. Sooner or later you're going to have to give up. I'm warning you that if I have to regain control of the situation by force, I cannot guarantee that you will not be badly hurt, or worse. However," here he tried to adopt a compassionate tone, which to my ears sounded deeply sinister, "if you will surrender the weapon I will undertake to cause you no physical harm. We have a task to complete and that is my only interest."

I heard Naomi clear her throat. "Yes, and I know all about that task. *Seagate Trader* leaves this dock tomorrow afternoon for South Carolina, and as far as I am concerned it will take its plutonium cargo with it. Your plan was to break into the warehouse tonight and with a forklift truck and lorry seize the crates and take them off to a small coaster you have chartered. I don't know where, but we would have followed you.

"We also know who you were selling to. The Yongbyon nuclear complex in North Korea is set up to produce weapons-grade fissile material, and that's your market.

"I know your game. I have no intention of dying of plutonium poisoning like that brigadier general from Ukraine you murdered during your last attempt. That was a sale to the east, wasn't it? This time your dirty goods would be heading westwards, then across the Pacific.

"Well, I know my duty and you are staying just where you are."

"My, my, you are well informed." Lovat-suit's sneering voice had gone up in pitch and was losing its polish. "I wonder if I know any of your colleagues. A pity you didn't drown off Spithead after all. You'd have saved me a good deal of trouble. Perhaps that lad who was nosing about one night on our island base is one of yours? We nearly caught him, you know.

"As for Commodore Penrose, where does he fit in? Innocent bystanders don't as a rule arrange clandestine meetings in country vicarages with senior officials from MI5. I always thought there was more to the Commodore than met the eye."

Through the gap in the doorway I saw Naomi look disconcerted at that remark, but for me it sparked just the resolution I needed to see a way out of this impasse.

The light from the gas lantern on its low packing case shone down on to the floor, its all-round beam giving an adequate illumination to everything below waist level, and a discernible glint to faces and limbs. The space above the heads of those sitting was, however, in almost complete darkness. I picked up off the floor what I had nearly tripped on moments earlier – the corroded remains of a chunky steel bolt or rivet that had once been part of the iron door frame. Gauging as best I could that part of the open doorway not in direct line of sight of the men inside, I suddenly hurled the rivet at high level into the storeroom with enough force, I hoped, to hit the back wall.

My aim was true, and the result more effective than I could have imagined. The rivet took a graceful arc through the overhead darkness and soared at speed into the pane of a blacked-out window I had not known was there. The glass shattered with a most impressive splintering and crash, turning all heads instantly around in acute alarm, but not before I had with one arm grabbed Naomi by the wrist holding the gun, hauling her backwards out through the doorway, and with the other simultaneously heaving the old door shut with a grinding of hinges, and slamming the latch bar home into its iron housing with only a momentary unwillingness on its part.

Against the muffled tumult of voices that then arose from within the room, on the far side of the thick steel door, I shed all concept of where I was, abandoned all thoughts, fears and purpose, and wordlessly wrapped my arms around the stunned form of the girl I had come to rescue, burying my head in her shoulder. In a moment I felt her tense frame slacken and collapse against me. She lifted her face to mine and burst into long, drenching tears of relief and release.

The automatic rifle clattered to the floor and Naomi lifted both arms around my neck, hanging there with all her weight, such as it was, as we leant against the old brick wall and rocked gently to and fro in euphoric silence for what seemed a space beyond time.

* * * *

The faint sound of more breaking glass coming from the room beyond brought us both back to reality. The men trapped inside were evidently exploring the possibility of escape out through the small window that had so neatly received my projectile.

We were on the first floor, but each storey was at least thirty-five feet in height from floor to ceiling. The iron-framed windows were almost flush with the external wall, and had no exterior cills. It would be a long drop to the ground from that window opening, even supposing they could reach it internally. It was a good ten feet above the floor. However, a pile of packing cases would solve that problem.

More worryingly, I had no idea whether the old storeroom contained coils of rope or chain by which at least some of the men might slither down the outside wall. I very much doubted that Lovat-suit was in a position to attempt it. Far too many five-course dinners at Brown's Hotel; and his bespoke suit (today in tasteful grey flannel) with leather-soled handcrafted oxfords were hardly conducive to mountaineering.

While Naomi was still recovering her breath, and between gasps asking me how on earth I happened to turn up in a Liverpool dock at such a propitious moment, I dug out my mobile phone. Mercifully there was an adequate signal and I dialled the number that Delta had given me.

He responded instantly.

By this time I had recovered my equilibrium a little, and was determined to enjoy this conversation.

"That you, Mr D?" I asked cheerfully. "Naomi and I have a surprise package for you on the first floor of Warehouse B14 in Gladstone Dock. You can't miss it. Its number is in large white letters over the main entrance door. You'll find us on the first landing passage outside the locked door of a room containing five very cross and frustrated criminals, including a certain renegade member of the Secret Intelligence Service."

Delta knew his job. Before even responding to me on the phone he had immediately turned away and given crisp instructions to a colleague, as I could clearly hear. He then returned to the phone.

"We're on our way, Robert. You can fill me in later, but well done you and Naomi. What else should I know as we approach the building?"

"The door is secure against any attempt to escape," I replied, "but they are armed and also have a stash of heavy tools. And by the sound of it they are attempting to get out of the window, so I suggest the building should be surrounded. Oh yes, and we are armed ourselves out here in the passage, as Naomi has an automatic rifle, which is loaded."

I raised my eyebrows at Naomi for confirmation of this latter assumption, and she nodded.

"We will expect you shortly," I concluded.

The huffing and puffing from the prison cell had subsided,

and all we could hear now was the occasional voice raised in anger. They had started bickering with each other, no doubt passing the blame for their new predicament. Notably absent was the voice of Lovat-suit. I felt sure that he was trying to think ahead, to adapt his strategy in the light of changed conditions. He was not one to give up, or doubt that he could always be one step ahead of the game. What he did not know, of course, was that his SIS/MI6 cover was blown to smithereens. Maybe he was banking on claiming a double bluff – an undercover secret-service officer who had infiltrated this international gang in the service of Queen and country – and still hoping to salvage that role, at least for as long as it took to disappear once his fellow room-mates had been arrested.

But hang on – what if that was indeed the true state of affairs? In his dealings with Naomi, and with me when I was kidnapped, he would have had to maintain his 'nasty' image and treat us as his cronies expected. It would be vital that their confidence in him remained unshaken at all times. The proof, one way or the other, would rest with an inquiry at very senior level in MI6 itself.

I gestured to Naomi to follow me back along the corridor the way I had come, so as to be well out of earshot. The large storage room at the head of the stairs would also be our rendezvous with Delta and his colleagues. I put to Naomi my thoughts on Lovat-suit's alternative allegiance, for her reaction. We sat on a pile of old sacks and tried to think this through.

Delta had not yet met Lovat-suit, although I had given him a description. Without knowing his name, it would have been difficult for D to pursue enquiries with his opposite numbers in MI6. Perhaps we were all in for a surprise.

Naomi was unconvinced of Lovat-suit's service loyalties. So was I. There was something creepy and snake-like in his whole demeanour: smooth and glittery with hooded, unreadable eyes – utterly untrustworthy. But my doubts persisted. Maybe those were just the qualities that constituted an outstanding intelligence officer, the more so, of course, if they were assumed by a brilliant actor to fit a particular character.

We could only wait and see.

In under ten minutes we saw the daylight cast a beam into the stairwell from the opening of the entrance door downstairs. What appeared to be dark shadows glided briskly up the stairs, quite soundlessly – half a dozen of them, closely followed by Delta, whose clicking footsteps rather gave the game away.

The 'shadows' proved to be men in dark soft clothing and balaclavas, wearing black gym shoes, with small rucksacks on their backs and a variety of weaponry strapped to their torsos and limbs. Their commander gave instructions by signal, and never said a word. He was unquestionably in charge of this exercise. Delta was merely tagging along behind.

While Delta and Naomi remained in the storeroom and whispered to each other their recent activities and updates, I led the soldiers (if that is what they were) along the corridor and pointed to the door of the room in which their 'target personnel' were caged.

"They are armed," I mouthed to the commander, who nodded and summoned one of his colleagues forward. He then signalled to me to retreat down the corridor.

As I neared the end of the passageway, I turned in time to see the soldier whip back the door latch and open the steel door just enough to lob something from his rucksack into the room. He then shut and latched the door again, and they all waited.

Instantly there was uproar from within the room. Firstly yelling, and then a cacophony of coughing, spluttering and retching. Wisps of what looked like smoke began to drift out into the passageway from around the edges of the steel door.

By this time all the soldiers had donned masks and lightweight breathing gear. Still they stood around and waited.

After a while the noise of distressed humanity tailed off. The commander nodded, his colleague threw open the door, and the other four soldiers rushed into the room. In barely twenty seconds the occupants had been led or dragged out of the room, handcuffed behind their backs and stumbling half blind from streaming red-rimmed eyes, their mouths and noses running with saliva and mucus, through the dense grey fog.

I was myself beginning to blink rapidly from a most unpleasant sensation in the dusty air – whatever it was that had been in the smoke bomb curling its way down the corridor.

I withdrew to rejoin Delta and Naomi, and firmly shut the intervening door.

CHAPTER TWENTY-SEVEN

The three of us descended to ground level and flung open the entrance door on to the dock hardstanding, taking gulps of clean, fresh air. As the soldiers appeared with their charges contained within a ring of weaponry heading for their prison truck, we waited for the commander to join us.

Having briefed his men and ordered the truck away, the commander strolled over towards us, enjoying a relaxing cigarette with the air of a job well done.

"Well, sir," he reported to Delta, "a satisfactory outcome, I think. We'll take them to the police station in St Anne Street and they can cool their heels in the cells there while formal charges are decided. That's us done, then, and we will return to base. Four very sorry-looking individuals out of harm's way."

He turned and started to walk towards his dull-green Land Rover parked nearby. We gave him a mock salute in acknowledgement.

"Hang on!" suddenly Naomi exclaimed in loud alarm. "Did you say FOUR individuals? But there were five of them in that room!"

The commander stopped and faced her with an expression of stone. Then in less than three seconds he had sprinted back into Warehouse B14, unstrapping his pistol holster as he ran. Delta, Naomi and I, exchanging determined glances, rushed in after him and followed back up the staircase two treads at a time.

Through the first-floor storeroom and into the long corridor.

The smoke from the disabling bomb, heavier than air, was dissipating in the draughty spaces at ankle level now, irritating but tolerable. We reached the open storeroom door together in a bunch. The commander stopped us and entered the room, gun drawn, slowly and purposefully swivelling his outstretched arm in an arc from right to left.

The room was empty. Empty, that is, of anything remotely human. The detritus of packing cases and old sacks lay around us as it had done before. The window remained shut, its glass shattered but unpenetrated.

We wandered around, looking rather hopelessly for a body or some other clue.

Naomi had climbed over a pile of old timber baulks in the far corner, and was lifting the edges of a heap of dusty hessian bags when she instantly and excitedly exclaimed, "Hey – come and look at this!"

We all dashed over and peered into the gloom. There under the heap was a small, hinged trapdoor, lying open and flat on the floorboards. The commander whipped out a powerful LED torch and shone the beam down into the void.

The trapdoor served a wooden chute, running diagonally below floor level to what looked like a similar trapdoor, presumably in the ceiling of the storey beneath. The lower trap was clearly shut. The sides of the chute were shiny with decades of use, sacks of grain, coal or whatever for import or export having been jettisoned down here to a belt conveyor or similar on the floor below in their thousands.

The chute was just long enough to take the bent form of a man standing on the bolted trapdoor underneath him. Of any such man, there was of course now no sign or whisper.

The commander was already on his radio to his colleague in the prison van. "Immediate, repeat immediate, physical description of the four prisoners in your charge."

We knew the answer well enough before those descriptions were relayed through. The van contained Blackbeard, Gingerhead and the two scruffs I had earlier followed into the building.

Our friend Lovat-suit had bested us. He must have discovered the chute when he was choosing this storeroom as a final centre of operations, and with his quick wits used this to his advantage during the chaos and disruption of the smoke bomb hitting the floor. Somehow he must have endured the smoke there under the floor (perhaps the trapdoor was reasonably well fitting) and made his escape once everyone else had left the vicinity.

He had not, of course, come out through the entrance door or we would have seen him. He must still be in the building unless he had slipped past us in the last three or four minutes.

The commander (an army major – I had now spotted his breast-pocket insignia) certainly had fast reactions. Again he was on his radio, summoning a backup team to race to the dock and surround the warehouse ready for a room-by-room search for an armed man.

He ordered us abruptly to stay where we were and jogged off down the corridor to hold the stairwell and main entrance covered with his pistol in case Lovat-suit tried to make good his escape before the new team of soldiers arrived.

This left Naomi, Delta and me to investigate our surroundings at leisure. The heap of ironware abandoned by the gang included heavy wire cutters, a mobile electric disc cutter, sledgehammers, long bar levers, two (unloaded) Kalashnikovs and a carton of ammunition. A couple of old donkey jackets lay discarded on the pile of packing cases. Idly I lifted them to check their pockets and there underneath revealed a transparent-plastic document wallet, the uppermost paper inside being instantly recognisable as the bill of lading glimpsed by Naomi on the window cill of the hut on Lone Isle. I passed the wallet to Delta without comment.

He emptied the contents and began to rifle through the sheets of paper, his brow furrowing with each new revelation. Suddenly he froze, reading intently from an official-looking document. His face drained of colour.

"Excuse me," he muttered, stuffing the papers back into the wallet and making for the door, "I must go. This can't wait."

And with that he was gone.

I felt very tired. The day's excitements had caught up with me and the last vestiges of energy and adrenaline seeped away. I sat down heavily on a packing case, put my head in my hands and closed my eyes. I felt a light, quiet form sit down next to me and put her arm around my shoulders. A lock of hair and a soft cheek rested against my ear.

"Bless you for saving my life a second time, dear Robert," she whispered. "I'm not sure I could have fired that gun."

I put my arm around her waist and gave her a wan smile. "Let's jolly well hope there doesn't need to be a third time. I'm not sure you're very good for my health, you know."

She was certainly playing havoc with my emotions. It was just as well that these were at present swamped by my exhaustion.

Naomi and I sat there in seeping drowsiness for some time, until I suddenly came to on sight of a pair of black sneakers on the floor in front of me, followed by a courteous little cough from their occupant. I looked up into the face of the army major, expressionless except for what I suspected was a slightly amused raised eyebrow.

"Sorry to disturb you both," he said, "but it would be safer if I escorted you from the building before my team commences what could be a cat-and-mouse search through the building for the missing man. No sign of him yet, I'm afraid."

Naomi and I meekly followed him back down the passage and stairs, and out into the open air. Arc lights, and the flashing red and green lamps of the channel buoys revealed to my surprise that it was dusk. The whole day had passed. I realised that I was extremely hungry and, more particularly, thirsty. Naomi, whose recent story I had yet to hear, admitted that she had eaten almost nothing for two days.

We left the commander and his men to their search for Lovat-suit. That was his business and not ours.

Fine dining was a rather unlikely proposition anywhere near Seaforth and Regents Road. Our best bet was to return to my hotel in Linacre Road, which had displayed a promising menu.

Although we could have walked it, the Major kindly offered a Land Rover and driver to convey us, and so we shortly arrived back at my billet in style.

I badly needed a wash and a change of clothes after all the coal dust, cobwebs, smoke-bomb residue and perspiration accumulated since departure that morning.

Naomi confessed that she was in a worse predicament, having been held captive in the same clothes for several days without any washing facilities beyond a small cracked sink with a single cold-water tap.

The polite young lady at the hotel reception passed me my room key. I couldn't help noticing her glance rapidly from me to the pretty girl next to me and back again, but her professionalism won through. She wished us a pleasant evening with a bright smile.

Upbringing and natural justice almost prompted me to offer the receptionist an explanation of our situation and relationship before leading Naomi upstairs, but it only took a couple of seconds for me to acknowledge that this would probably be digging an even deeper hole for me in the estimation of the hotel management. I said nothing. Let them think what they liked, dammit. Bootle was not a town on which I was likely to rely for my future reputation.

None the less, having let Naomi into my room for first turn in the shower, and to blow-dry her washed undies with the hairdryer, I ostentatiously returned to the hall lounge for the newspaper and a single malt in a comfortable armchair in direct line of sight of the reception desk.

After a while a thought occurred to me, and I tried to analyse why it had not done so immediately on our return to the hotel. Surely the obvious thing would have been to enquire if the hotel had a room with en suite that Naomi could have moved straight into. Why had I not done so sooner?

I put it down to exhaustion, frayed nerves and yet another day's experience well outside my comfort zone. I pushed to the back of my mind what else might have been going on in my subconscious that I preferred not to see the light of day.

I heaved myself out of the chair and approached the desk.

Yes, sir, certainly they could accommodate the young lady. The receptionist drew out a room key and the hotel register, and offered me a pen.

"If sir could kindly enter her name and address?"

Well, I had walked into that one, hadn't I? Naomi something-or-other, of – of what? Should I enter her flat address off Bermondsey Street, or did she as an officer of MI5 keep that to herself?

The receptionist had turned away to attend to another guest, and so I had a moment or two to collect my wits.

I found myself writing 'Naomi Penrose' and my own home address in Church Knowle, Dorset. So far as the hotel was concerned, she was apparently to be my daughter.

That might have salvaged my immediate reputation. What my subconscious made of it, goodness knows.

I returned to my glass of whisky and the routine headlines of international bickering with the regime in North Korea. Thanks to my dear and wonderful ersatz daughter, and indeed perhaps to my own unintended intervention, there would at least be one less cargo of weapons-grade fissile radioactive material heading to that country's nuclear arsenal. It would have been quietly slipping away from Liverpool Docks on the following day, and Lovat-suit would no doubt have slipped just as quietly back to his role at MI6 to await his next act as traitor and money-spinner.

Just where was he now? He must have realised that the game was up. Naomi and I had too good a description. My friend at the Admiralty, on his return from leave, would soon establish from his colleague the name of the MI6 official who had visited him that day. Delta may have found something personally incriminating in that sheaf of papers he had hastily dashed off with from the warehouse. The net was closing.

Naomi appeared at my elbow, refreshed and restored. I explained the latest subterfuge I had landed her with, and handed over her room key. She laughed and playfully ruffled my hair. At least I had been right to avoid entering her home address in the hotel register. She never did that – always using a fictitious address supplied by MI5 that was set up to receive post through a PO-box arrangement with Royal Mail.

I then remembered the state of her flat in Bermondsey. Tentatively I asked her, as we tucked into our hotel restaurant dinner an hour later, if she was aware of the devastation of her home. She nodded grimly. She had watched Lovat-suit's gang trash the place in search of that original document case, while being held painfully with her arms behind her back by Blackbeard himself, before being carted off as their prisoner. She had wept at the destruction of her books especially.

Since then she had been held captive in a couple of places en route to Liverpool. Although of no value to them without that document case (which, she had stoutly maintained, must have perished after her kayak was capsized), they had dared not let her go. At least they had not had the stomach to get rid of her permanently. In any case, Lovat-suit had fancied himself as an interrogator, and no doubt with future ventures in mind had been trying to trick her into revealing wider information about her MI5 role and those of her colleagues. But Naomi had been well trained and had said nothing.

It was only the distraction caused by the arrival of the two scruffs I had followed into Warehouse B14, diverting the other three momentarily from their close eye on Naomi, that had given her the chance to seize the loaded rifle and turn the tables on her persecutors, only minutes before I had arrived in the building myself.

We toasted one another silently with the rather good claret that accompanied our dinner, and set to in earnest to relieve our hunger pangs.

CHAPTER TWENTY-EIGHT

We retired to the lounge for coffee, and I thought that this was a good moment to phone Delta and ask how things were going at his end.

"We lost him, Robert," he responded glumly.

"There are two or three side entrances to that warehouse, which is a complete rabbit warren. He must have been too quick for us. The Major and his men searched the place from loft to basement. Two of the side doors out to the dock were insecure, so it wouldn't have been difficult.

"However," he continued more cheerfully, "his two main fellow conspirators we have in clink are proving most cooperative. They've thrown in the towel. I guess they'll turn Queen's evidence and tell us all we need to secure top-of-the-range convictions. They've given us names in surprising places – including my own service, I regret to say.

"And, of course, thanks to you and that first-rate colleague of mine who is so devoted to you, a serious international state-security risk has been averted and its organising cell revealed.

"No," he continued as I digested this last remark and glanced across the coffee table at my apparently well-known devotee, "my main problem remains. Those papers you uncovered this afternoon in that warehouse room are dynamite, quite frankly. I ought not to be telling you too much, but suffice to say that we need to find and detain that escaped ringleader, who you rightly say is an SIS officer, MI6. He may or may not be the mastermind, but he has inside information on a particular international situation" – here he paused – "that makes plutonium theft pale into insignificance.

"I shall need to brief Naomi on this, and cancel her leave, but not tonight. She deserves a good rest for a day or two. Look after her, won't you? Thanks, old man."

I relayed this information to my yawning companion over the coffee pot.

She smiled in resignation at the news that she was back on duty. "As usual," she said.

I then phoned home. Sarah answered, and yelled to her mother to pick up the extension phone upstairs.

"You've found her!" she exclaimed in excitement. "Gosh, Dad, well done! Is she OK? Let me speak to her."

I handed my mobile over to Naomi and left the two girls to it for five minutes while I sat back in the low club armchair and closed my eyes. I thought for a moment and then interrupted their conversation.

"Tell Sarah I'm coming home, and you're coming with me. Back tomorrow evening."

Naomi blinked back a sudden tear, and nodded.

I held out my hand for the phone. "Sarah, my love, if I can get a word in edgeways let me speak to Mum." I gave Anne very brief particulars of that day's adventure and said that she could expect us home late the following day.

She took it all in her usual indomitable stride, but I did detect a slight note of relief.

"Do be careful, Robert dear; if that man is still at large he could do you and Naomi some mischief. Just get on the train and don't be distracted into any other shenanigans on the way. I'll have supper ready for you both tomorrow. Give Naomi a hug from me."

I needed no further encouragement. Leaving my chair and settling on to the two-seater sofa next to her, I reported and obeyed my wife's instruction and put an arm around Naomi's shoulders.

"You know," I reflected after some minutes of companionable silence, "I wouldn't have missed these last four or five weeks for anything. I feel I've shed about twenty years, back to the days with a single ring on my cuff charging around the Med, showing the Egyptians and Libyans that they mess with the Royal Navy at their peril. Our number one was a chaotic individual, utterly delightful and great fun, forever misinterpreting instructions to squeeze the last drop of excitement out of the situation.

"This has been just as exhilarating, but with an added diversion that has made the old heart beat a bit faster – you. I can't analyse it, or justify it, except that we were thrown together and something clicked. That's a banal phrase, but what I mean is that an electrical switch has been thrown by someone, or something – Fate, I suppose. God moves in a mysterious way.

"I don't think it has hurt anyone. Anne has seen through me, of course, but seems to understand what has happened. Maybe she knows well, better than I do, that nothing ever *can* happen."

I turned to look into the eyes of the girl beside me and met her gaze. This was almost too much to bear and I looked away again.

"Sorry," I laughed, the moment over. "I am rambling incoherently from lack of sleep and too much cloak-and-dagger excitement. I'm a complete idiot."

But Naomi restrained me with a hand and put mine in hers. "Robert," she said so quietly, "circumstances brought us together – when you were saving me from hypothermia, much closer together then I was really conscious of at the time." Here she gave me a mischievous smile. "Your determination to look after me has saved my life at least twice, probably more. Before I left your home to come back to London, Anne gave me a good talking-to when we were alone in the kitchen one morning. She told me that you had tried to explain to her your sense of devotion towards me, a responsibility between one generation and another, an attraction that was protective and paternal but which isolation at sea on a boat had also made closely companionable.

"Do you know what Anne said then? She said to me, 'Of

course all that is true. But I know perfectly well that Robert has a commitment to you that he is incapable of describing. Don't let him down, Naomi. Don't hurt him.' That's what she said to me over the kitchen table.

"Then Anne went on to say something like this – I can't remember her exact words – 'My husband and I are an inseparable unit. I can say these things to you because I know full well that this will always be the case. His relationship with me, and with our family of daughters and son-in-law, is as secure now as it ever was – in fact, possibly enhanced by your having come on the scene. Sarah looks on you as a new sister. I do not look on you as a rival for Robert's affections. Just treat him gently.' "

Here Naomi giggled and dug me in the ribs.

" 'Men are such sensitive creatures,' Anne said as she left me there in the kitchen feeling a bit stunned that morning. A wise lady, your wife, Robert."

Well, I sat there in the hotel lounge feeling a bit stunned myself, I don't mind admitting. Was I really so transparent?

But Naomi had not finished. "One more thing I want to tell you, Robert, and then I'm off to bed." She stood up and stretched, then leant down closer. "I'm really very fond of you too."

She kissed the top of my head and was gone.

* * * *

Our train journey home was uneventful. We had breakfasted early and on reaching Victoria Station I thought it would be fun to make a diversion to Brown's Hotel for lunch before catching the Wareham train at Waterloo.

I had asked Naomi if she wanted to stop off at her Bermondsey flat to collect anything, but she couldn't face it. Her wardrobe there was probably unspoilt, but she preferred to buy a change of clothes or two at Victoria. As she pointed out, the cost would be borne by Her Majesty's Government in the circumstances.

We took a taxi to Albemarle Street, and Naomi took advantage of the luxurious ladies' cloakrooms to effect a sartorial transformation from the T-shirt and jeans that had been her constant companion for four days. The T-shirt did not again see the light of day.

Brown's Hotel had proved to be a convenient changing room for both of us on our adventures, and was no less accommodating as a watering hole. Anticipating Anne's idea of a light supper that evening, we lunched on an excellent salad and Chablis and resumed our journey south-west.

I had half hoped we might spot Lovat-suit in Brown's dining room, but I guess he knew that his high-profile membership of the London establishment was now a thing of the past, and that he was on the run for his very liberty. As I gazed out of the window of the train while we swept through the Hampshire countryside, I became more and more determined that we could not in all conscience return to normality until we had nailed that smooth blighter. I suddenly laughed out loud, and had to explain to Naomi what had passed through my mind. It was the juxtaposition of Lovat-suit's appetite for fine dining and a misprint I had recently read in a newspaper referring to some miscreant who had 'received his just desserts'.

"I know what I would feed him for dessert," she said with a scowl. She did not elaborate.

"Where do you think he might have gone?" I asked. "His only hope surely is to flee abroad. He doesn't seem to be a foreign political agent, just a mercenary interested solely in his own pocket. His customers have been Eastern European (possibly Russian) and North Korean; and now I gather from D that he has a new and much bigger game afoot."

"Yes, D briefed me before breakfast," Naomi replied. "Through his MI6 work that snake has names, locations, bank-account passwords, encryption codes and identity proofs – next of kin, you name it – for all US intelligence personnel currently engaged in Russia. There would be a keen market. Russia would buy, but so would Ukraine, Poland and Turkey. China would be interested too. Of course, now we know this we will have tipped off the Yanks and they will already be busy salvaging the situation. Unless he can make a very quick sale, in a matter of hours or days, all that information will be worthless."

"If he has no political allies to shelter him abroad, what might he do then? A new identity would be my guess," I said. "Fake passport and so on will not be a problem. He has the contacts for that kind of thing. If I was him that's what I'd do, and take a flight to somewhere in South America a bit quick."

"Yes, I agree," Naomi nodded, "but it would be too risky trying to fly from any UK airport. My people have recognition systems that no fake passport could cheat. They're expensive and not used often, but they will be used for him. He might try getting away by boat or ship – easier, but still he would be putting himself in the hands of others."

"He might first be making his way back to our part of the world. That's where his base was – Poole Harbour – and he knows the area," I suggested. "He may have reliable associates locally."

An idea was beginning to form in my mind as we drew into Wareham Station. I kept my own counsel for the moment.

* * * *

We had a rapturous reception on arrival home, principally from the dogs, but closely following from Sarah, who flung her arms around Naomi's neck and dragged her off upstairs. Anne came out of the kitchen, wiping floury hands on her apron, and smilingly gripped my shoulders. She looked me squarely in the face and quizzically in the eye.

"It's all OK," I said, "as you knew it would be." And I kissed her full on the lips, pulling her to me around her waist.

"Robert! You'll get covered in flour," she riposted, struggling to extricate herself from my heartfelt embrace. "You complete lunatic. Do go and change while I put on the kettle."

Home at last.

Over tea, and then supper, Naomi and I regaled Anne and Sarah with our respective adventures since leaving Church Knowle. Naomi was inclined to make light of her experience, but I could not easily forget her chalk-white face and trembling hands clutching that rifle as I peered through the open doorway into the storeroom scarcely more than thirty hours ago. One tiny false move, and both she and I could now have been bodies gathering coal dust on a Liverpool warehouse floor rather than very much alive tucking into a shepherd's pie in deepest Dorset.

Anne was appalled at my vivid description of the Bermondsey flat. She felt keenly for Naomi's loss of the few possessions – books, pictures and ornaments – that had linked her to her now alienated and dispersed family. To that extent she was more alone than ever.

"Now, when this is all over," Anne declared, "you and I, Naomi, are going to drive up to Bermondsey in Robert's car, take a deep breath, march into that flat to collect all the things that are still worth keeping, bundle them into the car, slam the door shut and retreat to somewhere suitable for a stiff gin and tonic, then head straight home here and forget the whole thing. That's my advice."

Naomi smiled up at her with rather glistening eyes. "It's very good advice, Anne," she replied in a small voice, "and I shall take it. Thank you."

"And then", chipped in Sarah, "you can come and live with us here!"

Was I a little too quick in my reaction to this sweet offer from my daughter? I could think of two fundamental reasons for that concept to be wholly impossible, but expressed only one of them.

"Lovely idea, darling, but you know Naomi has her own life to live, her own circle of friends and colleagues, and she works in London. Besides, she will want to find a new home of her own – she's an independent spirit, you know."

"Yes, s'pose so," Sarah said sadly. "Still, she can stay here for a bit, can't she?"

"If you'll have me," answered Naomi softly, looking at Anne and not at me.

"I think we could cope, couldn't we, Robert?" my dear wife asked so innocently.

"Guess so," I said, trapped by a pair of deep-blue eyes directed towards me across the table. "I wouldn't have to go chasing her around the country then, would I?"

CHAPTER TWENTY-NINE

The following morning I put to Naomi the idea that had come to me on the train the day before. It was more of a hunch, I suppose – an image of the possible means of escape that Lovat-suit might now be contemplating, to evade the authorities watching for him at airports and seaports. It was a route that required local knowledge and immediate access to the necessary means of transport. It also mirrored a high-profile precedent that had made national news many years ago.

First of all, we needed to do a little detective work once again, and this needed the services of our erstwhile home from home – trusty old *Peggotty*. Naomi and I drove to Redclyffe and boarded the boat with some provisions and warm clothing. Autumn was coming early that year, and there was a distinct chill in the air.

We spent the afternoon on the Frome river mooring, tidying up after what seemed a lifetime since we had last been on board. I had left her in some haste, and *Peggotty* needed a fair old sort-out to restore her to shipshape order: coiling rope, refilling the diesel tank from large cans, stowing everything properly away, and sweeping the recent accumulation of crisp brown leaves from the riverside willow and oak trees off the decks and cabin top.

We were glad to go below for some tea to warm ourselves, and to light the oil lamps as dusk began to creep down the river. It was not long before we had a cosy fug around us as we worked out our plan of action at the saloon table under the warm glow of the lamps. We double-checked the essential equipment – dark clothing and woolly hats, small torches with new batteries, and a working mobile phone. Our little escapade should prove to be short, all being well, but it had to be efficient.

Before long, darkness had enveloped the river and its banks. I fired up the old engine and switched on the navigation lights. We slipped the mooring and at minimum revs followed the ebb tide downstream, with just enough light in the sky from the orange glow of Poole ahead of us to steer an accurate course between the withy stakes marking the deep water down Wareham Channel. Once in Balls Lake, we stole as quietly as possible up the creek to our old familiar anchorage off Shipstal Point, where Naomi lowered the heavy CQR and its chain on to the mud bed without a splash or a rattle.

We extinguished all our lights and sat tight, sitting together in the cockpit trying to keep warm and alert to any sound or sight from over on the far side of the creek, where lay the black outline of Lone Isle, and away off to its right the larger shape of Rand Island, on which the solitary white light of its pierhead shone over the cluster of little boats moored there.

At this late stage in the season, we were alone on the water. No friendly lamps glowing from nearby yacht cabins were there now to relieve the isolation. A brisk north-easterly wind ruffled the surface of the channel and set up luminous little white horses of breaking wavelets that slapped rhythmically against *Peggotty*'s exposed flank.

Naomi shivered despite her layers of dark-blue and black fleece and gloves, and shifted position to use me as a windbreak, curling up on the locker bench into the small of my back, to which I raised no objection.

I had borrowed earlier that morning a pair of expensive 'night-sight' powered field glasses from a pal of mine in Swanage, and every ten minutes or so swept the shoreline of Lone Isle with them for the slightest sign of life.

There was nothing to be seen or heard. Even the birds were now silent for the night, except from far-distant Brownsea the occasional incongruous faint screech of peafowl high in their tree roosts.

We shared a Mars Bar.

At about midnight I shook Naomi out of her chilled and uncomfortable doze, and signalled that the time had come for our little expedition.

We clambered down into the dinghy that we had laid alongside earlier, and used the oars as paddles to ferry ourselves noiselessly across the creek on to the sandy shore of Lone Isle. We were on the sheltered side of the island, but the increasing wind in the scrubby trees exposed around the rim of the old crater was roaring now, sending bits of foliage as well as sand into our faces as we scrambled across the beach and up the slope.

We could move with confidence here, as there was no chance of our footsteps or inadvertent snapping of twigs underfoot being heard above the howl of the north-easterly, which was just beginning to carry spits of icy rain to add to our discomfort.

Naomi and I reached the fence around the rim of the hidden and sunken bowl. On this occasion the tall wooden gate was no longer padlocked, but swinging wildly in the growing gale, posing no obstacle to our entering the palisade and edging our way down the steep inner path until we had a good view through the undergrowth to the base of the bowl below us.

The timber hut was just discernible in the deep shadow. There was not a flicker of light from its windows, and the front entrance door was slightly ajar. The place looked abandoned.

And yet what we had come for was amply rewarded. There on the crumbling hardstanding next to the hut, swaying slightly against its webbing ground anchors in the eddying spiral of wind penetrating the depth of the crater, stood the faded black form of the little helicopter – that sinister unidentifiable menace that had buzzed us on *Peggotty* as we had lain off Freshwater Bay all those weeks previously.

If my theory was correct, here stood friend Lovat-suit's intended means of escape. My plan was to spring a trap so that Delta and his police or army personnel could catch him unawares. But Lone Isle was not going to be the theatre stage on which that last act was to be performed. It was no part of our scheme to attempt any heroics of that nature here in this desolate spot.

In any case, Lovat-suit was patently absent from the scene below us. We had established what we were hoping for, and a prudent withdrawal was now our best plan. There were some arrangements to be made urgently with Delta to set up the denouement that I had envisaged.

The next questions, of course, were where was Lovat-suit, when could we expect him to make his final move, and how could we keep a lookout for him without scaring him off? If he were to see *Peggotty* in broad daylight anchored once again off his island, would he not smell a rat and rethink his escape plan altogether?

In the event, these questions were all answered for us that very night, even before Naomi and I had left the island. Fortune was certainly to smile on us then, in no small measure thanks to the atrocious weather that had escalated even while we stumbled our way back down the slope from the ridge of Lone Isle on to the sand and mud of the beach.

The wind by now had risen to a good force 6, gusting 7, in my estimation. The rain was coming across in horizontal sheets, whipping around the northern point of the island and battering us from along the beach. Visibility in those conditions and at one o'clock at night was down to about five yards, and we could scarcely make out the form of the dinghy we had pulled up on the foreshore.

The glimmer of white light from the Rand Island pierhead to the south was just discernible through the murk. Indeed that was the only direction in which we could at present face with open eyes, as the rain was turning to sharp sleet and blinding us from several points of the compass.

I turned to trudge down the beach to the dinghy, but Naomi grabbed my arm and shouted something that the wind whisked away before reaching my ear. She pointed back down the shoreline to the south. I screwed up my eyes to try and discern what had caught her attention. For a brief second the rain squall eased and I could see it. A faint yellow light just penetrated the darkness for a moment and then vanished again.

Keeping hold of the arm that she had seized, Naomi led me a few yards nearer and we stopped again. Yes, a flickering lamp, probably an old hurricane lantern, formed a perfect disc in the side of a much darker shape that was now just visible – a long, low structure, half in and half out of the water.

Of course! Here was the old houseboat, drawn part way up the beach, her stern just afloat in the ebbing tide, her bow high and dry on the sand. Years of neglect had allowed straggling weed growth to form around the rusting steel hull in a dark-green curtain, while brambles had even begun to twine themselves up the old mooring warps and on to the foredeck well, which was thick with an accumulation of dead leaves, twigs and blown sand.

The stern well, with its companionway down into the cabin, had been opened up, and its pair of rotten timber doors stood slightly open.

We crept up to the side of the houseboat towards the lit porthole. On tiptoe I could just reach up high enough to see in through the dirty glass. There, inside, in deep shadow from the lantern, was revealed the familiar head and shoulders of our old acquaintance Lovat-suit.

Even in those conditions I could tell that this was not the suave, dapper and self-assured individual we had come to recognise. The yellow tinge of the lamp added a sick and ghastly pallor to his haggard face, which had a couple of days' growth of beard. His normally sleek and glistening hair was now an unkempt tangle down over his forehead. He had lost his tie and the collar of his shirt was ripped.

Rather more to the point, so far as I was concerned, I could just peer in far enough to see what he was doing. He was poring over a large coloured map. I did not need to squint very much to identify his area of interest. The map quite plainly revealed the English Channel and the north coast of France, well down through Normandy to Paris and Le Mans.

Cold, wet and uncomfortable as I was, in that moment I smiled to myself. Things were patently coming together just as I had visualised. Nothing was now more obvious than the fact that our old adversary was gearing up for an early departure from these shores – a quick flit across the Channel to land somewhere, anywhere, and to vanish from the record until re-emerging in due course as a new persona. I have no doubt that the adoption of a wholly new identity in a foreign country would be an easy call on his underhand talents. In the meantime, however, I believed that I was still one step ahead of his game.

As I think I have mentioned before, my naval career had given me a fairly robust working knowledge of helicopters of one kind or another, and I was aware of their various merits and of their limitations, especially in comparison with fixed-wing aircraft. When choosing a small two-seater to fly any distance from A to B, a helicopter suffered an inherent disadvantage every time.

In a word: fuel.

It had given me a glow of satisfaction, therefore, to spot just now through the rain, down in the crater basin below us, not just the little black helicopter but also two additional objects that had confirmed my suspicions. In front of the hut had lain a pair of alloy tubes, like huge cigar canisters, fitted with brackets designed to attach to the runner frame beneath the belly of the machine. They might perhaps have been floats, to enable the helicopter to land on water; but more likely in my view was that they were supplementary fuel tanks, which could be connected to the inbuilt tank as inherently provided for in its design.

With three tanks full, that little craft could make it into the French countryside without difficulty, provided it could get airborne with the weight. (That would take some skill.)

And so the question on which my plan now rested was this: *where could Lovat-suit obtain that quantity of aviation fuel?*

I let myself down off the gunwale of the houseboat, but not before I had noticed one other object lying on the table inside the cabin close to the man's hand. A heavy automatic pistol.

Time for Naomi and me to slip away into the murk. I signalled to her that we had seen enough, and we turned back into the teeth of the gale.

To recover the dinghy and paddle back to *Peggotty* took but a few minutes. We clambered aboard from the lee side, but the old boat was beginning to roll in the severe disturbance of creek water generated by wind against tide. With some difficulty, by subdued torchlight only, we raised anchor and crept away down Balls Lake before boosting throttle and planing at speed back up Wareham Channel with the wind behind us, and into the relative shelter of the river.

Once secured back at the mooring, *Peggotty* reassumed the role of campaign base. It was now three thirty in the morning. The phone call to Delta could safely await the dawn. Naomi and I tumbled down into *Peggotty*'s welcoming cabin, shed our soaking woollens and retired to our respective bunks wrapped in everything that we could find to restore warmth and guarantee a deep sleep. I set the alarm for six thirty.

CHAPTER THIRTY

I still remember my dream that night. In retrospect now, it forms an analogy of what was to come – a kind of prophecy of the culmination of this story. Like so many dreams, it was a bittersweet affair: a combination of an achievement (this was easy to interpret) with a measure of loss and heartache of a quite indefinable nature.

Encompassing both of these contrasting emotions overlay an occasion of celebration in which I participated with a joyful sense of peace, and sadness beyond words. The location of the dream events was all too familiar to me – a little village that lay on the approach to my prep school. I had not been there in reality for forty years, but to a small boy the scene had for five formative years heralded an almost overwhelming emotional severance from all that was dear to me, as I sat dismally in the back of my parents' car on the first day of each term. I had flourished at the school – indeed had been head boy, and it had been a place of accomplishment – but the impact of that village appearing into view never left me.

Peggotty's alarm clock burst the silence in due course, shattering dream or sleep. I rolled out of the fo'c'sle bunk and found my phone. Delta answered my call with his usual briskness, and I related to him our overnight discoveries. He was in complete agreement on the proposed course of action, and we talked through the likely scenario. On the opposite saloon bunk, Naomi had awoken and was listening in, head propped on elbow under the bedclothes.

"What's our role, then, Robert?" she asked, sitting up and wrapping her sheet around her like a kimono to preserve her modesty as she moved to the stove and the kettle.

"From here on in, old partner-in-arms," I said, "you and I will be spectators – mere hunt followers in at the kill. I think we are entitled to that satisfaction, even if we leave the professionals to do the work.

"You're much too young to remember, but many years ago a chap who had run a business called Polly Peck successfully achieved what we are now hoping to prevent Lovat-suit from repeating. He too was evading arrest, and managed to fly out secretly in a small private plane from a little grass-strip airfield run as a club for amateur recreational flyers. It became a cause célèbre in the newspapers.

"That airfield is only a few miles north of here, up near Shaftesbury. It's got to be Lovat-suit's best bet. It has fuelling facilities, hangar space and, above all, it's completely isolated. Aircraft landing and taking off up there would not be seen from any official monitoring station.

"Of course, the airfield office would record any flight and aircraft particulars and comply with the usual aviation-authority rules, but you can bet that Lovat-suit will have prepared false papers and identity long ago for just such an eventuality. All he needs is fuel.

"Mr D will have other southern counties airfields on the alert as well, but we can't be in two places at once. Wingreen Abbas is my best guess, so let's get up there."

"Wow!" was the response from the sheet-clad form busy with the kettle and teapot.

Dispensing with breakfast, we took the dinghy tender back upriver to Redclyffe. The wind had eased in the early hours, but low cloud still hung over the Purbeck Hills, dull grey and threatening more rain. I just hoped that visibility would not deteriorate too much, or our friend on Lone Isle would be deterred from making the helicopter flight we were all expecting.

Regaining the car, Naomi and I drove into Wareham and

up north to Blandford and the top road towards Shaftesbury. Before long we spotted the green steel hangars of the airfield and pulled into the car park.

It was an enterprising little flying centre, perched high up above the north-facing escarpment over Melbury Down, with the hilltop town of Shaftesbury away in the distance. The proprietors ran an excellent café, which had panoramic views of the airstrip and countryside beyond, and this had just opened as we arrived. With one or two other early visitors and a small group of obvious aviators, we sat down and did justice to a hot breakfast and a mug of coffee.

An interesting assortment of aircraft stood in a long row outside, the lighter ones tethered to the ground, and one or two with canvas hoods over their cockpits and noses to keep the weather out. There were single-seaters, a couple of splendid old biplanes, a few 'executive' six- or eight-seaters with gleaming paintwork, and several frankly rather battered-looking craft that were no doubt dearly loved but in which I would have been a very reluctant passenger.

The orange windsock on its wooden mast was hanging fairly limply, I was encouraged to note. Visibility, even at this elevation, was reasonable that morning. Conditions looked promising.

The door to the café opened behind us and there was Delta himself, with another man in a dark suit who, to my eyes, had 'senior police officer' written all over him. Nor was I mistaken. They sat down at our table and the introductions were made.

Chief Inspector John Trevelyan, a fellow Cornishman, impressed me from the outset. He had the calm, unassuming manner of a professional who is confident of his own competence and comfortable in his own shoes. He seemed very young to have reached that rank, as indeed he proved to be, but he possessed a maturity beyond his years.

He was also a very good-looking chap – a quality that did not escape Naomi's notice as soon as he and Delta had settled in their seats. The appeal was clearly reciprocated, judging by the continual exchange of glances and smiles between them as our conversation got under way.

Trevelyan was the lead officer for the firearms unit in the Dorset Constabulary, and had arrived at the airfield earlier that morning with his team in response to the alert which Delta had issued immediately following our phone conversation some hours previously. His armed colleagues were already deployed and out of sight, some in the shadow of hangar doorways, and one or two in unmarked vehicles parked innocuously in the visitors' car park.

The agreed tactics were to maintain as normal a routine at the airfield and in its public areas as possible while the expected arrival of Lovat-suit was awaited. None of us knew whether he had arranged to meet other accomplices there, perhaps to join him in his escape by air to the Continent. It was vital that no alarm bells were raised in the meantime. Any one or more of our fellow breakfasters could be one of the conspirators. I kept trying to avoid looking repeatedly across the room to the corner where the group of flyers was seated. Could one of them be Lovat-suit's co-pilot for the long, slow helicopter flight down into France or beyond? They appeared to be relaxed and acting naturally enough, but in my imagination I suspected each of them in turn.

The public was not permitted beyond the open-air veranda of the café, and the plan was to ensure that any police action should take place either well out on the airstrip, or in the hangar area, where the fuelling equipment was installed.

Delta was determined that the operation should 'mop up' (as he put it) not only Lovat-suit, but any accomplice as well. It was anyone's guess as to how many of them possessed the explosive knowledge of the national-security secrets that had caused Delta such anxiety in Liverpool. Some, to his certain knowledge thanks to the cooperation of Gingerhead and Blackbeard, were people in senior public positions. Most were now already under constant MI5 surveillance, but it only needed one to escape the net for the international role of the UK to be severely jeopardised.

We waited. Twice in the next hour or so our ears pricked up

at the sound of an aero engine approaching into the wind from the north-east, but on each occasion it proved to be a private plane landing on the grass and puttering off to the sidelines to be tethered to the ground. Their pilots entered the flyers' lobby next to the café for the formalities, and came in rubbing cold hands in anticipation of a hot drink.

The customers of the café came and went. We drank more coffee. Only Trevelyan and Naomi found enough to keep a lively conversation going. They had migrated to bar stools at the counter.

Delta looked bored. I felt – well, what did I feel? A little bereft, if I am honest. I consulted my watch for the nth time – eleven fifty.

If Lovat-suit intended to make it to France in daylight, he was running out of time.

The clientele in the café was growing in number now. The nearer lunchtime approached, the older it was growing too. A sea of white-haired heads, respectable citizens of a certain age, and accompanied by small dogs. No aviators, as far as I could tell.

"I guess he's on his own, then," I said to Delta, breaking a long silence.

"Looks like it, doesn't it? Damn!" he responded. "I was hoping for at least two birds with one stone."

"He's cutting it a bit fine," I added. "Maybe he's chosen another airfield after all."

Delta shook his head and patted his jacket pocket. "If that helicopter lands at any airfield in Southern England, my phone will be red-hot."

He paused. "Something's not right."

As if on cue, his mobile phone buzzed softly.

"Delta," he answered, and said no more as he listened to his caller giving a fairly lengthy message. "Understood," he concluded abruptly, and, returning his phone to his pocket, beckoned Naomi and the Chief Inspector back to the table.

"That was my man at Lake Boatyard in Poole Harbour. I had him there with binoculars to keep tally on Lone Isle opposite

207

on the far shore, to phone me if and when he saw the helicopter lift off.

"What I hadn't bargained for was the radio interference and jamming technology at the Royal Marines base next door at Lake. My man has had to relocate several times to get a signal for our closed-circuit phone system. Anyway, he's got through at last." Here Delta ran a hand over his forehead and looked up at me. "He reports that our target helicopter left Lone Isle just after 0900 and headed north, across Wareham Channel and the railway line, and over Upton, when he lost sight of him in cloud."

Three hours ago. And surely we had been right – he was heading north, up towards Wingreen, as we had anticipated. A flight of twenty minutes or so.

Delta sat back in his chair and frowned.

"We can't hang around here doing nothing. John, if you and your team can remain here on the alert in case he appears out of the blue, it's time for the rest of us to take to the air ourselves. We'll follow a line back from here southwards and see if we can spot the helicopter on the ground. He may have landed somewhere en route – I dunno, maybe to pick up an accomplice or something. It's a slim chance, but if we're going to see anything at all, it will be from the air. John, are you authorised to summon a copter from NPAS on an immediate basis?" The Chief Inspector shook his head. "I would need clearance from Dorchester."

Delta whipped out his satellite phone, a hefty object with an antenna I recognised from our meeting back at Corfe Castle Rectory. He pressed a number. "Get me the NPAS – Dorset, Wiltshire or Hampshire. Excuse me," he added, getting up and moving out of earshot.

The National Police Air Service was quick to respond to Delta's instruction. In less than three minutes he was back at the table.

"An MD902 is on its way. Naomi, can you nip next door to the control room and explain? They already know we are here, of course, and expecting to arrest an armed flyer. Say we need clear airspace and landing strip for the police helicopter and to ground all private aircraft until further notice. Robert, would you like to accompany us? Entirely up to you."

"You bet, Mr D," I responded enthusiastically. "I've always hankered after a police chase in the air."

In a matter of minutes, the drone of a small helicopter penetrated the café walls and we stared up out through the glass. Maybe this was Lovat-suit after all.

But no, a dark-blue-and-yellow craft hovered into view and dropped gently on to the grass sward in front of the airfield buildings. We grabbed our things and dashed out through the lobby. The police pilot gestured with his arm for us to approach with our heads well down. Delta, Naomi and I quickly boarded – Delta into the crew seat in front, and we two through the flank openings into rather basic passenger seats behind. This was not going to be a particularly comfortable ride.

Within seconds we were airborne and accelerating diagonally forward – a most disconcerting manoeuvre that gave me the distinct impression that we were aiming for the ground.

Delta opened the intercom. "Now, we need to keep our eyes peeled. I will look out ahead and left; Robert, please scan out to the left, and Naomi to the right. We all know what we're looking for."

He gave directions to the pilot, and we settled along a steady straight line just east of south. Over the top of Ashmore Wood, and across the road to the Tarrants and the open farmland towards Pimperne, we flew low at about 200 feet at a slow pace.

I am what they call a good sailor, in that I can be in a boat in all weathers and not suffer from seasickness. However, this kind of motion in the air, with the obligation to concentrate my gaze out sideways instead of ahead, soon began to play havoc with my internal gyro, and after about five minutes of this I was starting to feel a little queasy. I glanced across to Naomi, who caught my eye and grimaced back. We were fellow sufferers.

We were about to cross the main road from the east into Blandford, and the pilot had gained height in order to avoid inflicting sudden loud noise on the passing traffic. Pimperne Wood was behind us. Suddenly Naomi let out a yell and instinctively pointed down through the glass of her window. She pressed her intercom.

"Down there, just to the right. Do you see that grassy earthwork on the corner of those two tracks? There's something black on the edge of it."

The pilot took the helicopter around to starboard in a tight turn and with a roar of engines. Immediately below us was an oblong hillock that we later identified as Pimperne Long Barrow. Three rough farm tracks converged on one corner of it.

Long scrape marks were freshly furrowed along one of them, culminating in a dusty black metal machine hard up against the grassy bank.

CHAPTER THIRTY-ONE

Delta instructed the pilot to land, and for a few moments the machine was hidden from view. Slowly we made vertical landfall further down the track on its hard gravelly surface, and climbed out on to the ground.

What immediately caught the eye ahead of us, now that we were on the same level, was one of the rotor blades of the black metallic beetle on the hillock before us. It stuck up into the air at a twisted angle, its companion rotor bent downwards, touching the ground.

Delta held up his hand to stop us walking any nearer. He pulled an automatic pistol from an armpit holster under his jacket, and, signalling us to stay still, crept forward towards the machine, his pistol arm outstretched in front of him. He reached the tail of the helicopter and peered round along its side.

Instantly we could see his shoulders relax, and his arm was lowered. He restored his gun to his person and waved us forward. We walked towards him in some trepidation. I felt Naomi unconsciously take my hand in hers.

The police pilot had not left his seat. How many curious sights had he witnessed through his windscreen, I wondered, in the course of his career. One had the impression that nothing could possibly ruffle the surface of his impassive face behind the UV visor of his helmet. Sangfroid personified.

The two of us joined Delta alongside the black helicopter, and he pointed. Naomi suddenly tightened her grip on my hand

and pressed her shoulder into mine. She let out a gasp.

The front of the machine had completely caved in. The Perspex dome of the windscreen lay in shards all over the grass. The alloy body of the cabin had concertinaed back into the motor compartment, the pilot's seat squashed down half under the engine block. Blood that was now congealing had run all over the collapsed cabin floor and through the door cill on to the ground. The cabin door itself had literally been blown like a cork from a bottle of fizz out on to the bank of the hillock, where it lay virtually intact some ten yards from the machine.

A great deal less intact was the erstwhile pilot of the craft – Lovat-suit himself. He was very dead. I will spare the sensibilities of my readers and forbear to offer any more detailed description of his fearful injuries. Suffice it to say that I turned away on to the grassy bank and resolutely threw up my substantial breakfast. I made no attempt to blame this on my airsickness.

Having recovered her equilibrium, Naomi proved to be of sterner stuff than I, and had gone around to the other flank of the mangled old beetle. She was tugging at the crewman's door on the other side, but this was evidently jammed shut. Delta and I went to join her when we had both taken a few deep breaths. Between us, and with the help of a length of steel rod that had come away from the landing skids, we jemmied the door open. I immediately saw what Naomi had spotted. On the empty crewman's seat lay a briefcase. Delta hauled it out and sat down on the platform step.

The case was locked, but the leather strap was no match for his sheath knife. Honestly, I marvelled at the sheer scale of armoury nonchalantly carried around in the pockets of the nondescript lounge suit of this equally nondescript middle-aged ordinary chap – a man who would not merit a second glance from anyone in the street, and therefore presumably the perfect secret-service intelligence officer.

I could not help reflecting that perhaps Naomi was never likely to reach the same professional perfection. Anonymity in public places would be a perpetual problem for a young woman who could not fail to turn heads wherever she went. As may have become apparent during the course of this narrative, this was amply demonstrated in my own case – indeed hardly confined to my head.

I digress.

I suppose we were, each of us, keen to divert our minds from the dreadful picture of the ruptured corpse seated behind us. Delta opened the briefcase with Naomi looking over his shoulder. I walked back to the police MD902 to report the position and let our pilot stand down from the alert. He was also to radio the airfield and get Chief Inspector Trevelyan on the line. Police and security services throughout Southern England could now stand down. We had our man, albeit in diminished condition.

By mid afternoon our police pilot had taken off once more, his role completed. In place of the MD902 the field track was obstructed now by Dorset Constabulary Land Rovers, and a white plastic tent erected over the wreckage of the black helicopter – no longer a malign and sinister object of vice, but an innocuous, sad and vulnerable canopy of the dead. Pimperne Long Barrow suddenly had one more cadaver alongside its 5,000-year-old inmates, however briefly.

The site was now, officially, merely the subject of an air-accident investigation. With the briefcase removed, the matter could be left to the usual channels.

In due course it was established that a distinguished gentleman in a senior position in Britain's intelligence services had died tragically after a terminal malfunction of his private helicopter during a recreational flight over mid Dorset.

His funeral, reported in *The Times*, was attended by senior government ministers and minor royalty and held in Sherborne Abbey, of which he had been a notable benefactor.

The funeral was also attended (unreported) by representatives of the domestic security service MI5, whose attention was concentrated not on the solemn liturgy but upon the members of the loyal congregation. Several discreet arrests closely followed the recessional organ voluntary, the Sedulius chorale 'From East to West, from Shore to Shore'.

Lovat-suit will remain anonymous in this story, at the particular request which a certain government department made to my publishers.

* * * *

It was some weeks later that I received a handwritten letter from Delta, signed 'D', in most kind and generous terms thanking me for my part in the adventure that I have attempted to describe in these pages. The leather briefcase salvaged from the helicopter wreck had proved most revealing. Several people in certain quarters had subsequently been 'helping him in his enquiries' and it seems that a major international incident had been averted – no doubt the same incident from which Lovat-suit was expecting to enrich himself through the ransom of inside information.

I have not seen Delta again from that day on Pimperne Long Barrow to this. He has simply melted back into the obscurity in which he no doubt flourishes.

Naomi and I had hitched a lift back from Pimperne to Wingreen Airfield in the back of Chief Inspector Trevelyan's Volvo, both of us very dazed with the day's events and quite exhausted, especially after the previous night's tramp over Lone Isle, and our disturbed sleep back on board *Peggotty*.

Back in the airfield café Naomi, John Trevelyan and I enjoyed a much needed pot of tea and some excellent home-made cake. I left the two of them to recount that afternoon's experience, went off to pay the bill and suchlike, and returned to find them much restored and in happy mood together.

"I must dash," said Trevelyan. "All my colleagues will think I've deserted. I ought to get back to base for a debrief. Usual story with the firearms unit: we turn out bristling with weaponry and on high alert, stand about for hours in the rain, and then get stood down because nothing's happened. It's really not the most exciting job. It's been good to meet you,

Commodore, despite the circumstances."

We shook hands. He rose from the table.

"I'll see you off," said Naomi, and they went out to the car park together.

* * * *

She and I were very quiet on our drive home to Church Knowle. Heaven knows what was going through her mind, but my own was largely a blank. I was too tired to think. I had a feeling that I was going down with a cold, or a bug of some kind. The prospect of a comfortable bed was becoming very appealing.

By the time we turned off the Swanage road on to our lane to the village, I was beginning to shiver and felt rather light-headed. Anne on the doorstep was a welcoming sight. One look at me, and she hustled me off upstairs to a hot bath and a pair of pyjamas. I was soon prone in bed, with a raised temperature and a prickly throat.

In contrast, as Anne reported when she came to bed some hours later, Naomi seemed to have thrived on the experience of the last twenty-four hours. She had regaled Anne and Sarah with our return visit to Lone Isle and the events that had followed, and was positively sparky.

"It's well enough for a girl her age, of course," my dear wife remonstrated, "but you really are a nitwit, Robert, gadding about in the small hours in the pouring rain with no foul-weather gear on. You are fifty-four, you know, and should act your age."

"Fifty-three," I answered weakly from beneath the sheet, and then sneezed twice.

"Hmph," was the response from the other pillow, but she did reach over and give my hand a squeeze.

I managed a smile of contentment in the darkness.

* * * *

Thanks partly to some medicinal whisky when I took to my bed, I slept quite well, but was in no fit state to get up in the morning. My throat was raging, my nose dripping and my forehead thumping. It was two or three days before I felt human again, and pottered around the house in my slippers. On the fourth day of our return, with Sarah to look after me, Anne made good her promise and drove Naomi up to Bermondsey to salvage what they could from the vandalised flat.

Naomi's smart neighbour in flat 4 of her building heard them arrive and welcomed her home with huge relief, commiserating warmly over the disastrous burglary.

"And do you know," the lady continued in disgust, "the police were so dilatory. That nice Inspector Jameson I met here was very prompt, but it was another week before the local police arrived and re-secured the front door. And another thing – they had never heard of Inspector Jameson. I mean – I ask you! The left hand doesn't know what the right hand is doing half the time these days."

She returned into her own flat to make coffee for the three of them.

Anne and Naomi retreated behind the front door of flat 3 and burst out laughing. This helped lighten their mood as they surveyed the dismal scene.

"Come on, dear," said Anne, "let's get this over with."

An hour later, punctuated by an elegant coffee break over in flat 4 (which was immaculate), they had filled the back of the car outside with Naomi's few prized possessions and as much ordinary useful stuff as they could fit inside. Without a glance back, Naomi closed the door behind her and pocketed the key. Collecting a quantity of post accumulated in the entrance hall, she and Anne walked around the corner to fulfil their other promise to themselves – a stiff gin and tonic in the garden of the Woolpack, where they decided to stay on for lunch in the sunshine.

Instead of bringing it all back to Church Knowle, which had been the original plan, they drove to the address of a friend of Naomi's north of the river and unloaded the contents of the car into her capacious warehouse maisonette in Docklands, returning home later in the afternoon.

I think Anne and Naomi must have had a heart-to-heart talk most of the way back to Dorset. They seemed to understand one another, and to know something that I did not.

CHAPTER THIRTY-TWO

The evenings were beginning to draw in now. I am not an all-seasons sailor. My life in the Royal Navy had been too soft. Open-air bridges on ships had long-vanished by the time I joined up. *Peggotty* would be hauled out of the water at Ridge Wharf later in the winter, but I needed to bring home unused provisions, spare sails and valuable equipment. The engine needed to be 'winterised' with its coolant system filled with antifreeze. The boating season was over for me, and would not resume until the following Easter.

One bright sunny morning, a few days after she and Anne had returned from London, Naomi and I took the dinghy downriver to the boat to 'put her to bed', as I termed it. We bagged up all the stuff to take home, and then made ourselves thoroughly mucky changing the engine oil, drying out the bilges and fiddling about in *Peggotty*'s bowels, renewing water-intake washers, engine filters and impellers.

It was just such a happy working partnership that day – I have never forgotten it. Sharing the tasks in such closely confined spaces, laughing at each other's grimy faces and tangled hair, and reminiscing over our adventures on *Peggotty* that summer; and when all the jobs were completed, sitting together in the cockpit in the still-warm sunshine sharing hot coffee from the one remaining china mug and Anne's cheese sandwiches.

The autumn fall was well under way. Brown and gold leaves from the riverside oaks and willows floated in leisurely fashion on the surface of the water, gathering and separating in the ever changing eddies of the slow ebb tide. The river and harbour lakes and channels were now barely disturbed by boat wash or outboard motor; recreational craft were all being taken into their various forms of hibernation. Only the hardy, oilskin-clad professional shell fishermen carried on their business unperturbed by any weather, chugging endlessly round and round in circles on the end of their anchor warps, hoovering up their valuable clams and mussels from the muddy shallows in their flat-bottomed Poole 'canoes'.

Somehow, as I sat there in silent reverie, leaning against Naomi's forgiving shoulder as we shared the narrow cockpit locker lid in mutual contemplation, there descended on me a calm awareness of cadenza, the unutterable poignancy of the last few diminished chords, the closing and fading notes of the oboe in rallentando, drawing the elation of the inexpressible to its natural conclusion. But what was it that was ending exactly?

We locked up the companionway hatch and piled the canvas bags and wooden boxes into the dinghy amidships. Naomi rowed while I sat in the stern trying to prevent our teetering cargo from falling overboard. We were rather low in the water, our freeboard reduced to a few inches. Windblown ripples slopped occasionally over the gunwale. We made alarmist faces at each other over the mountains of bags as we made our way carefully back upriver.

* * * *

That very afternoon, Naomi received a call from Thames House, her HQ in Millbank. Delta needed her rather urgently, and she was to make her way to GCHQ at Cheltenham with all haste.

She quickly gathered all her things into a suitcase, gave Anne and Sarah a prolonged hug and leapt into my car, her mobile phone to her ear.

With a strong sense of déjà vu, I drove her down through the village and out on to the Wareham Road towards the station. Until we had passed the last roundabout, Naomi was engrossed in the instructions she was receiving over the phone, making notes with difficulty in a pad on her knee.

As we approached the station forecourt, however, she pocketed phone and notebook and turned to me. "Robert," she began, "I . . ." She stopped and blinked, running a brown hand through her shiny black hair. If she was lost for words, what was I? Just lost, I guess, at that moment.

We drew to a halt. Her train was due.

She put her hand against my cheek. "I'll never forget – never, ever" were her parting words to me.

I jumped out, hauled the suitcase from the boot and we both rushed into the ticket office. Mercifully, no queue. The train pulled in as we walked on to the platform. Naomi found a window seat and I soon found the window. We waited for the whistle. The carriage began to move slowly forward and I kept pace for several yards until impeded by a cast-iron pillar.

She blew me a kiss and pressed her hand then against the pane, my own hand matching hers but with unattainable touch, isolated now by so much more than the sheet of plate glass that slipped away from me into the distance.

EPILOGUE

I am sitting at my desk in the study window, the spring sunshine warming my back from the south-east way over Studland Bay and Old Harry Rock. Several times I have taken a seat here and drawn a pad of paper towards me, intending to embark on the story of my encounter with the girl in a wetsuit and all that followed; but somehow until last week I seemed at a loss to know quite what to say.

Anne and I rattle around in this house these days. Sarah is starting her MA at Cambridge reading modern languages, and even in the vacations we seldom have her company, gregarious daughter that she is. Caroline has long left Exeter University and has taken a teaching post in Cardiff. She and her partner, a shy and rather intellectual academic, come down to stay every so often. We now have two noisy but delightful grandchildren in Windsor, and usually spend Christmas with them. Mary is head of her department at Exeter.

Almost seven years have passed since those momentous events in our domestic life over that extraordinary summer and early autumn. I am rapidly approaching my sixtieth birthday. Anne and I now jointly run the church cleaning rota, old Mrs Brownlow having long since moved away to live with her daughter in Bournemouth. Frankly, not a lot has changed in Church Knowle otherwise. We carry on much as we did before.

But, as I mentioned when I first put pen to paper a few days ago, I have never really been the same since that life-saving encounter in the shipping channel off Spithead. What began – what hit me between the eyes – was an enchantment, a captivation. I am not so naive as to imagine that my readers detect in the early pages of this tale much more than an old man's infatuation with the perfection of youth. However, the adventure which followed soon cast such shallowness aside.

What has until now discouraged me from literary revelation is the difficulty of describing with any semblance of credibility the mutual bond of allegiance which so thrillingly developed between us from that very first day. Whether I have attained that understanding I can only leave to the discernment of my critics. It has been my steadfast good fortune and blessing that my wife, Anne, recognised the true nature of this affinity and respected it. My relationship with my better half in these seven years has, in consequence, deepened and matured.

It was Anne who, last Wednesday while going through piles of papers, came across the photograph and brought it to me as I was cleaning shoes on the kitchen floor.

"Remember this, dear?" she said. "I think it's the only photo we have of Naomi."

There she was, standing on the front doorstep of this house, smiling up in the summer sunlight into the lens of Sarah's camera, one arm over Anne's shoulders and the other over mine, there between the two of us in jeans and T-shirt, her dark hair still rather short from her temporary transition into a boy. So incredibly full of life and vitality.

"You ought to write down your adventures, you know, Robert," Anne continued. "Your grandchildren would be fascinated to read the story one day. You did have some exciting moments with that girl. That Liverpool warehouse. You both made my flesh creep when you came back and told us about it."

Yes, I did have exciting moments. The photograph brings some of them rushing back as I look at it now, framed on my desk. That excitement needed no warehouse in Liverpool, no Lovat-suit, no Delta.

Mr and Mrs Trevelyan live in Norwich now, John having had enough of firearms and opting to transfer back to general duties.

He was promoted again a year ago to chief superintendent. Naomi is expecting their second child; she said so in their Christmas card.

Over these last seven years I have so often found myself thinking of that *Brief Encounter* parting on Wareham Railway Station. Our farewell had been all too rushed. There had been no time to express what needed to be said, no breathing space to linger under the conductor's baton for that closing sequence of slow chords. Only the lonely single note of the oboe plaintively in the air as the train disappeared around the curve of the track eastwards. Neither of us could have recognised this for the final bar, nor wondered if it merely signalled an introduction to the next movement of the concerto of our experience together.

In any case, it was only the sound of the locomotive horn.

I always promised myself that one day I would write a long letter to Naomi, going back to those exalted summer days, standing again in our place and blessing her for the memories.

I have never done so.